SEAN THOR CONROE
FUCCBOI

WILDFIRE

First published in 2022 by LITTLE, BROWN AND COMPANY a division of HACHETTE BOOK GROUP, INC.

First published in the UK in 2022 by
WILDFIRE
an imprint of HEADLINE PUBLISHING GROUP

1

Cataloguing in Publication Data is available from the British Library

Hardback ISBN 978 1 4722 9310 7
Trade paperback ISBN 978 1 4722 9311 4

Offset in 11/15pt Minion Pro by Jouve (UK), Milton Keynes

Printed and bound in Great Britain by Clays Ltd, Elcograf S.p.A.

HEADLINE PUBLISHING GROUP
An Hachette UK Company
Carmelite House
50 Victoria Embankment
London EC4Y 0DZ

www.headline.co.uk
www.hachette.co.uk

For
R

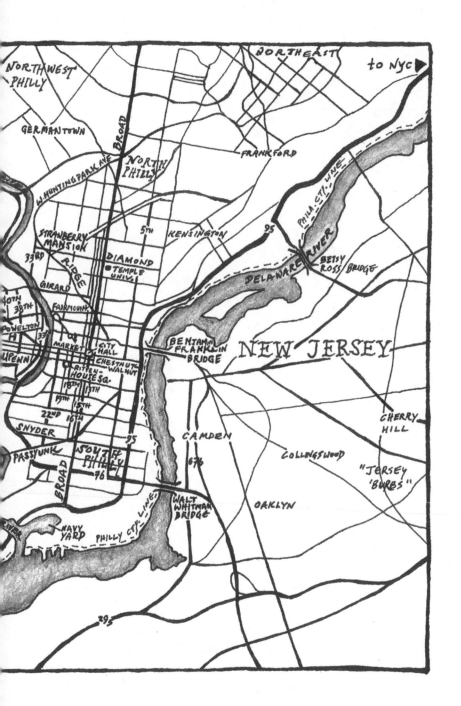

Misanthropy comes of an all too greedy love.
                    —NIETZSCHE

I

Winter

1

POSTMATE

December 2017

Got into a thing with the Fresh Grocer lady over coffee filters.

It honestly wasn't a biggie, but why say they're on sale if they aren't, all I'm sayin.

She was like *This* muhfucker. What aisle.

I told her what aisle and we went and checked. Together.

Well we started to, but then she told me not to follow her when she noticed me following her.

I was like Aite, fasho, putting my hands up. Like I'll hold it down. Man the reg'.

When she came back and said No du', they ain't on sale, I snapped.

That's why I tried to come with! I said. To show you they are.

So we checked, actually together this time, she hemming and hawing the whole way.

Honestly can't remember whether they were or weren't, but I'll never forget that incident. It connected us. It marked the start of a long, fruitful, and strictly nocturnal friendship.

Too fucking cold out.

Too fucking cold!

I balaclava'd up and put my head down, weaving through a herd of incoming undergrads.

Shitfaced.

Not I; but they, very much so by the looks.

Saturday night!

I'd started shopping at 2 a.m., and the pod I listened to while shopping was almost through, so had to be 3 damn near.

Right before I hit play again, one of the undergrads yelled "Water! I need water!" and another yelled "Lacy! You can't drink that!"

Caught a glimpse of Lacy squatted like she was pissing, chugging from a 2-gallon guy on display in the vestibule there, laughing and spilling most of it, stance wide so it missed her feet.

Takin a piss.

Takin a piss in the Fresh Grocer!

Pulled my Nike Dri-Fit snapback I found in the street down low, over my balaclava, under my hood. Unlocked my bike and got to walking.

My thing lately was sticking to 41st.

Walking down 41st and only 41st, whenever possible.

Doing so was how I managed to leave my house.

My room.

My bed.

41st was my block.

Forty-one hunned.

Gang.

Fuck you, high-30s UPenn motherfuckers with your dorms and well-insulated jackets and bike cops and senses of purpose.

Eat all the dicks.

And you, mid-40s kombucha-guzzling hippies with your communal housing and fermented foods and jars and senses of purpose.

The fuck y'all know about 41st Street.

That shit ain't even straight.

It zigged east a half block at Market, zagged west a quarter block at Walnut, and was paved for shit all along.

Ran one way one block and the other way the next.

Wasn't respected as a thru street.

But walking it.

Kept things interesting.

Turned on Postmates and started unloading groceries, back at the spot.

The lights were out and roomie's bike was gone, which meant he was at the wifey's.

Probably cuddled up, spooning.

Netflix auto-playing atop their shared covers.

Just like the rest of the simps: accepting affection from others to mask the pain of themselves.

One pound russet potatoes ($2) on the counter, in the corner. One pound cooking onions ($2), next to that. Seven-grain soft white presliced loaf ($2) and Bustelo tin ($4) in the cabinet, above. And eggs ($1.50), Vermont sharp white cheddar ($1.69), and bag of clearance, overripe avos ($1) in the fridge.

Got a ding right when I least expected it.

Right when I'd forgotten I'd logged on.

When I'd settled into the couch and opened YouTube.

3:37 a.m.

Pizza spot in south.

Way south.

South of Snyder south.

The fuck.

Hit accept before fully considering the logistics.

Fuck it.

This was my life now.

Was it even open still.

Would they even be awake still by the time I got it to them.

Would my prepaid Postmates Fleet credit card even work, like it hadn't been lately.

Were my thoughts as I huffed it — wheezed — across the Schuylkill.

Mellow but popping still somewhat, somehow, once across.

People still out tryna fuck or get home or not get home just yet.

Folks passed out on cardboard, in nooks, on Market approaching City Hall.

Could feel the Under Armour rubbing against the rash below my right pec, extending into my right pit.

Shoulda vaselined that bih.

Forgot to vaseline that bih.

Gotta remember to!

Next time.

For now, less upper-body, side-to-side movement.

All legs.

Yelled "Yo fuck your lights!" as I ran my third red and *skrt*-ed right down 16th.

Loudly I think but hard to say over the Kodak blaring in my balaclava-compressed earbuds, wedged deep into my earholes.

Gassed by the time I arrived at the pizza joint.

Right at their 4 a.m. closing time.

Drunk folks huddled out front, inhaling slices off paper plates. Mopping going on, inside.

Retrieved the package from the bada-bing bada-bang mobster types working counter.

Guzzled down the cig roach I'd stashed in my pant-leg roll, while waiting for the drop-off location to load, side-to-side shimmying to keep warm.

They didn't tell you the drop-off till after.

How they got you.

Sneaky fucks!

Whattayagonnado.

One of the girls in the outdoor pizza-eating crew eyed me from beneath the fur of her parka, through the glitter/tears of her eyes/lashes. Chomping with her mouth open.

Or maybe not tears.

Maybe it was just cold.

I don't know.

I looked away, but understood her gaze.

This guy.

Who tf is this guy.

Why is he here now.

Babe, I'm right there with ya!

No clue.

My whole vibe, of a sudden, seemingly: so serial killer-y.

Terrorist-y.

When did that happen.

Feel like it had to have been fairly recent.

Feel like it can't have always been like that.

Definitely wasn't before —

Ohp!

Drop-off.

Finally.

Just devouring data, this app.

Ayyy, West!

OK, 48th, little further than ideal.

But I'll take it!

Took her a sec to come to the door; but she did, eventually.

In jammies.

Like she'd stayed in, couldn't sleep, and got hungry.

Coulda sworn it woulda been a shitfaced bro.

Can't guess em all, innit.

She was light-skinned but in a way that made me think college transplant versus intergenerational local.

Plus this block, Cedar, despite extending this far out west, was one of the whiter ones.

I worried she'd think I was considering overpowering her with my maleness, forcefully entering, and having my way with her — which I wasn't considering, not even a bit, beyond the possibility of her thinking it — so I pulled down my balaclava, below my chin, to show my face, and removed my hat — before putting my hat back on since a bare-balaclava'd head looked weirder, I decided.

But she didn't seem scared.

Not even a bit.

Hit me with a thanks.

A smile.

Then closed and locked the door.

I shuffled down the porch steps a step at a time, back to my bike, looking at my phone waiting for my payout to load.

Three drops of snot dripped off the tip of my nose, one after the other.

...

...

...

$6.43.

$6.43!

Plus tip!

2

SUSBOY

New Year's Eve 2017

I pulled up early to the house I used to live in.

For the New Year's party my ex roomies were throwing.

I showed up on time, but no one besides my ex roomies were there, since on time was early at parties.

I hadn't been drinking or going to parties for months now, so I'd forgotten.

But here I was.

At a party.

So I started drinking.

Last year's New Year's got ugly.

Happened here, at this house, only back then I still lived in it.

Had just moved into it.

Into the third-floor 'closet-room.'

I had, since, graduated into a new 'closet-room,' across town.

Well... 'closet-sized.'

This new room itself had a closet.

Which I think disqualified it from being a closet.

But same feel.

Same claustrophobia.

Same shitty ventilation.

———

But last year.

The beginning of the end.

Or end of the beginning.

Or maybe just beginning.

Of everything.

Of the sadness.

Of Reality.

When ex bae and I decided to open things up.

Polyamorize.

Or maybe when ex bae got a firsthand look into how I polyamorized when she wasn't around.

Before we'd agreed that polyamory was what we were doing.

Side bae coming on strong, all of us coming up, and me shrugging like Hey, ex bae, whattaya want me to do?

Side bae tryna get it.

That's her right.

All about equal rights here.

Just like it's my right to be a spineless fuck with no loyalty or resolve.

Molly, y'all.

That dang molly!

Ex bae, though.

She'd be back.

I was sure of it.

Just needed time.

To 'explore.'

To hammer home that she wasn't fucking around.

11

She was waiting it out, making me suffer, forcing me to reckon fully with my Destiny, without the buffer of her affection, so I'd be left with no choice but to 'make it.'

Hit it big.

Show em all.

And then. Only then would she return.

But this year.

This year wasn't last year.

This was a New Year.

Side bae showed up around eleven with the beans, like she'd promised.

I'd insisted No, not this time around, I was done with that.

Right up until the moment she procured my double-dose capsule.

Till she handed me the beer to wash it down with, watching to make sure I swallowed.

Right up until then, I resisted.

But how assertively she asserted.

Yes ma'am, I said, swallowing.

Too much activity going on, all around.

I returned to the middle-room couch.

Next to the roomie, who showed up with his wifey not long before side bae did.

We fit in due to our education level, but also remained slightly outside, due to our hapa-ness.

Our introversion.

Our shared misanthropy.

He was on something too, wasn't sure what. But we

started talking faster and faster and more emotionally and less judgmentally.

I'd cut my hair, dolled myself up, and washed for tonight.

Felt prettier and prettier the more people showed.

Still didn't interact with anyone besides the roomie and those who approached me — in the corner, on the couch — but began conducting myself in a more and more performative way.

Not performing for anyone.

Just aware of being watched.

Laughing more.

Once the bean kicked in I started wilding.

Flirting up a storm.

Up and off the couch.

Roaming.

No one was off-limits.

Anyone could get it.

Whispered into peripheral bae's ear "We both know we both want it. Have wanted it. Tonight's the night. Tonight you can get it."

Then winked and backed away, into a crowd.

Told ex-roomie bae's out-of-town, pretty-boy bestie "No you're right, I guess I *don't* know until I've tried it. So what are you gonna do to try *me*?"

Went up to unfamiliar bae, in the middle of a convo, and corralled her into my dancing vortex when "Starboy" came on for the umpteenth time.

Went "Ayyy, college!" when ex-roomie bro said "Her?! She's still in college, bro!" after I asked him if he knew unfamiliar bae and, if so, what her deal was.

———

Side bae was less than impressed.

Cornered me in the packed kitchen, by the drink station.

Said You need to focus.

Gestured circularly in her face area.

On this.

On me.

Then put her hand on her hip and cocked her head like And? What do you have to say to that?

Oh side bae.

Side bae, she was a grown-ass woman.

Had two years on me.

Sexy when she told me what to do.

She knew what she wanted, and how to make known her terms and conditions.

Thing was, that was only the half.

I knew what I wanted. I'd made known my terms and conditions.

But getting them...

"Hahaaa, ayyy, woah," I said.

"Whattaya want from me, bae?" I said.

"Skiddly doot pop?" I said, handling her hips, touching groins, and smelling her all over — neck, pits, tummy.

Side bae said: "Dance floor."

Grabbed my wrist and led me two rooms over, through a crowd, to the front room.

To the dance floor.

Danced with a coy pout on her face, directed towards me until I gave her my full attention; then away from me once I did, but dancing for me, wanting me to watch; and then towards me again when she noticed I wasn't watching.

Confusing.

Sexy!

But confusing.

I couldn't stay focused.

So many baes.

Too many feelings.

Multidirectional feelings.

And never enough to fill the hole inside.

Got ensnared in unfamiliar bae's dance vortex.

Got sent spiraling her way.

Wasn't two two-steps in when I felt myself yanked another way.

Side bae pulled me into a corner. Hard.

Harder than she meant to, maybe, because immediately after she went small again.

She'd initiated it; but somehow, I felt like the dominant one.

Like she wanted me to be the dominant one.

Like she was testing me.

So I did the only thing I could think to. What I coulda sworn she wanted.

Grasped her by the neck — firmly enough for her to feel it, gently enough to not leave a mark or obstruct her breathing, just like she'd taught me — and pinned her to the wall, leaning in to nuzzle her ear.

She grabbed my wrist. Hard.

Said No.

Not here.

Not in front of people.

Not unless I say to.

•

Around 2 a.m.

Big Indian dude I didn't recognize, hovering in the front room. By the piano.

Swaying slightly.

Looking lost.

"My guy," I said. "Doin arite?"

He looked at me surprised, like Me?

Yeah you, pal.

Oh yeah, me, doing great.

"Fuck yeah!"

"..."

"Drink?"

I poured him and myself a shot of the sake I'd brought, that I'd been lugging around, then lost, then found, then was lugging around again.

He looked around skittish, eyes bulgy and unfocused.

We cheers'd.

"Yo so you Indian, huh?"

"Yuh."

"Lit. Born there?"

He told me he was born in Baltimore. Where his parents immigrated to.

"Ah," I said. "B-more."

Made a *Wire* reference.

Side bae entered the front room, looking tired.

Gave me a cryptic, mostly frustrated-seeming look.

Went upstairs with her bestie.

To re-up, probably.

"Well here's to our respective Asian brethren. Holding down our respective motherlands," I said, pouring and shooting another shot.

Started rolling a cig.

"Y'know," I said. "I was actually born in Tokyo. Lived there till I was five. Been back a few times since.

"Recently, as I learned more about my family history — white dad's dad a U.S. Air Force pilot, mom's dad's entire fam besides him bombed out and merked by U.S. planes — I started to wonder why my mom moved us. Why she let me lose my Japanese. Why she let me get so detached from Japanese culture.

"Can't even speak to my *baba* hardly!

"But what I realized —," I began.

Before side bae started tugging on me again.

"This way."

I looked at Indian homie like in slo-mo.

Like 'Nooooooo!'

Like 'Brrrrrbbbbbbbb!'

He receded past the wall and out of sight as I fell back, through the middle room, into the kitchen, and out the back door. Down the back steps, to the backyard. Where side bae fed me more drugs.

Commotion in the front room, when I returned.

Front door wide open, wind billowing up the curtains.

Weird contrast between the fluorescent streetlight outside, emanating off the snow in the yard, and the blacklight of the front-room dance floor.

"Starboy" blasting again.

Forged ahead, to close the door.

Partiers adjacent to it, talking like discussing versus talking like flirting.

Not closing the door.

Why weren't they.

Right when I was about to, Indian dude came barging in.

"Ayyy, woah," I said, arms wide in welcome before, a split second later, realizing this wasn't one of those barge-ins.

This was a different kind.

"Bud, bud, hey," I said, blocking his path and spreading my arms, but now to stabilize him.

"Where ya goin."

"Fuck you motherfucker," he yelled. "All o' yous."

"Bud, what happened."

He flailed to his right, to a group of white girls.

"Ohhhkay," I said, grabbing him by his shirt collar and pushing him back.

"And you!" he yelled over my shoulder. "Fuck you too, white motherfucker!"

Jeez.

Dude was heavy.

Pushing him, I felt like a lineman pushing those dummy linemen linemen push in football practice drills.

Ex-roomie bro—whom he was pointing at—was like Wha?—before Indian dude grabbed the coat rack over my head and tried to blitz past me—before ex-roomie bro hit him with a linebacker tackle and pushed him back to where I'd gotten him.

Back into the doorway.

I threw all the coats off me like "Ohhhkay, done playing nice." Pushed him through the boot room and down the front steps. Like *Fuck* outta here, bitch.

Was pissed now.

But also hyper-lit, euphoric almost, given the adrenaline plus molly.

Indian dude hit the pavement like thwack.

Slid some feet on the ice.

Then popped back up, eyes bulgy and crazed, like he was on bath salts or some shit.

"The fuck, dude," I said. "Thought we were cool."

"Fuck you," he said.

"Fuck you and fuck you," he said, pointing at ex-roomie bro and other ex-roomie bae's boo, T, who lived around the corner. "Fuck all you white motherfuckers. Colonizers, all o' yous."

I started laughing.

"Bro — what are you even talking about? Weren't we literally just talking about — "

Before one of the girls from the whitegirl trio he'd flailed at, who'd followed me out, cut in like "Dude. Chill. You need to go. You're making it worse."

"*I* need to chill?" I said, feeling gaslit. "I — "

"Yeah you. Back inside. We got this."

Speaking to me like a grade school teacher.

Ex-roomie bro and T were hovering in front of Indian dude, crouched and hands raised, like animal trainers coercing a tiger back into its cage.

What I was going to continue saying to Indian dude before side bae yanked me away was,

"But what I realized was, for however much I want to

19

rep the motherland, be bitter towards America for merking 1/20 of Japan's population, I actually know next to nothing about Japan.

"About Japanese culture.

"Japanese homogeneity.

"Japanese gender roles.

"Like, my mom had to have had her reasons for not only *not* wanting to raise me and my sisters over there, but for leaving herself.

"Like, every other nation has an *ethnic* identity. America is the only one that doesn't.

"That takes on, as its national identity, the task of working through ethnic differences.

"Of uniting them.

"To assume it was all my dad's idea to leave Japan is like weirdly patronizing to my mom...

"Y'know?"

Partiers inside explained that Indian dude was 'coming on to girls too strong,' so ex-roomie bro had stepped in.

Told him he was 'making girls uncomfortable.'

That he 'had to cool off.'

At which point...

Heard yelling out front.

Plus needed to smoke.

So went out front.

Sat on the top step.

T had Indian dude in a headlock.

Was going "Chill! Chill!"

Ex-roomie bro was on the ground also, hugging Indian dude's legs together like a koala on a tree.

"What. In. The," I said.

Lit my cig.

Unable to not laugh.

"I know! I'm sorry about my ancestors! I hate myself for my ancestors!" T yelled. "Now *stop resisting*!"

"You white motherfuckers," Indian dude kept yelling. "Murdered my people!"

"Dudes," I said. "What are y'all doing? Bro is clearly blackout and needs to get home, all there is to it — "

"Not now, dude!" said white girl from earlier.

I put my hands up and zipped it.

But she seemed to hear me.

"You guys, I'm calling him an Uber," she said. "Let him stand!"

"You gonna chill?" T said.

Indian dude wriggled, then stayed still.

"OK," T said. "I'm letting you go now."

T and ex-roomie bro backed off slowly.

Indian dude stood, swaying a sec.

White girl approached.

"Just gimme your address, K?" she said in a baby voice.

Indian dude looked around like he'd just been teleported here and was gathering his bearings.

Before looking around horrified suddenly.

Like this was the wrong teleportation stop.

"Look," white girl said. "I just need — "

Indian dude swiped the phone out of her hand. Sent it bouncing down the walkway, out the yard, to the sidewalk.

Then flung her back, over the row of potted plants, against the chain link fence.

Like a rag doll.

"Bro!" ex-roomie bro and T yelled, tackling him.

"Gonna be some medical bill," ex-roomie bro said.

"What other choice did we have?" T said.

He gave a thumbs-up to the ambulance driver as he pulled away, lights flashing but siren off.

"I had a bad feeling about tripping tonight," ex-roomie bro said.

"Yeah, me too," T said, rubbing his forehead.

3

SHAWN

January 2018

Went out to my stoop to smoke.
    To stimulate the stimulants I'd just railed.
    Parka'd up.
    Clear night.
    Cold as shit, still.
    But clear.
    Moon full.
    Second of the month.
    The first was on the first.
    This happened infrequently, I'd read.
    Something in the air.

Had a round of edits on my Walk Book manuscript from editor bae to get to, but first had to figure out what my name was.
    I had too many names.
    'Sean Conroe' my American legal.
    'Sean Thor Conroe,' full American legal.
    Either worked, with the middle adding a tad of writerly pretension.
    But so Anglo.
    All Anglo.
    Ignored the yellow half.

Its passport—the Japanese, birth country's—read 'Sho Kamura.'

Could take the first or last.

People did that, I was pretty sure.

Could go Sho over Sean.

What I was most leaning towards.

Only, 'Sean' was what I responded to. In the world.

They called Sean and I answered.

So then: the matronym?

That was woke.

She who raised me.

Why should he get all the names?

Not to mention, as I'd only recently learned, Conroe wasn't even my birth great-grandpa. That was Rucker. Only Rucker hung himself when grandpa, Rucker's son, was one. Step-great-grandpa Conroe came later, when grandpa was eight. And only for four years. Conroe left grandpa's ma when grandpa in his teen years.

Rucker, though.

Crank out your first son.

Baby suddenly hogging all the wifey's attention.

Fuck this... I'm out!

At least he just hung himself.

Bullets are messy.

Wouldn't wanna make a mess.

So I guess Rucker would be the last option.

The pure-blood, patronymic.

But no.

Fuck Rucker.

Bitch ass.

Bowed out before the game even started.

———

Ahhhh.

This coffee hitting.

Moon peaking!

Bursting.

Stubbed out my cig.

Started rolling another.

Sho.

Had to be.

The writing self was the private self.

The hidden self.

Fa shoooo.

Guy I hadn't seen before, coming down the street.

Walking quickly.

Not carrying anything.

Timed my 'What up, man' head nod with when he passed.

He'd already been looking up at me when I looked up.

Held his gaze.

Lingered.

I lingered.

"Got another of those?"

"Suuure," I said, beckoning like Pull up a chair.

He sat on the top step leading up to the stoop.

Level with the stoop.

"Here, have this one," I said, handing him the one I'd just lit.

Sat back down on my chair wedged between the dresser drawers and bedside table I'd found, separately, in trash piles.

Started rolling myself another.

When I looked up again he was looking up at me again.

Dragging, head tilted, gaze intense.

Like 'checking me out' intense.

"Ah, this moon though, huh?" I said.

He looked up at the moon.

After some moments, once I'd gotten my cig going, "What you doing out and about this late, anyhow?"

"Shoot," he said, shifting. "You know."

I looked up. Like No, not really.

"Just out here trolling?"

"Just out here. Tryna get it."

"It?"

"That fire. I need that fire."

"I see," I said. "That fire, yes."

I dragged.

He dragged.

"You stay around here?"

He indicated a direction.

"OK," I said. "Well hey, what's your name."

"Shawn."

I looked at him eyes wide.

Like Gotta be kidding me.

"Bro mine too!"

I stood, walked over, and dapped him up before, not knowing where else to walk, returning to my seat and sitting.

"Ess aitch? Ess ee ay?"

"Ess aitch."

"OK. I'm ess ee ay. But hey. Sounds the same, innit" — observing, based on the acceleration of my speech, that the stimulants were hitting.

He smiled, amused.

Dragged.

I dragged.

"So you just out here—"

"Hey," he said, serious suddenly.

"You hung?"

"Whassat?" I said, cocking my head like Come again?

"I said," he said. "Are you *hung*?"

He was smiling again.

"Liiike..."

He nodded down.

"Ah. Like that." I dragged. "You know. Not so much, honestly."

"Can I see?"

I let out a laugh. "Nah, bro. Nah."

"I'm really good," he said. "The best."

"I believe you."

He gestured like So what's the problem?

"That's just...not my mode right now," I said.

He stared at me blankly.

After some moments: "So that's how...You able to survive like that? Doing that?"

He looked down. Shook his head. Sighed.

"I'm able to get," going quiet a sec, rubbing his face, either itchy or distressed I couldn't tell. Then looking up, grinning, and saying, "I'm able to get what I need."

"Food?"

"Not food," the moon and his crackling ember appearing, seemingly suddenly, like the lone lights in a sea of darkness. "But that fire. When I need it, I do what I gotta to get it."

I considered this.

Then said, "I feel you, bro. I fucking feel you," taking one final, greedy drag before stubbing out and stuffing the butt into the overflowing butt jar on the bedside table.

4

HORSE RIDER

February 2018

Got a ziplock of shrooms from V in the mail.

For my birthday.

Bday shrooms.

With a melted stick of fair-trade chocolate to chase em with.

Received the package two days before my birthday, but opened it anyhow.

On my way back inside from my 1 p.m., morning smoke.

Partway through my morning coffee.

I was on a tight schedule for my day's first shift, but I took a sec to read the card.

It was a quote.

Just a quote.

Characteristically cryptic stuff from V.

When art, become independent, depicts its world in dazzling colors, a moment of life has grown old and it cannot be rejuvenated with dazzling colors. It can only be evoked as a memory. *The greatness of art begins to appear only at the dusk of life.*

By some guy Guy.

'Guy Debord.'

Hm.

Nice.

—

Espresso from coffees numbers two through four started spewing steam, so set down the shroomies and attended to it.

Turned off the stove, dumped the espresso into the mason jar with the dented lid from that once it went flying off my bike on Market. Added equal parts half-and-half and ice. Sealed the lid shut and stuck it into my bike's bottle holder.

Same espresso pot V and I kept on deck in Humboldt, dangling off the backpack strap. To spark up with the single-burner camp stove for that trim-break quickie.

Handle melted and misshapen from that once we got too stoned and forgot about it.

1:17.

Lunch rush waning.

Grabbed the messenger bag ex bae gave me two birthdays ago, that was now my designated Postmates bag, but that I'd never used when ex bae was still main. Checked that there was still Saran wrap in the Saran wrap roll.

That there were backup drink carriers.

That there was my emergency poncho. On the bottom, beneath my interior, Postmates Hot/Cold Bag™.

There were.

Would any liquids be spilled on this day?

Fuck no they wouldn't.

Filled my empty smartwater bottle with water from the Brita and stashed it aside my Postmates Hot/Cold Bag™, inside the messenger bag.

Grabbed Ferrante's *The Story of a New Name: My Brilliant Friend Book 2* (2013), and stuck her, my notebook, a pencil, and a uni-ball in their designated ziplock.

Which I then positioned beneath my Postmates bag, above my folded poncho, to create a flat surface for the drink tray. And to furnish me with between-delivery entertainment.

Between-delivery Work.

The Work I'd do during 'work'-breaks.

Wallet and phone inside a ziplock, inside my fanny pack; above them, Bluetooth speaker, also in a ziplock.

Ziplock in case it rained, which it looked like it was gonna.

Synthetic neon-yellow snapback on my head. Bike chain around my neck.

Good to go.

"Well—almost."

Nabbed the shrooms, stuck em in the fanny pack, and hit it.

If one wanted consistent work, this job was trash.

Some hours one got up to five deliveries; others, none.

If one waited around, hunting for deliveries, one lost patience real quick.

One had to *choose* to be available, strategically stationed, on one's own terms.

Find the most popping area. Sit. And wait.

Commit to already happening to want to be in the area that was most popping.

The area that was most popping, I'd assessed, was Rittenhouse. Rittenhouse Square.

Benches, pillars, and grass upon which to sit, read, and write.

Reading and writing, sitting on benches or pillars or grass, then, was my job.

With occasional, reading-and-writing-encouraging bike excursions to break up the reading and writing.

Not too shabby! I reminded myself as I *skrt*-ed down Lancaster, picked up Market, crossed the Schuylkill, cut south at 22nd, and posted up on my designated pillar in the square.

———

Had I gotten a delivery immediately, I mighta been able to help myself.

But I was ten pages into Ferrante, and it was already 2 damn near.

Still no dings.

So I did what I'd been trying not to. What I knew I was inevitably gonna.

Made a melted fair-trade choco-bar sammie, shroomies in the middle, swiveling one time to ensure no one saw, and railed that shit.

Was at the part where things were getting spicy between Lenu and Nino.

Had me wet.

Artist bae, who'd read all four books, when I mentioned how lit Nino was, had said "Nino's a fuccboi. Fuck Nino."

"What?!" I'd said, not understanding.

But now I was curious.

Reading quickly.

I wanted to know how/why.

They were flirting on the beach.

Lenu getting tanner and sexier every day.

Feeling herself.

I was feeling myself, basking in the muted midday sunlight on the Rittenhouse lawn, waiting on the shroomies to start hitting. Poncho-wrapped backpack beneath my butt, to prevent body-heat loss to the ground.

"Just like me and V!" I thought after reading the part about Lenu getting the letter from Lila.

About how all the writing Lenu, the protagonist/writer, had ever written was, ultimately, mimicry of her bestie Lila's writing.

How unbridled and unaware of being art, and the best kind, Lila's writing felt.

V was whom I sent my first book, on Bolaño and the Juárez femicides, the minute I finished it.

Not published, but completed 'book.'

Semblance of.

The one to tackle all the Qs.

About why men were men, women women, and fathers rapists.

Thought he'd be impressed.

If by nothing else, by its ambition.

Ninety-K words, 12 monthly chapters, set and written over a year.

But no.

He'd evaded me when I'd harassed him about it.

Had said he was still thinking on it. Still digesting.

But after X times of harassing him, he'd caved and admitted he only got 11 pages in before bowing out.

This right after I'd finished trying to walk across country.

Failing to.

Back home barista-ing.

Renting a room out of my high school home.

V living out of his Vanagon.

One-upping me.

Showing me how it was done.

How to live outdoors successfully.

Sustainably.

Ex bae, after saving my broken ass on day 100 of walking,

at the base of the Rockies, was living over the hill in Red-wood City.

V's (now ex) bae living in Santa Cruz.

V leaning on her somewhat to sustain the façade of out-here-ness. For showers, etc.

Not admitting it.

Me flexing like I'd walked across, even though I hadn't.

Basking in others' convincings that Still! 100 days! To the Rockies!

Even though. Still. I hadn't.

I'd gotten saved.

Both of us flexing, leaning on our baes, jerking each other off for how woke we were.

How Out Here.

Except not, somehow, when it came to my Bolaño book.

"The writing is clunky. He tries to say too much in each sentence," I deduced he'd said to S, his college friend and acquaintance of mine, when S commented, on a blog post I'd posted about my walk: "Love this! His writing isn't clunky! He doesn't try to say too much every sentence!"

•

Got a ding right when I'd forgotten I was waiting on a ding.

After I'd stopped tasting the shroomies' aftertaste.

Chipotle on 15th, five blocks over.

Mounted the steed and started pedaling, wobbling initially.

Weaving through picnickers on the grass, in the square.

Insinuated myself into eastbound Locust traffic, behind a 21 bus.

Sustained-exhaling out of my nose so as to not inhale its fumes.

You didn't need to wait in line for Chipotle pickups.
　　You could just go to the front.
　　To the reg'.
　　How it felt, pulling up, was bank robber-y.
　　Especially on colder days when I was balaclava'd up.
　　Like Fuck it mask on.

I got there so quickly the order wasn't ready yet.
　　So rolled a cig and posted out front, on a cement pillar.
　　Took in my surroundings.
　　There was a girl about my age, sitting across from me, also on an elevated cement thing.
　　Also smoking.
　　As I remember it, I started feeling tingles / heightened self-awareness at this point.
　　I remember bc I couldn't handle how *close* to me she felt.
　　How defined her features.
　　Mesmerizingly so. Like once I looked, I couldn't look away.
　　How I was convinced she thought it weird I'd sat across from her, on such a similar perch.
　　Like it was too symmetrical, how we were sitting.
　　Dishonestly symmetrical.
　　Disrespectfully ordered.
　　Disrespectful to the Chaos.
　　Of the city; of the World.
　　Everything quiet of a sudden.
　　Pin-drop-y.

Which seemed strange.

Bc cities are loud.

A year after my walk I moved to North Oakland / Berkeley / Emeryville — on the intersecting intersection — with ex bae.

With ex bae's cat, even though I was allergic.

Working on my Walk Book. About my failed walk.

V went to Senegal.

To join his mom on a cob-house-building mission that was Christian missionary–like even though it wasn't.

To bike across, from site to site, eventually to Cabo Verde, on Africa's western coast.

It was the Walk Book 2.0.

One-thousand-point-O.

Actual otherworldly exploration/investigation.

No septic.

Poop fields/shores.

No lights at night.

Muhfuckers out here slanging kerosene.

Real world shit every self-hating woke American would do well by acquainting themselves with. That self-hating woke Americans didn't have a clue about.

Which fact made his record — blog posts, unlike mine with pictures and less pretentious, if written/inspired by my initial 165K-word Walk Book draft, which he was reading and would read in its entirety while writing/biking — infinitely more important.

Which cast my project as an inefficiently paced view of what any road-tripper could get driving to Bonnaroo: rest areas, highways, trash-strewn shoulders.

And all this to say nothing of the writing.

———

Reading his posts as posted, sitting in my NOBE studio, railing Benadryls, getting progressively less attractive to ex bae due to domestic overexposure, I was rapt.

Heart beating.

Palms sweating.

His syntax was different.

Sentences shorter.

Pacing effortless.

No theories of writing grafted onto the recounted events.

Flowing in a way in spite of, or maybe even more so due to, typos.

The sense of it being a living record of someone genuinely trying to share about totally new and novel events so apparent in the writing.

Not obstructed by anything technical.

Like mine, I was forced to admit, just like V had said, had been.

Cruising down Ridge after picking up at a burger spot on Girard in Fairmount I'd never been to.

Neither the burger spot, nor the neighborhood.

Ridge ran SSE from Philly's NW corner to its SE.

Cut diagonally across the grid.

Hypotenuse-d the grid.

Went against the one-way flow discouraging folks from outer hoods from entering.

Allowed someone out of the game, off in the northwest corner, near Strawberry Mansion and other wastelands up there, to get back in with relative ease.

Like, say, a bike courier blown off course, out into the outer reaches of Fairmount.

He could get back in the game.

What I'm saying is I fuck with Ridge.

The burgers were for someone in a hotel / convention center–type place on Broad.

Some event going on, in the lobby.

Folks dressed fancy but also some with name tags.

Seemed lit but possibly professional.

On my way up, two girls about my age followed me into the elevator.

Both falling over themselves / catching each other.

I stood in front of them so they wouldn't be weirded out by me standing behind them.

Kept my earbuds in and eyes forward.

On floor three of five, removed the burger bag from the Postmates bag inside my messenger bag.

Lil greased but not too bad.

Seen worse.

On floor five, as I was exiting, one girl yelled "Where you going? Come party!"

I turned back and caught a glimpse of what looked to be one of the girls undressing the other, untying her dress's neck strap, behind the closing elevator doors.

Six months ago, last August, V had been living out here. In Philly. With me and roomie bro.

He'd pulled up for the three-month, seasonal stint.

Working as a compost pickup driver.

Working on our follow-up mixtape to the previous summer's.
Roomie bro even hopped on a track.

Then we got into a fight about dishes and tidiness.

We'd been splitting a room with a makeshift divider down the middle, tryna stretch out the weed bands we'd saved the previous fall.

The money I'd chosen to spend cohabitating with V rather than with ex bae, whom I'd followed out to Philly, and who had just started grad school.

Shit got too close.

He tried to tell me how to live, to mom me, I told him fuck off, then he dropped a diss track clearly taking shots at me, that I heard on SoundCloud even though he was upstairs when he posted it. I sneered at him next I saw him, leaving for his 4 a.m. composting shift, and told him Bro you got it twisted. I don't know what you think this is. But it ain't that. We ain't in a relationship bruh, stay in your fkng lane.

He copped a plane ticket back to Cali the next day.

When I got back to the elevator, I pressed the down button. The door dinged.

It hadn't moved.

The girls were still in there.

One was in her underwear, tryna pull on a dress that was snagged on her heel. The other, seeing me, tried to human-shield her from my sight.

"What in the actual — " I started to say, before the human-shield girl, giggling up a storm, jabbed at the door-close button.

The door closed.

"Just a sec!" I heard her yell. Like this was a goddamn bathroom I was waiting for.

After more rustling and laughing from inside, one asked the other if they should let me in, the other agreed, and they yelled You can come in now!

I hit the button and entered.

Two Augusts ago, same shit:

V and I were up in Humboldt doing freelance weed work, and the first break we got after a big payout, about a month in, he was tryna throw down five hundo-plus on a music festival and drugs. I was like I'm not tryna do that, I'm tryna save, I'm done with that life, he was like Whatever bro and copped the ticket anyway. But he was living with me. In my van. Shit blew up the next day, at a campground north of Arcata. I told him What are you gonna do about getting there. You're totally relying on me. You're pulling audibles that aren't in sync with the gang. You're wilding.

He was like What do you mean how am I gonna get there?

I mean all your shit's in my van. I'm your ride rn.

He was like How you mean? I got legs.

I was like Oh so you gon' walk outta here?

I'll walk outta here. I'll walk outta here tomorrow morning.

OK bro. We'll see about that.

The next morning, he packed it up and hit it.

This like a 30-minute drive north of Arcata. Directly off the 101. On the ocean.

This fool actually walked his ass to Arcata, crashed out in the woods by Humboldt State there. Then caught a rideshare down to Santa Cruz.

I went north, to an isolated campground on the border of Oregon, and read *Don Quixote* (1620) for a fortnight.

Right before the festival weekend, before we had to go back

in for the next work stint, I caved. Copped a ticket and hit him up, breaking the silence.

We linked up and were good again.

The one girl had changed into a different-colored dress.

Musta spilled something on the first.

Half expected them to re-invite me to whatever party they were hitting.

But, once dressed, they were calmer.

Asked me some questions about Postmates.

"So you're saying I can order McDonald's and have a dude on a bike bring it to me?!"

"Bro pretty much," I said, grinning.

•

The intersection out front was where Broad hit Ridge hit Fairmount, plus a couple side alleys there.

Lil isosceles island in the middle.

More a jacked-up asterisk, or tree, than an intersecting T, from bird's eye.

Sat on the steps facing out onto Broad and this side street Potts, for a smoke.

Sun descending ahead.

Nippy, still.

I considered how best to get home from here.

Fairmount, if driving.

But there were all these mellow one-ways to hit, to avoid this sort of congestion, on Broad.

Melon, Mount Vernon, Green.

One-ways only those living on drove down.

Highly coast-able one-ways.

Employing the full lane.

Guide hand barely touching.

Posture erect.

Slaloming slightly, as potholes dictated.

But otherwise.

Cruising.

Fanny-pack Bluetooth slapping, still.

But something mellow.

Something scenic.

I thought about how this mode was prehistoric, to the first horse riders of the north, who'd figured this out. How to harness Nature without disconnecting from it completely. In contact with the unmediated, unscreened Outdoors.

The evolutionary discovery of Out Hereness one step above walking.

Out Hereness in technological motion.

"I'm a muhfucking horse rider bruh!" I yelled at a passing F-150, observing a light drizzle coming on but not caring.

5

SIDE BAE

March 2018

Went over to side bae's to fuck.
    Or sleep, conceivably.
    Or neither.
    But how she'd framed it, via text, last time.
    Come over lemme blow you like you've never been.
    A masculinity challenge.
    I'd gotten shook.
    Excited/shook.
    But mostly shook.
    Could I live up to whoever she thought I was.
    Was I the dude she wanted me to be.
    Was I that savage.
    Honestly didn't know.
    Didn't think so.
    Same time, wasn't about to pass up on finding out.

This time, though.
    I wanted things to go different.
    Didn't leave me feeling great, how they ended, last time.
    Never said I was gonna sleep over.
    Nor did I know that that was what she'd wanted.
    But she had.

She felt she was owed this, for what she'd done, it seemed.

I wasn't going to sleep over for anything though.

Not last time; not this.

I didn't do that.

Didn't sleep at night when alone even!

Damn sure wasn't gonna with another.

Not to mention, her dang cat, I reminded myself, popping a Benadryl as I pulled up to her stoop.

Side bae was in coy mode.

Coy and pretty.

She wanted to watch a show together.

Like we were OD booed up.

I was game, I said, my manhood recoiling inside me slightly.

She had her laptop open on an ottoman.

Love seat set up with pillows, blanket.

"Gotta go to the bathroom, brb," she said, bounding upstairs.

I unbundled.

Sat on the love seat.

Tapped her mousepad to see what she was thinking, show-wise.

YouPorn.com's privately familiar homepage lit up the screen.

Caught me way off guard.

Heart pounding, I looked around to see if anyone saw me see, even though I knew damn well no one did.

Didn't know what to do so just left it, acting like I hadn't noticed as I heard the toilet flush upstairs.

I'd jokingly proposed watching porn with ex bae before.

But she'd never been down, always jokingly declining.

Honestly assumed no women watched it, besides curiously once or twice.

Tried not to, but saw side bae differently now.

"Oh whoops," she said, noticing the screen.

X-ed it out and sat.

Also acted like I hadn't seen.

After an episode of *The Marvelous Mrs. Maisel* (2017), with her feet up on my lap — digging the contact but also feeling slightly and literally held down — we went upstairs.

She started undoing her clothes.

Lay back on her bed and gave me a look like Come get this.

Wasn't feeling it though.

Wanted to be.

But wasn't.

Unable to get myself to.

I cuddled up next to her.

"Gonna be the accommodating one this time," I thought, and conveyed with my actions.

Sat next to her and held her hand, touching myself noncommittally as she lay on her back, eyes closed touching herself.

With quick circular movements just around the clit, without going inside, in a way I'd never realized was a way to do it.

Thought you always had to go inside.

After she came she seemed tired, but nestled up to me, on her knees, on the mattress, and sorta cupped my balls.

Unsure whether she felt obligated to bring me to completion since she had herself, or if she genuinely wanted to; either way, I sensed it wasn't gonna happen.

Was at maybe a quarter mast and dropping.

Had I been hard and into it, I probably woulda let her do whatever she wanted.

But I told myself that even had I been, I woulda done what I did.

Which was nudge things away from the direction they were headed.

Tucked myself back into my boxers—I was protruding out of my right leg hole, unable to commit to full nudity—and lay on my side, by her side, playfully.

Like we were girlfriends telling each other secrets during a sleepover.

Before, playing off of a convo I had with my lil sis the other day about pressure points, improvising and flipping over.

Sixty-nining, but without the oral sex.

Grabbed her still-ankle-socked foot and pressed.

"Ahh," she said, first relaxing but then, as I pressed elsewhere, flinching.

"Ooh, ow," she said.

"The parts that hurt are the parts we gotta press, I'm pretty sure," I said.

I was feeling so woke.

I'd passed up on oral sex to provide medical insight/practice.

This was wrong; I knew that seeing her bring herself to completion so outside of me, with me as a mere accessory to the event, unhinged some default ability to objectify I relied on to get off with women.

But ignored this—blocked it out—and focused on my wokeness.

Felt intoxicated by it.

Was almost turned on by it, were my manhood responsive.

Was turned on egoistically.

"OK, here's where hurts worst?" I said, pressing this one spot just inside and in front of her heel.

She nodded, finger between teeth.

"K, let's work here then."

I pressed, harder now, less hard then, responding to her bodily and vocal responses.

Meandered around her foot a bit, but always returning to the same spot.

Side bae's kitty, who disappeared behind furniture on the far side of her room whenever we were fucking, sensed something was different with this type of touching.

She hopped up onto the bed, purring like she wanted to get in on the action.

Side bae stroked the kitty as I pressed her feet.

"So each spot actually corresponds to an organ or body part. An organ or body part that's ailing," I said.

She stayed silent a sec, squinting and going Ow-ee as I pressed.

"What body part does that spot relate to?"

"I think insomnia," I said.

Since that's where it usually hurt for me.

I had this glass foot massager with a handle my mom gave me long ago, that I used to hit my own pressure points with.

You could massage yourself, but it was better when someone else did it. To push you past your limits.

And if you did do it yourself, it worked better when you had some sort of external device.

"But that's actually a little lower. Here, lemme look it up."

I looked it up, while continuing to press with my off hand.

"Oh damn," I said when I saw what it said.

"What?" side bae said. "What does it say?"

"Uterus. It says uterus," I said, showing her.

46

6

BROKE BOI

Spring Equinox Eve 2018

It's been two months since I've thrown down on anything besides tobacco and rolling papers since I'm two months behind on rent and it's been two months since I got my SNAP card approved and my check from my construction gig has yet to arrive and every bike delivery payout I get goes straight to keeping my almost maxed out credit card almost maxed out, but tonight I'm making a concession since my next credit card payment isn't till the end of the week and I can't, haven't for the life of me been able to, find any of my goddamn uni-ball pens — need me my uni-ball pens — despite all the room-cleaning and organizing and item-culling I've been doing for when, once my check arrives, I will leave this godforsaken city I don't even know why I returned to, or no I do actually, I came back to mend things with X, then still O, so I could be near her, fake woke-ly 'be there for her,' since her recurring gripe was always 'her being there for me' while I ran all over the country in my van or on foot, only now I'm near her, much too near, and need to get out, away, long gone, especially so since the book about running all over the country in my van or on foot I wrote for her is complete, has been submitted, is out of my hands until further notice, if ever, after much self-destructive, responsibility-shirking, job-dodging, mostly nocturnal and consistently manic dedication, meaning it's now time to write *again, only I can't find any of my goddamn*

47

uni-balls, all I have is this U-Haul ballpoint that keeps dying on me every third word, so I've decided, have been left with no choice but, to break my abstention from copping anything besides the entirely essential, to bite the bullet and trek out to CVS late-night to cop a uni-ball two-pack, only if I'm to do that, figure I might also grant myself the concession of copping one candy item, something chewy or chocolatey or nutty, since during these past two months with zero or negative money, of doing without all amenities beyond the entirely essential, I've also been deprived of cannabis and stimulants and psychedelics, one of which, at separate points since I stopped running all over the country in my van or on foot, I'd self-prescribed in micro- or perhaps-not-so-micro-doses so that I'd be optimally equipped to write the very best book about running all over the country in my van or on foot, which was, at root, an apology to X for running all over the country all those years when I could have Been There, with Her, Working on Us—all of which strategic self-medication of course had nothing to do with her deeming me unfit to remain her O—all to say, I've been such a good boy of late, the least I could do is grant myself one dose of sucrose, yes, that's what I'll do, only by the time I gear up, decide on which podcast I'll walk to, walk, and get to the CVS candy aisle, the kind I'm eying, turns out, are 3 for $3, 2 for $3, or 1 for $1.50, so I mean, sure I could just get one like I said I would, only Reese's Pieces or Milk Duds, who's to say which is better, neither is since both are best, except both is $3 and both plus another is also $3—damn right I'm looking at you, Charleston Chew—so fuck it might as well cop all three, and stat, the way this graveyard security guard keeps eying me, pacing up and down this aisle like I am at this hour, making jerky, juke-like movements each time I change my mind, forcing him to look up from the YouTube video he'd been pleasantly enjoying before I had to pull up and kill his vibe, so now I'm

48

at self-checkout, clutching my movie-sized candy boxes like I'm prudently prepping to save a buck or two at the concession stand at, say, the Black Panther (2018) *premiere I've bought tickets in advance for, like I'm a regular ole twentysomething doing regular ole twentysomething things, off to a movie with a couple pals, coworkers or classmates, all set to surprise em by providing em their choice of Pieces, Duds, or Chews so they can save a chunk of their hard-earned paycheck or stipend or grant money on this weekend outing they've been looking forward to all week, only it's not the weekend, it's Monday night, technically Tuesday morning, and there are no pals, is no paycheck nor a movie, there's only this 3 for $3 deal and this pain I will try to sugar-coma my way out of once I get home, if I even get home before finishing all three, I'm not even at Walnut and my Pieces are dust, and come Market I'm combo-ing my Dud dregs with my all-but-chewed Chews, chomping like a cow or mouth-breather how moist my mouth is, jeez I'm damn near home already, pump the breaks a sec would ya, the whole point was to* deliberately *ingest the sugar* in conjunction *with caffeine in order to optimally spearhead* the new writing *Jesus fuck the goddamn uni-balls —*

II

Spring

1

EDITOR BAE

Last Easter (2017)

BoltBused to NYC to link with editor bae.

    Met her at school, when I went back to graduate.

    After 'dropping out.'

    Then returning.

    Then failing to fulfill graduation requirements.

    Two years late.

    Right after ex bae got pregnant.

    After ex bae terminated the pregnancy.

    Bc, regardless of how she felt (could I ever know?), how could she not have.

    How much of a broke boi I'd been.

    Shit, still was.

    When I'd been feeling hella un-sexy.

    Hella guilty.

    Ex bae tired of my shit.

    Of my 'books.'

    My 'art.'

    Lol art.

    Editor bae was about it tho.

    Outta nowhere.

    Like Books? Fkn *books*?! You write books!

    Get naked.

    Of course, never told her about ex bae, then not yet ex.

Not even fully main, given we hadn't yet cohabitated.
I mighta sorta told her.
Mumbled it, then petered out.
While she was tugging at my belt.
Then told myself I totally told her.
And ex bae.
Told myself I totally told her, too.
About editor bae.
But of course: only mumbled it.
When she wasn't listening.
Ex bae was squarely ex now though.
Time to dive back in.
To 'date.'

Pulling up to 11th Ave & W 34th Street still lit from last night.
Off the addies and last of the rocks V threw me.
That pure shit.
That I took alone.
Enough to be humming — to be immersed in the Lil Peep I'd been banging to all night, all ride — but not so much that I was grinding my teeth.
We met at an ice cream spot in Greenwich Village.
Hella date-y, this mish.
Only time I ever ate ice cream was alone, at night, after the 3 a.m. Fresh Grocer run.
And this wasn't even ice cream.
This was mfkn gelato.
With flavors like cashew and salted caramel and honey basil.
Bro honey basil!

———

But editor bae.

Looking fly the minute I pulled up.

Partially erect within seconds of seeing her.

She looked different than I remembered.

But fly.

Indisputably fly.

Started rambling about myself off the rip.

Wilding.

Tryna impress her, and to a degree maybe succeeding somewhat.

But not listening.

Not really.

Not until she'd drop the bomb about what happened to her in college.

Only then would she, as a person, register.

As an evolving human beyond however she appeared to / affirmed me, in the moment.

And even that was difficult to fully register, with the last of the rocks I was dealing with.

That I railed, in the bathroom of the coffee shop we pit-stopped at pre-dinner.

For 'staying awake' purposes, I told myself.

But this much later.

First we had to eat our ice creams.

Our gelatos.

Popping day at Washington Square.

Sun blasting.

Everyone out, about, and lowkey naked.

All places to sit sat upon.

Not only the benches but the concrete railings.

The grassy patches.

Folks chatting.

Looking around watching people watch other people watching them.

Or, if not watching, aware of being watched.

Or maybe only I was.

Told editor bae about the mixtape I'd just dropped with V.

She told me what she'd been listening to.

Impressed me by citing Smino.

My salted caramel was perfect: not too sweet nor salty.

We sampled each other's.

When we finished our gelatos, we roamed, in search of more food.

I started out confident, proposing places we passed, till I started seeing the prices.

Not cut out for dating in the city, on my courier salary.

Courier 'salary.'

But it was all good; she said she didn't mind.

At a diagonal intersection, I removed my unbuttoned button-up.

Dangled it from the backpack strap.

Underneath was my Gal Pal Softball League cutoff tank.

Guns out.

Flexing.

She acted unaware but noticed, I noted.

I asked her what drugs she did, considered telling her which I was on.

Adderall and weed.

Occasionally both.

I told her I'd dabbled when she asked whether I'd ever tried that combo.

By the time we made it to the vegan burger spot in the East Village, on her rec, we were hangry.

She looked exhausted.

It ended up no cheaper than the fancy spots we'd passed up on.

Finally mentioning editor bae to ex bae was the nail.

The straw.

The spine-cracker — all 'at.

What unleashed the rage.

The desire, on ex bae's part, to break me.

What was craziest was I coulda sworn I'd told her.

This was early spring, when things were still salvageable.

When ex bae only humoring women.

Me microdosed and in my feelings.

Coming through like "A woman. Really. Who."

Ex bae being like "Bae, it's a phase. A curiosity. Just sit tight. We're obviously gonna end up together. Just can't trust you rn," here referencing side bae.

How I'd told her side bae and I had made out during mine and ex bae's 'break,' weeks after this past shitshow New Year's.

"Ah," I'd said, flagrantly clueless. "That seems to be the trend."

"What does."

"Women not trusting me."

I'd told her I'd gone and visited editor bae. That editor bae had agreed to edit my book.

"Why doesn't she trust you?"

"I mean. You know."

" . . . "

"Bc what happened. Back at school. But you already know about that."

She hadn't known about that.

How she cried that day was different. Not resigned, like before, but furious.

Fury-like.

Tears not focal, but witnesses to the rage.

Accessories to the primary thing.

She squinted her eyes, compressed her body, and lashed out.

Like FUCK you, bro.

Disgusted.

Before hitting the burger joint, editor bae and I pit-stopped at a coffee shop.

To recoup. Revaluate our plan.

And to re-up, literally, for me.

I'd started rolling the night before, around 9 p.m.

Hadn't particularly wanted to, but had this thing about having uningested drugs on deck.

Doing them all, in one sitting, was part of my recovery from them.

Once I did em, would no longer be able to do em! How I saw it.

But come 2 a.m., it became apparent I wasn't gonna conk.

And my bus was at 8:30 a.m., for our 11 a.m. meet time.

Only way out was through!

Re-upped near sunup, pre-shower and -final packing of things.

Leaving me a key's worth for the day in case I started crashing.

Which I did, right about the time we evaluated our third, too-expensive menu.

Might've even proposed the coffee shop stop *specifically to* re-up.

And, to add sus-ness to injury, I not only killed the last of it but snorted it.

In the bathroom, without telling editor bae, while she thought I was peeing.

Then licked the bag like a fiend.

Tf was wrong with me.

"What do you mean non-consensual?" I asked editor bae, trying to calibrate my vision.

"I mean I literally said No. There was no ambiguity."

"Je-zus," I said.

"What the fuck," I said, earnestly furious.

As furious as one could be on five points of uncut MDMA.

I didn't know why she was telling me this.

Hearing her tell me what she told me, I didn't not empathize.

I wanted to protect her.

I felt rage.

Racked my brain for who it coulda been.

Considered how I might track down and inflict pain on him.

But I misunderstood her.

It wasn't about me.

Her telling me this didn't preclude me from those very same tendencies that made him do what he did.

Those very same potentialities.

But that's how I took it.

"I'm one of the good ones!"

2

SEYMOUR

Good Friday 2018

Postmates was piloting a new alcohol function.

You could pick up alcohol, so long as you scanned the customer's ID.

Only, they hadn't figured it out according to the specific order, just to the restaurant type.

I didn't figure this out till I'd biked from Rittenhouse to a bar in the Gayborhood, then 5 miles north to the Temple dorms. So Broad and like Diamond. Way up there. To deliver an order of fries.

Just fries.

But bc these fries were from a bar, my phone kept refusing payment unless I scanned the customer's ID.

"I mean, I only have my school ID," the girl said, shrugging. "And anyways I'm only 18."

She looked at the precautionary friend she'd brought down with her, who shrugged back.

"Jesus fuck this fucking app," I said, pacing, tryna figure out the move.

Undergrads in sweats and slides, shuffling in and out the vestibule, through the security turnstile.

The guard on staff eyed me.

Put his hand on maybe a Taser.

Gave him a look like Don't even with me, bro.

60

Before going, "OK, know what? Just take em," handing over the paper bag. "I'll figure it out."

Postmates made me bike all the way back to the bar before paying me out.

Another 5 miles.

To 'return the item.'

Their GPS stalked me all the way there, to make sure.

Payout turned out decent, like $13, since the mileage was so bananas.

But now I was fucking beat, and people were raging their asses off in the Gayborhood.

Friday night.

I dismounted. Walked some.

Passed a club I'd never passed, MilkBoy, on 11th. Open side wall, house music pounding, muhfuckers dressed fancy turning up.

Veered onto the street to shimmy past a group of girls shimmering in glitter, taking up the whole sidewalk.

Stepped in a puddle of possibly vomit.

Rubbed my shoe on a pile of gravel, in a construction zone, going FUCK SHIT MOTHERFUCK.

Going Yeah yeah yeah, to the stares.

Plunked down on an elevated, sill-type platform of a vaguely financial-seeming building on Walnut, across the street from that Chipotle there.

Plugged in the earbuds, took out my notebook, and started transcribing what I'd meant to earlier, from Bolaño's *The Return* (2010):

Summoning some ghostly courage, I told myself that if it was a dream, the best (and the only) thing I could do was to go on dreaming. From experience I know that trying to wrench yourself out of a nightmare is futile and simply adds pain to pain or terror to terror.

I'd just been interrupted by a fuccboi-ass-lookin bro rolling deep in a bro-crew rocking designer, hair slicked smelling sexy, who made me stop writing and remove an earbud to go Weed? Pointing at my rollie, before going Oh, never mind, and walking off when I said Nahh bruh, 'bacc-y —

So was already keyed up when, not five minutes nor a paragraph later, I got interrupted again.

"Bus?"

I looked up.

Einsteinian-looking old dude rocking a faded dad hat and baggy dress clothes. Carrying two trash bags full of what looked to be more clothes.

"Here? I dunno dude. I'm just sitting here," making a show of holding my earbud outta my ear.

"So you're not waiting for the bus."

"I'm not waiting for the bus."

"But a bus *could* come here," he said, sorta to himself.

"A bus could," I conceded.

He nodded. Started pacing, craning his neck down Walnut then coming back.

Right when I hit play again he approached again.

"You know, these buses. You never know with these buses."

I stared at him. Looked around like Yo — *whose mans is this?*

"Oh. Excuse me," he said. "Seymour."

Like my indignation at him not letting me write JUST ONE FKNG SENTENCE before interrupting me again had been bc he hadn't introduced himself.

"Sean," I said.

I shook his hand.

"So tell me, Sean, what are you up to this evening? Night ride? Journaling?"

I closed my notebook.

"Working."

"Working?"

"Delivering things. Food, mostly."

"On that?" indicating my bike.

I nodded.

"Oof. Yeesh."

" . . . "

"And you're writing? What're ya writing?"

"You know. This and that."

"Stories?"

"Something like."

He nodded like Hm, OK.

Like OK, fair enough.

Like a 'Larry David scrutinizing nod.'

"Well hey, you know they have schools for that. An old friend of mine, Jerry, he used to write for, what's it called...*Harper's*! Used to teach at, uh, not Haverford—"

"Bryn Mawr?"

"The other one."

"Swarthmore."

"Swarthmore!"

I thought about whether or not to say what I was about to say. Then said, "Where I went."

His eyes lit up.

"Noo!" he almost yelled, not believing.

"Class of thirteen," I said, not mentioning the extra two years it took me to graduate.

His gaze and stance 180'd.

"You went there...and you're writing...but" — gesticulating, brow furrowed, like he was piecing together the damn Da Vinci Code — "now you're doing" — gesturally dismissing my bike — *"this?!"*

Sure, homie was a curmudgeonly fuck. But he was also so old and enthusiastic.

I wanted to know what the trash bags were all about.

He kept asking me if I'd been published in this or that mainstream-ass mag.

Going Man, if only.

Wouldn't that be something.

"You'd be able to quit...*this!*" cackling hoarsely.

"I mean, it ain't all bad," I said. "Gets me outside."

He looked at me like I didn't know what was good for me.

"Bro what *you* been doing? Shopping?" I nodded to his bags.

"Shopping? Ehhhh — "

But then the bus came.

"Oh man, here we are," he said, picking up his bags and indecisively turning back and forth, between me and the approaching bus.

The bus stopped. The door opened.

"Hey — Sam was it? I'm headed down to the Wawa on Broad for a coffee. Why don't you bike on over, we can keep talking a sec."

"At the Wawa?" I said.

The bus driver gestured like Tf bro.

Like On or off pal, chop chop.

"Yeah I wanna tell you about my friend Jer — "

"OK OK, meet you over there!" I said, shooing him so he'd get on the dang bus.

———

But then I actually did meet him over there.

I hadn't gotten a delivery in twenty minutes, it was almost midnight, and shit wouldn't pop off again till drunk folks started ordering Taco Bell around 2. Plus it was on my way home.

This Wawa was the belly of the beast.

Blown af.

A fkng shitshow.

I held the door open for a trio of yelling drunk girls: one wobbling and crying, eyeshadow streaking down her face; the other two stabilizing her.

I turned to see where they went.

Into an awaiting Uber.

I let the door go.

Two huge lines to either register, extending to the back sammie station.

Seymour about two-thirds the way back one of them.

Seeing me, he pointed frantically to the standing-only bar table facing Walnut.

Where, I noticed, he'd stashed his trash bags.

'Saving us a spot.'

Hit him with a thumbs-up and went over to the table, setting my bag beneath and leaning against it.

He kept wanting to tell me about MFA programs.

"You heard of the Iowa Writers' Workshop? My friend Jerry, the playwright..."

But I wanted to know what was good with him.

Took a good twenty to pry it out.

How he'd lost his spot a little while back.

Had been crashing with a friend, but then his friend moved.

Now he was just floating, waiting to hear back from places.

"That all your stuff?" I asked, eying the bags.

"Just about," he said. "But you know UPenn? I think UPenn might have a good writing program. Jerry used to read at the... Kelly Writers House? Was that it? Something like — "

I finally had to go "Dude, I don't give a shit about MFA programs. I'm not interested in writing for people who already read. Who consider themselves 'literary.' More 'literature' means more insulated, masturbatory bullshit completely irrelevant to the culture. I'm tryna write for people who *don't* read. Who don't give a shit about books."

He opened his mouth. Closed it.

"All these things you're harping on are *dis*advantages. All an MFA writer bio credit signals is that you're churning out more derivative crap. That you're out of touch with the people."

"What people?" he asked, genuinely clueless.

I actually rambled to this dude about 'the book I was working on.' About 'the time I almost walked across the country.'

That I had an 'editor-agent-friend' editing it.

At this Wawa. At midnight. On a Friday.

He was like That's great. But stories. You need to write stories. To *get your name out there.*

It was almost 1 a.m. by the time I'd heard Jerry's Yaddo story for the third time and turned Postmates back on, hoping to get saved by a ding.

Some show had just ended and a new wave of drunk folks filed in.

One group was three girls, three guys; fly outfits and 'dos, kicks and lineups, respectively.

The girls horseplaying about something or other as they passed, through a narrow corridor of space amidst the mayhem all around.

One playfully pushing another like *Shut up, you fkn stoopid,* the pushed girl sorta brushing against my big-ass Postmates bag, which I'd put back on since I was about to dip.

Seymour lifted up his coffee and stepped back, exaggerating 'trying to not spill it,' even though I took the entire brunt of the hit.

He looked back at the crew as they headed for the sammie counter, his face a fear/indignation combo.

Leaned in conspiratorially.

"Tellin ya, that's what's wrong with this city. With this country. Look at them! Animals, all of them."

"All of who?" I said.

But I knew how he meant it.

"Alright bro," I said, tugging on my backpack straps.

"Wait — you're going?"

"Gotta hit it. Deliver these drunchies," I said, untangling my earbud cords.

"Wait — where do you live?"

"Out west. Why?"

"By yourself? Housemates?"

"Housemate."

"What's your rent?"

I told him.

"Well is he leaving any time soon? Do you think you'd want to share an apartment?"

Oh boy.

"I don't think so, man. Sorry."

"Well OK," he said, looking so small and sad. Mousey face contracting around its snout, hunched back hunching.

I turned to leave.

Turned back.

"What about Jerry?" I asked. "Can't you crash with him?"

"Jerry?" he said. "Oh no. Jerry died in oh nine."

3

ICED-OUT HOMIE

May 2018

Sure I was a lil confused when my phone dinged for a pickup at the Vans store on Walnut.

Didn't know Vans slanged food, or that Postmates did kicks.

But didn't bat an eye. I hit accept. I did as I was told.

Ankle a softball since I ate shit last week, biking back from the beer spot, sixer in tow. To celebrate the arrival of my one-off construction gig check, all of which went to backlogged rent to the roomie.

Not even Postmating.

Going 5 m.p.h. in a light drizzle, turning onto 41st off of Haverford.

Getting distracted by a posse of youngins wheelying past on dirt bikes.

Looking right when turning left.

Before hitting the trolley tracks and doing a slo-mo somersault.

The slowest ever crash-out.

It had been two weeks and the Advils I was railing daily weren't doing much.

But shit bro. Had to do what I had to.

Refilled my smartwater bottle at the filtered tap at the Shake Shack oasis I was posted at and hit it.

•

Editor bae wasn't responding to my emails.

To my texts.

As of a week ago: voicemail.

She'd wanted to change this, rewrite that, and nix every part about ex bae. I hadn't been sure, but then just did what she said to.

Just doing what they said to was never the move, I had yet to learn.

We were seven months and twenty rewrites in.

Every rewrite the last, till she'd submit it to her agent-boss and we'd both get rich.

Till we'd become the ultimate power couple.

•

After navigating past two police blockades for an anti–Proud Boys march, I finally found a sign to lock my bike to.

Turned out the pickup was shoes.

SK8-Hi's, lit concrete grey / street-sign yellow colorway. And the fancy ones that cost a hundo instead of sixty-five.

My size.

"Guess you could just nab em, huh," the cashier, pretty baby-faced blond boy with surfer locks, said.

I hadn't considered this. But then did, looking down at my discolored, misshapen ankle.

Coulda used these hi-tops when I skidded out, honestly.

"Yeeeah, but then I'd have to quit."

The cashier shrugged like Your call, struggling to pick up the receipt I'd signed. It had adhered to the counter like a sticker from all my sweat. He got it, finally, but not before tearing it some.

•

I sent editor bae the latest iteration of my Walk Book early on a Friday, mid-November last year.

Edited down from 120 to 75K words, over the six previous, addied up and anguished months, since I'd first sent it.

I'd been working on a query for days and had homed in on three agents who seemed like they might fuck with it. Who represented authors I fucked with. Like, for example, the writer Sheila Heti's agent.

I'd been up all that previous Thursday night, and shot it out at around 7 a.m.

Then, at 8 a.m., on an impulsive whim, I sent it to editor bae too, even though we hadn't spoken since last we'd hung, last spring.

Since she'd abruptly ghosted.

So was surprised when she got back to me right away, saying Just read over your chapter and query and can you send the whole thing?

She was an editorial assistant at an NYC literary agency.

Sure! I said, sending it.

The next afternoon, Saturday, she emailed me saying she read the whole thing, and loved it, and was I free to talk next steps tomorrow night.

The next night, Sunday, she called around 9.

Side bae was over, tryna Netflix and chill. We were like 5 minutes into the *SNL* ep she was tryna watch.

Ended up talking to editor bae, out on the stoop, for like an hour.

She first went over the things she liked. How she felt like she was right there with me, the whole walk. How my self-deprecation about my eventual failure made her laugh, and made my story unique. That my depiction of all the Bible Belt Midwesterners I encountered was so relevant to today's political climate.

I straight up almost started crying.

I couldn't believe someone had not only read, but had gotten it. This thing I'd toiled over so long and hadn't shown a soul.

No I definitely started crying.

I remember bc she stopped what she was saying, listened, and said Uhhhh — are you *crying*?!

Nah bro I'm not crying, I said quickly, wiping my face and putting an abrupt end to the crying.

She asked what other agents I'd sent it to.

I told her.

She asked if I wouldn't mind withdrawing them; she wanted to edit this with me and submit it to her agent-boss.

If it was accepted and did well, she said, this could be big for both of us.

I was speechless.

"I mean..." I said. "OK!"

I loved her so much right then.

"So. What next?"

"Well," she said, her tone shifting. "There are a couple parts we gotta cut."

"Cut?"

"Rework, let's say."

I was all ears.

"Well there are parts where you seem sorta entitled. Like when you steal the knife from the flea market in the Ozarks, for example."

"Well yeah," I said. "I *was* entitled — brash, clueless, self-satisfied — throughout. That's sort of the point of why I ended up stopping, innit."

"And then there are all the letters at the end," she said. "Thinking we cut those..."

"Cut? The letters?!"

"Oh and finally. The, uh...rape-y parts."

"Rape-y parts?"

"Well there's the time you...y'know...masturbate in the shower of that family who hosted you in Kansas. With the underage, Miss Kansas daughter."

"Well yeah, that was a precautionary—a preemptive—jerk-off, since walking and sleeping out on highways, under bridges, in cemeteries—not jerking it—for months really does make you a savage, and the whole point is to *look* at those impulses, to understand where they come from, that we all have em, so that they don't manifest in real life—that's all that matters, the real life actions, those that have consequences for others—"

"And again, when you say you were so full of lust when you finally saw R on day 100 that you...felt like you were going to...*enter her whether she wanted you to or not*?"

"Well, in my defense, she *did* want me to—"

"A little rape-y!"

Oh jeez.

R was ex bae.

Shit was getting complicated.

I should have seen everything that was to come coming, then and there.

I should have thanked her for her generosity, for reading the whole thing.

For the encouragement.

And then said: But this obviously won't work. There are way too many overlaps.

Like: This book is a result of me being so fucked up about ex bae; things are fucked between me and ex bae bc I cheated on her, with you; so now you wanna help me edit (and mostly nix) all the parts about ex bae; not to mention — I'm still definitely tryna enter you! I mean, only if you want me to. Obviously.

Just. Yeah. No.

Was what I shoulda said.

But shouldacouldawouldabruh.

"Y'know. OK. Let's work on it," was what I actually said.

•

Had to hit all kinds of detours, around the protest, to get to the drop-off.

Ninety-plus out and stupid humid.

Detours aside, just getting down the roads.

Walnut mazelike, how gridlocked. Even with the bike.

Engine exhaust stagnant, inhaling it unavoidable; horns honking louder than the fanny-pack Bluetooth; diesel grumbles groundshaking.

•

Back upstairs, side bae had finished the entire *SNL* episode.

She went Yay omg amazing! When I told her 'my book might be dropping.'

It felt like she got a hard-on bc I said that.

Which, who was I kidding, was why I said it.

But we started fucking around on my bed, all excited. Till she tried to get on top and one of the bed slats from the shitty twin IKEA frame I'd found on the sidewalk during Penn Christmas last year slipped, and the whole mattress went poof.

Dropped down to the ground like a lowrider with hydraulics.

I started laughing bc this happened all the time. Bc I was a broke-boi fuck with a bed so shitty that this alone should have disqualified me from any and all forms of intimacy.

But she got really hurt by this, and didn't believe me that it happened all the time.

She thought it was bc of her weight.

I told her No dude! It's definitely not, still laughing.

But the mood was dead. She looked around at my closet-room like, I can't.

Like You gotta come over to my house until you get a better bed.

A better room.

Then Ubered home, in tears.

•

Iced-out homie in a grey/yellow Adidas tracksuit, waiting for me when I pulled up.

Sorta purgatorial rando block, half of it 'bandos, north of Girard.

This was a cryptic flex, Postmating shoes.

Seeing him, I was glad I followed through with our contract. They were just shoes. And this, after all, was my job.

He was just tryna get drippy for the club.

In West the lines between the hood and where white folks lived were noticeable.

Traceable to specific streets.

I was just north of Haverford, for example.

Haverford the dividing line.

The outer barrier of the Penn/Drexel bike cops' domain.

Where the amount of trash on sidewalks spiked suddenly.

Where consistent streetlights stopped.

But college students weren't balling that hard.

The divide didn't seem as distinct in West as it did where the drop-off was, north of Girard.

It went: Logan Square, up 22nd, past the Eastern State Penitentiary, all nice, homey houses up to where College did this lil one-way fishhook north. Then the last coffee shops on Girard. Before going abruptly hood north of that.

More menacing without the college buffer.

Houses in the pre-hood part elevated, set back.

They seemed more vulnerable. They so blatantly had things to take.

So long as you could hold your own, the safer move was to live in the hood.

To stay in the hood.

To never have anything to take.

4

EX BAE

June 2018

Ex bae texted me a pic of the cutest lil black Lab.

With the caption *Doesn't he look like your aunt and uncle's dog Casey we housesat that once we housesat?*

Heart beating, palms wet, vision blurring, reading this.

What the fuck.

What was happening.

It was Thursday night.

I'd gleaned, from a previous check-in, that Z, her new boo, taught in NYC Tues–Friday.

Late week loneliness? An isolated lapse? Or something bigger.

Who were we kidding. Had to be something bigger.

Finally, after fifteen months, an admission of grave errors made on her part.

I was going to get back inside! I exclaimed, going half hard.

Linked for the seasonal check-in, the next day.

Initiated by me, went without saying.

At the Green Line on Powelton, a half mile away and equidistant from our houses.

Tried my best to stay calm.

To curb my excitement.

But I was already at half mast before I even arrived.

Erect within seconds of seeing her.

The breasts.

The demeanor, and shared memories, too.

But mostly: the breasts.

Couldn't imagine ever getting over them.

The attention she put into her appearance ('some'), however subtle, gave me hope.

Hope I would hold close.

That I would employ to fuel my purpose, and imagination-only masturbation, going forward.

We proceeded tentatively.

Housekeeping updates, to start.

Treading lightly.

Perfunctorily.

We'd go in, eventually.

I'd make sure of it.

Wouldn't leave till we did.

But for now.

I let her do the talking.

She referenced something I referenced in my most recent podcast.

I didn't say anything about it, and wasn't sure whether she'd even listened.

She must have.

But if I didn't bring it up, I couldn't be proven wrong in my assumption that she had.

Plus, not mentioning it coincided with the New Me: silent, attentive, selfless.

———

What I'd referenced in my latest podcast was something Sheila Heti had on hers.

On her podcast *Podcast with Raisins.*

She'd posted four episodes the past four years.

The first two were from the same week, in 2015; they were conversations with her brother, on a lake in Canada somewhere, about philosophy and the 'point' of art.

Possibly unserious.

But then, outta nowhere, she'd posted another. Last week.

A rant, really.

Going in about how critics misunderstood her most recent book, *Motherhood* (2018), as a polemic when what it was was a personal account.

How critics, in the U.S. especially, and especially since Trump, tended to politicize all art.

When art was that which specifically and categorically was not meant to be politicized.

To politicize art was to misunderstand its point.

To misuse its function.

How artists today were becoming more like entrepreneurs.

Not that there was anything wrong with entrepreneurs.

It was just...

Entrepreneurs were entrepreneurs; politicians, politicians; and artists, artists.

Everyone had their role.

The artist's role, Sheila reiterated, was not to be political.

It was to be honest and uncompromising.

To *shake* people.

To, as DFW via Rilke put it: disturb the comfortable and comfort the disturbed.

Ex bae reminded me of this; we used to tell each other this often.

———

When I first heard Sheila's take on the artist's role, it was revelatory.

Here I was thinking I'd botched all prospects, chosen a life-path outside of the one elders encouraged.

That women, ultimately, wanted me to take.

That ex bae dipping affirmed she too had wanted.

Social Darwinism.

By renouncing the political game, eschewing all entre-preneurialism, I'd...*proven myself unfit!*

Had fallen off.

Was washed.

But no.

Fuck that.

What Sheila was saying was: Darwinism didn't apply to individuals.

It wasn't that only the strongest man, the most fertile woman, survived.

Nah.

Groups had to survive.

This meant a group was strongest when each contingent member played their part.

The fact that everyone I encountered around the city— students at UPenn, ex bae's PhD cohorts, woke kids in West—the fact they weren't about That Art Life like I was didn't mean shit.

Didn't mean anything bad.

Not for them; nor for me.

It just meant they were fulfilling their role; and I, mine.

Someone had to make the art; others, to study medicine; and, still others, to figure out what to protest.

———

I didn't say any of this.

That that take made me feel so much better about how bad ex bae had made me feel.

Bc ex bae was on a roll.

Going in about this and that and everything she'd been going through.

With confidence she lacked before.

Or maybe she didn't.

Maybe I was just unable to hear it, over my neediness.

My rambling.

My need, like she spat at me during one of our last fights, to be blown by everyone. To only fuck with those who, literally or symbolically, blew me.

I could barely see ex bae's features how dark it had gotten at the dog park on 33rd and Powelton we'd walked to.

Lil pup kept digging into this hole with a construction cone in the middle.

Like that was gonna discourage dogs from digging.

Every time we tried to stop him, he sprinted around our reach and approached from a new angle.

Honestly didn't see what the problem was.

Dig away!

But the owner of another pup lil pup befriended kept getting all worked up when her dog joined in on the digging.

And join he did!

Once lil pup showed befriended pup how the digging was done, the box was opened.

Neither could stop themselves!

So she re-collared him.

———

Right when she sensed I was about to dive into the House of Resentment, ex bae proposed we walk.

"Better get this pup home. Shall we?"

I wasn't tryna head home.

I wasn't done walking.

But I'd do whatever was necessary.

Fetch any and all bones.

To accommodate a face-sit.

To earn myself that treat.

"Yes, let's," I said, cheerful.

A problem before was the pressure I implicitly put on her, when asking about where she was at idea-wise.

But this time, I didn't ask.

And was pleased/awed by how/that she came to it on her own.

Not there yet but the big diss was around the corner.

She was considering writing about Morrison Swift.

Morrison Swift was a canonically overlooked anarchist from the early 20th century.

Real Renaissance man.

Wrote political pieces, stories, novels even.

Was wildly misunderstood, when not ignored, by critics.

Wrote a list of culturally hagiographized thinkers who'd killed themselves.

Detailed how they killed themselves. How they left families, peers, and pals in the lurch. To clean up their mess.

Scathingly criticized those others unanimously dick-rode.

Got so wet — delirious — listening to her.

This is me.

You're writing about me!

Who I'll be.

Who, in past iterations, I was.

The wildly misunderstood genius the canon overlooked.

I couldn't even respond in words.

Just blushed, went coy, and repeated Bae, and What is happening? while going googly-eyed at her.

Started imagining scenarios in which I'd propose to her.

Considered proposing to her, then and there.

But no.

The wounds were still open / possibly infected.

Almost back to her spot.

Two blocks away, and she still hadn't initiated a parting of ways.

Z was out of town, I realized, and she was considering letting me back inside.

She wanted it, but was still undecided, I decided.

We were through the gate of her front yard before she showed any indication of reticence.

She lingered on the path, looking away and hiding behind the wall of hair she let get unstuck from behind her ear.

I was so erect, I was ignoring all hints.

Realizing this — that I was going to ignore all hints — she sat on the top of three steps leading up to her stoop.

Lil pup started sniffing yard plants.

Listened suddenly and intently for squirrels, but there were none. Just some dried leaves dislodged by a fluke gust.

I sat next to her on the stoop, bringing up something to distract her from the fact I was still there, sitting next to her on the stoop.

That I had no intention of leaving, unless explicitly commanded to.

Lil pup perked up his ears again and did this weird, vaguely marine-animal-like contortion, chasing what he thought was prey but was just his tail.

Ex bae and I both turned. Giggled.

Distracting me from whatever I'd been saying.

But I didn't try to pick it back up.

I sat still.

Let my legs spread naturally.

Leaned back and rested my hands on the porch, like I was readying myself to be blown.

"What's happening, bae?" I said.

"This really what you want?" I said.

"You know it will be different this time, don't you?" I said, my voice cracking.

"What do you mean, this time?" she said, either clueless or doing well to feign cluelessness.

Her eyes were glistening, with either sadness or happiness at being here, with me, who'd been more consistently inside her than any other person ever.

Right before I was about to say something I'd regret, that she wouldn't want to deal with having to respond to, she said "So what about the new Drake, huh?" with surprising authority.

"'Jaded,'" I said. "'Jaded' is the one."

"'Jaded'?" she said, scoffing. "The second, emotional half? I'm not about it. It's all about 'Mob Ties.'"

"'Mob Ties'!" I said, leaning back and erupting.

Our legs made contact.

I immediately had an impulse to move it, but then didn't.

To see if she moved it.

She didn't.

84

We stayed like that a sec.

But then, like clockwork, lil pup bounded in between us, face up close to hers, panting.

She looked at me, apologetic.

"Better get back to it."

Just like that.

"You sure?" I said, cocking my head.

"Think so."

She stood.

Raised her arms in farewell.

Going in for a hug, I tried to initiate groin contact.

But she was leaning forward, hugging me shoulders up, in the most professional, non-intimate way imaginable.

5

ROOMIE BRO

July 2018

Roomie bro was done with the spot.

Lease was about to be up, and he wasn't tryna re-sign.

He probably woulda been, had I given any indication I too was tryna.

But I'd been talking about how I was 'probably gonna skip town, any day now,' for days now.

Since the day I moved in.

"Oh you know, maybe hit my Humboldt plug and get back into the weed game."

"Or you know what — might move back into my van and just fkng *roam*, bro."

"Or fuck it: sell my van and just start walking again. Maybe probably through Mexico this time. Bro — you fuck with Mexico?"

I doubt he ever believed me; same time, he wasn't about to sign on for another year of counting on me as a roomie.

But roomie bro's wifey's friend from college had a beach house in Delaware.

They were headed out there for a July 4th weekend hang.

"Tryna pull up?" he asked on July 2nd.

"Shiiit, I'm down," I said. "Ain't got shit else going."

"Only thing," he added. "Is...you tryna drive?"

Roomie bro's wifey had gotten called into work; her whole crew had already caravanned out there.

They needed a ride.

"Ha," I said. "For sure," slightly hurt but also not caring. Just happy to be included.

Hadn't driven with two passengers for days.

Maybe ever.

Only with a sidekick.

A partner in navigation.

Had to see what was good back there.

I went out back, entered the back of the 6' x 6' x 10' box through the side door.

Folded down the futon couch into bed mode, wedging it into the back corner with my cooler and tub of roof paint I'd had since 2015 — that I'd been planning to paint my van's roof with, since 2015 — so it wouldn't jostle around.

After picking up roomie bro's wifey from her work, roomie bro agreed to ride in the back, lounging on the bed.

"Crack those Reflectix curtains it gets too dark back here," I said.

"But also maybe don't be too visible in the windows, you see a cop or whatever," I said.

"Or, you know what. It's whatever. I'm not trippin," I said, clearly trippin.

I slammed the side sliding door shut.

I reopened the side sliding door.

"And text or knock on the cab door, ya need to piss or whatever," I added.

The door to the cab was a legit house door, with a lock and everything.

Roomie bro waved me off like I got it.

On the drive, I learned things about roomie bro's wifey one only learns talking like you talk, unselfconscious and introspective, when facing the same direction watching the road fly past at 65 m.p.h. for some time.

Was proven wrong in things I'd assumed.

Her dad a military guy who kept bugging her about getting strapped.

When roomie bro went out to Cali to meet him last spring, he kept bringing it up.

"It's not about wanting to kill anybody. It's just logical, as a woman, to be armed in this day and age," was his case.

A thing roomie bro and I did regularly was get lit off the trees out on our stoop.

I'd be at the end of an addie cycle, all burnt and beat but unable to sleep, he'd be at the end of a long workweek, and he'd come downstairs proffering a spliff like,

"Splee?"

Splee Time.

It was never scheduled, but happened with a regularity like it was.

When it was time you just knew.

"Exactly what I fkng need rn bro," I'd say, slamming the Walk Book Word doc shut.

———

I used to get so pissed at him for conflating his past relationship with his ex with mine and ex bae's.

I'd always pull the same card. Always ride the line between helplessness and rage.

"I just don't understand," I'd say, looking out onto twilit 41st Street: Mount Olivet housing project across the way; the pyramidal silhouette, topped with a cross, of Church of the Living God, beyond that. "This whole thing of ceasing all contact the minute you stop fucking with someone. What is that? I feel like that's reverse-sus. Like counterintuitively sexist. It says, Sure, we *acted* like we were a lot of different things to each other: friends, fam, each other's cheerleaders, intellectual companions. But nah. We were pretending. We were *only* fuckmates. *Trial* mates. And now that you done failed the test—ain't got no more reasons to fuck with you bruh!

"It's so Darwinian, y'know?"

"Yeah but bro," roomie bro would say, "it's not that complicated. That all may be true, but it's not about that. At least not now. Not yet. Y'all may well have been all those things to each other, and might still be again. Down the road. But for now? No matter what y'all were to each other, the fact y'all *were* intimate is the only part that matters. That part is in a different category, not bc of some 'hidden sexism' at play, but bc that type of intimacy forms a bond y'all gotta actively break. That it takes effort and intention and deliberate separation to. Like, when things started going south with S—"

"That shit's not the same, bro!" I'd yell.

S was roomie bro's ex. I'd been homies with her too—the three of us kicked it hard that weekend I came back to school to graduate. She was in the class I eventually graduated with, and roomie bro had been living nearby at the time so came through.

They'd lived together — where we lived now — for the year before I moved in.

The wild thing I'm only realizing now, writing this, is that roomie bro had tried to live by that exact spiel I always made. About how the 'woke' move would be to see our partners as not only partners, but myriad other things also.

This probably why he was so adamantly against it. He knew where it got you.

Late in their year of living together, they both decided they wanted to see other people. To open shit up. S lived in the bigger room roomie bro lived in now; and roomie bro, in my current closet room.

Roomie bro started lowkey seeing M, a friend of both of theirs.

S started seeing this other dude, Roomless Dude.

M and S stayed friends.

I remember coming over two Marches ago and being so confused.

S and M were posted upstairs in the big room, stoned, watching random videos on their laptop.

Roomless Dude was in the kitchen, making soup, his shit strewn all over the living room. Bc he'd recently lost his room and so was now roomless. He lived there.

But roomie bro was the only one working a 9-to-5; and so, effectively, was holding down this spot for a whole gang of folks who only sorta fucked with him anymore.

After S moved out, roomie bro held down the spot on his own for like two months.

When he asked me if I wanted to move in and I asked when move-in was, he said Whenever.

He wasn't tryna live with anyone else.

"If you ain't tryna move in, I'll just hold this spot down solo till the lease runs out."

•

I slept out in my van the first night in Delaware even though there were mad couches.

We'd arrived late, it was dark already, and everyone, all of roomie bro's wifey B's friends I'd never met, were sorta mellowing. They'd gone hard the night before apparently.

Roomie bro and I and B and B's friend whose house it was hit the Henny and a J and mished it out to the water.

Like 100 feet away!

This whole area, beach houses and American flags and Ford trucks in driveways, felt like a slice of society I'd hitherto been excluded from.

That I'd somehow managed to sneak into.

6

LIL B

America Day 2018

The next morning I awoke early, like one does when sleeping borderline outside.

Tiptoed up the three flights that switchbacked the east-facing front of the house, inside, to the kitchen. To make coffee.

But there were so many people passed out on the floor and couches, I didn't wanna wake em.

So went back downstairs, to my van, to get the Coleman going.

Took the 2-gal. propane tank outta my van, onto the gravel driveway.

Hooked it up to the Coleman camper stove I'd placed on the entry step of the side door, sitting in front of it on my three-legged, fold-out stool.

Attended to my lil stove desk.

Packed the pot with Bustelo and sparked it.

Started looking at my phone.

Railed a banana.

Smoked a cig.

When I checked back on it, the espresso pot was only half full and was no longer spewing steam.

The flame was out.

I checked the connection.

The tank.

Everything looked/felt good.

Thought maybe the gas was out. Tried it with my backup, 1-lb. propane tank. Still nothing.

I inspected the stove more.

Everything was rusted out bc I hadn't used it in so long. Had left it out back in the rain.

I'd neglected it.

Whatever the pot had managed to gurgle up before the thing crapped out, till the rest awoke, would have to do.

Ever since roomie bro had hopped on my and V's last mixtape, the plan had been to drop one together.

But we were less than a month away from him moving out and I didn't know if it was gonna happen.

Didn't know whether we'd neglected the project too long to resuscitate it.

But this, rap, was what most connected us. Since way back.

When we lived together in college, we'd freestyle weekly in the empty room on the third floor of the Barn—the off-campus house we lived in—that was reserved for hotboxing and freestyling in.

And then, spring of my last year of school, before walking. Mished it up to the school V went to, to see Lil B the BasedGod perform.

Such a legendary and formative mish, I can't even.

Peak Lil B, when he was dropping videos like every third day.

Which, this aspect, the frequency of his output, was one thing.

A thing on its own.

The creative liberation necessary for output that consistent was revolutionary.

But the secret meaning of Lil B roomie bro and I mutually

understood, yet needn't ever state explicitly, was how he de-
manded the attention of every demographic, and forced each
to question their assumptions: Lil B's troll element — his outfits,
his apparent lack of artistic talent, his funny ad libs — made him
an internet phenomenon anyone seeking to 'understand the
times' had to pay attention to; his emotional/subversive songs,
like the "I Love You" video he cried in, the *I'm Gay* (2011)
mixtape, even weirder, confusingly subversive songs like "I'ma
Eat the Ass" (scrumptious!) made him someone woke kids had
to at least peep; but most — I repeat most — importantly, his
bars weren't separate from the 'vulgarity' of real street rap.

Songs like "Suck My Dick Ho," "Pretty Bitch," "Bitch Mob
Anthem."

What differentiated Lil B from rappers disconnected from
the actual risk of rap (de facto exclusion from 'proper society')
who were making funny songs poking fun at some of rap's more
homophobic or misogynistic aspects.

Lil B did do these things.

But he wasn't on the outside looking in.

Lil B forced hood kids and even suburban kids who idolized
hood kids for all the wrong reasons, to reckon with his 'no
homo'-subverting homo songs, his emotional songs, which
they wouldn't have HAD HE NOT ESTABLISHED THAT
STREET/HOOD CREDIBILITY.

While, at the same time, forcing proper, white, woke kids
to reckon with the puritanical, ultimately fascistically Western
roots of their apparently woke language-censoring.

For this, the subtlety of his subversion (where you couldn't,
like with Bolaño, quite decide 'whether or not he was an idiot'),
Lil B was the goat.

———

Yet this also made the fact that there was actually a group of protesters there, protesting that show—that *religious gathering*—so mind-melting.

The ass-backwards-ness.

Lil B, who mighta single-handedly killed 'no homo' as a relevant phrase in rap.

Who did so much for gender fluidity in ACTUAL MAIN-STREAM CULTURE by calling himself a Pretty Bitch.

Those protesters were the same kids who looked down on me and roomie bro for describing a Nietzsche or Heidegger bar as Lit or Fire in the existentialism class we met in. That I met ex bae in.

Who perpetuated, linguistically, the sort of classism they thought they were fighting.

Who was to say "Suck My Dick Ho" meant hateful misogyny?

You were the one saying that! if you were saying that.

And in so doing, excluding a whole faction of society from your gang—incidentally the exact group your causes purportedly sought to help.

To LIFT UP.

Yeesh.

Too fkng cringe, bro.

"Suck My Dick Ho" meant a gender-nonspecific feeling.

Meant whatever Lil Brandon's cheeky grin in the "Suck My Dick Ho" music video meant to you.

•

Around 2 p.m.

Sitting on a beach towel in a row of beach towels.

Squinting.

Tryna read but too stoned.

Edible-stoned.

Wasn't feeling just sitting, so went How about we walk.

Roomie bro was down.

Dried-out grass up by where the houses were, in clumps. A low fence running along it. Little openings leading to the road.

Clumps of families all over that blended together. White, occasionally overweight families, mostly — although that wasn't what I thought, looking at them, just what I think of now tryna remember them. Tryna describe them. Progressively more activity the closer to the water you got. Sand firmer, darker, more solid the closer to the water. Too much water and it got muddy and then you couldn't see it anymore. The sweet spot was where water met sand. That lil sweet spot stretch —

You're about this sweet spot stretch. You walk along it, even though it's where the kids you feel you appear a menace to to moms are. Even though the rest are walking higher up on the beach, just above the slight plateau that marks where the highest tide reaches. Doing your loner, off-on-your-own thing, but whatever. You've always been on that. Only with her were you not. But then it became about her having to be on that with you, in order to be with you. Till she wanted to be off with others and not on that off-on-your-own alone shit with you. She told you read Hannah Arendt that Hannah Arendt was the antidote to your Heidegger off-on-your-own alone shit. You tried. You did try.

You keep following this water's edge and you'll be OK. Too far either way and you're fucked. You want to record this somehow. To not forget it. You'd write it down but you're too stoned and anyway you're walking. You double tap outta Notes. Switch to Camera. Start taking photos, one after another, even though each is a Live Photo so is already a series. You've gotta catch every angle of every wave. Every new iteration. Every photo isn't quite it, but maybe the next will be. You stop after about twelve. Nine months later, you delete all of them to free up space on your phone.

Someone is flying a kite up ahead. Kids tryna bodyboard but just getting sloshed around. Couple bigger dudes in tanks shoulders torched lobster-y up on the plateau edge drinking beers in cozies. You almost step on a shell. Not a shell. A crab. A dead crab. Dead crabs everywhere suddenly. The wind whips harder the more the shoreline bends, you feel. Tank flapping like a flag. You flip your bucket cap's front up like Baba used to on vacations growing up, before Jiji passed. The dead crabs mean everything. Jiji in Santa Cruz that once before you moved there, when just vacationing there, crouching down sitting on heels dress pants rolled up like Asian dudes out front bodegas do, grabbing the crabs in the tide pools on the reef down the cliff path by where, once you moved there, drunk and wilding, you'd first enter another. Where you'd go down to sit at night, alone and sober, once entering others was no longer a thing you were concerned with. Once you'd done it enough times to not have to do it to say you had. Jiji not even stunting grabbing the crabs like that. Just doing it curiously, looking at em from all angles, indifferent to mine and lil sis's yadaaa exclamations to No what if it pinches. That memory tangible bc it wasn't just a mental memory but a body-experience. What you thought of / felt subsequently whenever something squirm-y happened.

But these crabs are different. Not squirmy lil guys flailing their pincers alarmed to be lifted outta the kiddie pool. These are big crabs. Football sized. And dead. Just parched-ass shells that look more like root vegetables. Turnips. White pinkish turnips. You start taking pictures of them bc now they are everything. Ex bae a Cancer. Roomie bro a Cancer. Side bae a Cancer. Editor bae a Cancer except cusp Leo — why you keep knocking on that door. The cusp Leo will save you. The Cancers are the moms that will take care of you. Continually being taken care of what keeps getting you. You're too receptive to being taken care of. Cancers accept you for your solo loner shit. They're down to go in on it with you. But your solo loner shit is the thing you gotta stop going in on. Your solo loner shit got you here. You stop taking pictures after maybe three. Top, side, bottom. That's enough —

Roomie bro and B and a couple pals approached from the plateaued region. They were tryna head back. I was tryna head back. It was time to head back.

Halfway back to the towels, B's friend whose house it was and another friend pulled up on four-wheelers. They weren't as grating as you'd think bc the wind whipping so hard. You could barely hear em. Everything blended in with everything else. Holding our hats on our heads was how much it was whipping. But they were going so fast. They drove out to where we'd walked, then U-turned, but it only took like four minutes, there and back. They didn't notice the crabs. Or I don't know. It was fun in a different way probably. Right when B pulled back up to the towel spot, it sputtered and ran outta gas. She toggled the accelerator a couple times. No dice.

•

That night roomie bro and I rolled and sat on the back balcony and recorded a pod on Sam Pink's *Rontel* (2013), which I'd given him for his birthday on the 1st and which he'd already crushed.

On why it hit so hard for him.

On the weird joy Sam Pink found in the absurdity/meaninglessness of everything.

How his style tapped into a sort of profound ego death: one went through the world responding to stimuli in a way that was, ultimately, out of your control; the passing phrases we perceived the world as — which he captured so uniquely with his line-broken style — even these were out of your control.

You weren't even in control of *your own thoughts/mind.*

Your own thoughts had minds of their own, determined by / in response to the stimuli you fed em.

Phrases and responses and even commands flashed past as you moved through the world, in an absurd way.

Like early on, when the narrator is watching a baby eating a small bag of chips, dancing to music blasting on a speaker in the subway, and is commanded by his thoughts to imagine stealing them.

To, if the dancing baby drops the chips, grab the chips and scurry off with them.

Lol.

This was a disconcerting realization, initially. How little control we had over our own thoughts/memories. Thoughts/memories that, arguably, constituted our 'selves.'

But was weirdly comforting, hilarious even, the more you thought about it.

Woulda posted the pod but the mouth sounds the molly had us making were a bit much.

III

Summer

1

MRA

St. James Day 2018

All fucked up, body-wise.
  Skin resembling an elephant's.
  Ankles cankled.
  No ankle bone, foot veins, nor ligaments to speak of.
  Wrists, neither.
  Golf ball–sized lump, side of my face.
  From my infected right tooth I hadn't been able to chew on for months, maybe.
  Honestly didn't even know.
  Everything cut up.
  Palms to neck to soles of feet.
  Not healing.
  Getting infected I thought but honestly couldn't tell that either.
  Lathered myself with Vaseline, caffeinated, and sat at my dining table.
  To write.
  Then read.
  Then, unable to do either, troll my Twitter feed.

A lot of activity on here, even though it was Friday night.
  Maybe bc.

Saw an interview with zero likes by the founder of a lit mag I'd submitted to.

With "banned/cancelled American Genius Savage Ckhild."

Lol what.

I clicked.

Homie had gotten a book accepted to be published by an alt-lit press before getting it revoked. Due to tweets.

Wild tweets.

Possibly/certainly misogynistic tweets.

Damn bruh, #metoo hitting the alt-lit scene too?!

Wild.

After reading the interview, which spoke of a 'psychotic break' after the cancellation and a name-change from his government to Savage Ckhild, I stalked his Twitter feed.

His website.

It had a collection of poems and essays that read like diary entries.

Photos I couldn't unsee, including a full-frontal bathroom nude.

Both savage and childish.

Ckhildish.

Twitter feed full of angry, occasionally poignant one-liners.

At least five a day.

The irreverence.

The sense of something having snapped and so clearing the way for the expression of real, unhindered-by-morality art.

Zero fucks given.

Gotta say, I respected it, even if I felt bad respecting it.

Even if it seemed possibly more a mental health situation.

A lot of talk of alpha and beta maleness.

MRA-type strategies to give no fucks about fucking women in order to, ultimately, fuck women.

About 'ONE-itis', which it took me a sec to figure out the meaning of.

ONE-itis: the affliction of viewing one lady as 'the one.'

Of viewing one's romantic arc as *destined* in one direction.

An offshoot of the Madonna-whore problem.

Did I have it?

It was so seductive, this path.

Give in to the view of sexual attraction as 100% a game.

Of women as mere responders to stimuli, as essentially manipulable, as incapable of acting outside of this framework.

Like volitionally, I mean.

I thought I was sure, that this wasn't the case, but now I wasn't.

Gotta think on this one, I thought, putting water on for another coffee.

I'd be lying if I said this didn't tap directly into what most fucked me up about the whole thing.

About ex bae.

That things, even with her, came down to those immutable rules 'ONE-itis' implied.

I'd been aware of such rules, but had dismissed, even ridiculed them.

And *to her,* specifically.

Had made an aloof stance to the basic rules the rest followed central to our relational identity.

I didn't need to 'keep her' with money and success bc we were above that. My draw was so strong I didn't care if she flirted with others; if anything, I wanted her to! To reiterate how lit I was.

I didn't own her; nor she, me.

The polyamory dream: communication can solve all problems. Only it couldn't.

Hadn't.

The narrative I had to avoid at all costs, lest I find myself unable to continue: you tried to show her all sides of yourself, to evade the paternal stance of unfeeling decider/owner, to let her evolve/act autonomously outside of you; only she, as a non-speaking female unable to find her voice on her own, turned to the first daddy available: Z, seven years her senior, even more committed to this role since she lacked the genitalia/T-levels to have to struggle against / mistrust paternal tendencies.

Z didn't know what it was to respect/fear where paternal impulses could lead.

To understand what paternal impulses have done.

She was play-acting at being Daddy.

Out-daddying dudes with her metaphorical strap on.

How convenient.

How fun!

In any case, she'd out-daddied me.

When, months after telling me Z had texted her saying I (whom she'd never met, even seen) "was probably just using you for sex" — told me this jokingly, like *haha hear how silly she is* — ex bae then repeated the same thing, that my affection seemed contingent on when we'd last fucked, and then pleaded ignorance when I brought up this fact, that "that's what Z told you months ago, remember?," this felt like evidence of the above.

When, late in the year ex bae and I lived together in Oakland, spring before she moved out to Philly for grad school and I didn't move with her, instead moved into my van and went to Humboldt to do weed stuff, abandoning her on her cross-country quest with our kitty Winnie all shook in her cage in ex bae's stuffed-to-the-brim four-door, and we visited lil sis, who lived across the bridge in SF with C, her ten-years-her-senior partner, and ex bae kept insisting that the way C spoke to lil sis, told her to do this and that, exercised power over her by providing financially "woulda been sus / controlling / lowkey abusive were she a dude, if she didn't have the immunity of being a woman," to which I kept disagreeing, saying I don't know, lil sis *seems* happy...

But no.
    Fuck that.
    It wasn't that simple.
    Nothing was.

2

OUTDOOR DUDE

August 2018: Week One

Big cuz E hit me with the gig deets.

Four days to a week at a farm just outside of Bennington, way up in Vermont.

Probably shouldn't have signed on, how fucked I felt.

How things didn't look like they were getting any better.

Cysts popping up on palms and soles, didn't know why.

Cuts on forearms aligned with skin lines.

Looking like a damn parched-ass desert.

With grooves that never healed.

So like hella infected-ass rivers running through em.

Woulda seen someone, but I had negative money and no health insurance.

Owed roomie bro hella bands, plus had been smoking all his weed since I felt I needed it, and couldn't afford any.

Till one day I snuck into his room to nab some and he had a Post-it on the jar that said *Bro! That's fkng sus! Stop!*

Now I couldn't ask for help; I was too embarrassed.

Generally hit the ma in situations like this.

But she left for Japan early July and wouldn't be back till mid-August.

———

Trump had passed some bill supporting farmers.

You a farmer? Need a greenhouse?

WE GOT YOU.

You find labor, we'll send parts.

MAKE AMERICA FARM AGAIN.

Only — gotta cash in on this deal by November midterms.

And the weather started to turn in October.

So one of big cuz E's ex-employers, a farmer, hit him up.

We were the labor.

E came through Wednesday night.

To peel out early Thurs.

I hadn't been drinking for a minute.

But the minute he pulled up, his energy dictated we were gonna drink.

We were Conroes, and drinking, whenever together, was what we did.

We walked along 41st, to the beer spot, zigging and zagging as 41st dictated.

My socks kept slipping down.

"Diabetes socks" I'd copped at CVS a couple nights back.

Suggested to me a couple weeks back by my neighbor, bigger older church lady across the street, when she saw me sitting on my stoop smoking in slides.

Cankled ankles exposed.

Glistening with Vaseline.

Face hella swollen.

"Oh baby, you gotta raise those feet."

"Raise my feet?"

"That's what I do, when my ankles get like that. From standing on them too long."

"Your ankles get like this? From standing on them too long?"

"Oh yeah."

"Like *this*?" I said, looking at them with horror, like they weren't mine. "Just from standing on them too long?"

"Well that. And the diabetes."

I didn't know whether I had diabetes.

But the elastic of my regular socks was making indentations into my ankles.

And the results from a 'swollen ankles indentation' Google search suggested, as an antidote, 'diabetes socks.'

Like regular socks, except without the elastic.

Kept having to stop every couple blocks to pull em up even though my ankles looked twice as wide.

E noticed but didn't ask about it.

Just said Aw man when I, unprompted, explained what was up.

Expressing or acknowledging or comforting weakness wasn't our relationship.

Autonomous bae came over with new roomie bae, who'd just moved into roomie bro's old room.

We drank and kicked it out back, beneath the makeshift cab-over gazebo E and I built last year.

When my thing was building semi-permanent structures to show ex bae I was here to stay.

Even though she'd never once been over.

We sat in a circle around the lopsided table back there.

I lowkey felt like I should be on a hydration IV, how fucked I felt; but everyone else was drinking so I did too.

E did the thing he did socially where he flexed his wit.

Autonomous and roomie bae were chipper.

I kept my head down and DJ-ed.

Took extended IG stories.

When the convo flagged / veered woke towards the patri-archy and how women, in America, in 2018, were held down, I felt a rage bubbling.

A rage I knew was sus but nonetheless couldn't suppress.

How tf was I privileged.

I couldn't do shit.

Not only that, no one allowed me to show/admit I couldn't.

Not men nor — if not especially not — women.

We had a fkng job to do; so, even though I couldn't, I was gonna do it.

Not to mention, every woman I knew — all my baes, both sisters, ma — had their shit together.

Effortlessly.

Had no issues integrating themselves economically/socially.

And even if they couldn't or didn't want to, they could always nanny.

Everyone needed moms; every woman could get paid to be a temporary mom.

Women didn't need to cross the street, when walking behind a woman or weak man, to show they weren't predatory.

Or keep their eyes down when traversing protected spaces like college campuses or playgrounds, so as to not ruin people's days.

Just last week I'd gotten harassed by a security guard for pulling up on my bike to the Penn dorm after 'curfew' with food in tow.

Who are you you can't be here tf outta here — how it felt to me, anyhow.

Like Bro — I'm doing *literally my job.*
The only job I can do.
The one way I'm able to feel of use.

I was only two beers deep but had the tolerance of a virgin drinker.
Felt belligerent.
OK anyways, here's a story I wrote, gonna read it now, I cut in.
It was 500 words and was basically a transcription of a rant I went on to a friend a while back about how writing was different now, everyone could do it, trying to write in a way that established an elevated stance above readers and other writers was fuckshit.
A fuckboy move.
Stop tryna be fancy; *share* some shit.
It was lowkey shots at E.
His poems were complicated.
Didn't realize it was till after I read it.
After I read it, roomie bae was impartial.
Autonomous bae said it felt unnecessarily literary/complicated.
E said he fucked with it.

I offered E my bed, but he chose to crash in my van out back.
We had an early start the next morning.

E had a triggering relationship with my van.
Two Christmases ago — right after I followed ex bae out east, right before she became ex — we — E, big and lil sis, and the ma — linked at big sis's spot upstate.

A month after I'd driven out from Cali.

After living outta my van the previous season doing weed work in Humboldt.

I'd secured a room by this point — my first closet-room in West Philly — but still considered myself a van dweller.

My closet-room more a home base / amenity spot.

Was still spending nights in my van.

Except awake.

Writing in my van at night with a propane heater.

Red Bulls.

Reds.

Weed and the occasional (honestly for some moons there daily) microdose.

Was sleeping inside — in my sleeping bag, on my mat — mornings till late afternoons.

So sleeping in my van for the Xmas mish was no biggie.

If anything luxurious since big sis had an off-street driveway.

But big cuz E, that Xmas, was living upstate also, with his on-and-off bae of ten-plus years — since college, like ex bae had been for me — working some sort of renovation construction of this old mill turned art space.

Hella isolated with on/off bae.

In the town adjacent to the one he went to college at in VT.

Seeing me, he felt like any domesticated bro would upon seeing one of his 'un-contained,' single bros.

Like tf am I doing.

Like this dude out here!

Masculinity challenge.

Even more insidious/challenging since I presented so woke

and self-aware and self-deprecating about how dumb ideas of alpha-beta masculinity were.

Purported implicitly to inhabit a new category, of alpha-beta immunity.

To sidestep this problem entirely, by pivoting the angle.

Although, ultimately, still tryna establish myself as above that shit.

Anyway, on the evening of that Xmas day—2016—we drank and smoked in arctic-ass upstate, in my van, Canadian hotboxing that bih, huddled around my propane heater, till we damn near couldn't sit up straight.

Canadian hotbox: regular hotbox except with cigs.

Listened to *Savage Mode* (2016) on loop, me telling E to listen carefully to 21's lyrics.

"He's in Savage Mode," I said.

"He's showing you what it feels like to be a 'Real Nigga,'" I said.

"Hear how sad he is," I said, cutting E off and demanding silence. "He's not proud of it. Or rather, it's not about whether he is or isn't proud of it. It's not even a choice. It's just how it is. How things are."

Less than a month later, E cut things off with his longtime on/off bae and jetted out to Hawaii, where his parents were posted. Where his pops, my uncle, a U.S. naval chaplain, was stationed. To 'start over.'

"That fateful Canadian hotbox," E said as I led him into the van, to set up his bed for him. "Changed the course of everything."

•

It rained nonstop the entire drive up.

Through NYC, along stretches I'd never driven.

Over bridges I'd never crossed.

E drove the whole way.

I DJ-ed.

Things mellowed once we hit the Taconic.

I slept the last two hours.

Forearms cut up, face swollen.

But I distracted myself by IG storying so much of the drive my feed was a bunch of dots.

The farm was something else.

Hill overlooking trees for days.

Head farmer S paternal but friendly and stylish also.

E spazzing a bit when we pulled into Bennington but mellowing once on the farm.

Hadn't slept in my tent for days.

Was missing three stakes.

So went on a Walmart run, into town, for some.

Which they, impressively, sold à la carte.

Also nabbed granola bars, gauze pads for my arms/feet, more Vaseline.

And a three-pack of cookies I merked on the way out to the car, in secret, even though I don't know why E would have given a shit.

When I was walking across country, sleeping out, tent life wasn't shit to me.

Unfazed no matter where.

In the tiniest of one-man bivies no less.

Under bridges, in ditches, behind bars.

FUCK IT.

I was that dude.

The tent dude able to withstand any and all conditions.

Unsure whether I was still that dude though.

Convinced myself I was, and said as much, when E asked Tent camping's cool with you though, right?

Was so sweaty inside my tent, once I got it up.

In the dark, with a headlamp, as the rain started coming down.

Set up my makeshift, tarp rain-flap like I did every night while walking across country.

But incorrectly.

It wasn't holding.

Still warm out so wasn't a biggie.

But wasn't gonna sleep with it how it was anytime soon either.

Tried to zone out by listening to a pod about a cult, by a dude who grew up in one.

Everything raw and cracked and chafing.

Putrefying.

Arms like I already said.

But crotch all fucked now also.

V on either side cracked and oozing.

Where either side of my ball bag met inner thigh cut up.

I lay on my side and listened to the disembodied dweeby NPR voice tell me how charismatic the cult leader his parents followed as a child was, initially.

Turned it up to compete with the assault of raindrops pattering on my tarp draped over my tent.

Couldn't believe I slept in this thing for 100 days, while walking 20–30 miles a day and barely showering.

Come 3 a.m. I couldn't take it.

Got out of my tent and smoked a cig sitting on the picnic table in between mine and E's tents, under my umbrella.

Went "Ayo E" a few times.

Nothing.

Stared at my tent lit up eerily in my headlamp-light, through the rain.

Tried to imagine re-entering it.

Couldn't.

Didn't wanna.

Wasn't gonna.

Recalling S's offer to "head down to the main house the storm gets too crazy," grabbed my pack outta my tent, draped my poncho over it and my head, and stumbled in its general direction.

Fuck this shit.

I wasn't Outdoor Dude anymore.

Head down, I followed the tire treads down the hill, to the huge field opposite the main house.

The field we'd be working on first thing tomorrow.

From there scaled its upper edge.

Past S's hollowed-out, windowless pickup with flat tires.

To the stoop.

The minute I pulled back the screen door, S's dog went fucking bananas.

S had said he'd leave the front door unlocked, so my plan had been to sneak in quietly.

But there went that.

How the dog was snarling between barking bouts, primed on its back legs.

Sounded like he really didn't fuck with me.

Really hated me.

Like personally.

Maybe he smelled my rotting flesh.

Maybe he smelled my cowardice in the face of the elements.

Or maybe he sensed that I wasn't a Decider, a Master, like the other humans he interacted with were.

That I was a pushover follower who bowed down and did as he was told, provided there was some dangled treat, like pussy or money.

That I was just like him.

And this unsettled him.

Whatever the reason, he didn't stop.

Even when S came downstairs, groggy, shirtless and di-sheveled, and yelled at him to fkng quit it would ya—even then, he didn't.

Based on S's expression, I could tell that the offer had been perfunctory.

That he hadn't expected us to actually take him up on it.

That, now that I had, his esteem for me, as a man, diminished.

Running on fumes and coffee from the pot S and his wife, K, sparked up at 5:30 a.m. sharp, E and I got to it.

Day one was laying out, measuring, and leveling the stakes.

Fifty on each side, at 5' increments, level and 30' from the one across from it.

Laying these down solid was critical as they'd mark where to plant the base beams that would support the curved-V cross-beams we'd assemble and erect last.

Once these foundational beams were set, they wouldn't be able to be moved; and the thing wouldn't stand up if they weren't set correctly.

We used string to get the layout of the preliminary stakes right.

Took about all of a sun-blasted morning.

Couldn't take off my long-sleeve synthetic pullover since it was holding the gauze wrap I'd wrapped my forearms with to absorb the ooze.

That, and shoddily wrapped medical tape that wouldn't hold without the sleeves, given the sweat.

Ditto with ankles/feet: gauze/tape held in place by diabetes socks, which in turn crammed into shin-high wellies E lent me.

A lotta squishing going on.

Inside bc the above.

Outside given how muddy the field, with all of last night's rain.

Come midday I was crashing hard.

E showing no signs of letting up.

I could see him on the far side of the field, going to town on a stake with a sledgehammer.

We'd started in the middle and were working outwards, away from each other. I was using a mallet.

Had too much pride to ask about lunch.

E rocking a beater, glistening statuesque.

S off in an adjacent field lower down the hill, pacing the rows, puffing on a yellow-pack American Spirit. Bandana tied around his neck.

Kept getting blasted by bugs.

They were going for the cuts.

For the eyes.

Threw my synthetic pullover's hood on; zipped it up to my chin and drew the drawstrings taut, creating a hole just big enough to see out of beneath the brim of my Nike Dri-Fit cap. Despite the heat.

Pushing 90.

Went at it a couple more stakes before I felt like I was gonna pass out.

At which point, barged up the hill, to E's tent.

Where I tried to hit it, protected from bugs by his tent's mesh, only it was too blasted out.

So laid down my tarp and crashed out beneath the picnic table.

E and I got into it the next day.

On the way to Walmart (for more medical tape) from the one coffee shop in Bennington we went for lunch.

Where E used to go, while a student here.

Where he used to go when he worked for S before, while living here couple years back, with his now-ex, then-long-term on/off bae.

"Bro what are you tryna prove? Never taking breaks and shit," I spat, feeling myself go mean.

E jetted his all-black Tacoma past some geriatrics doing 20 in a 45, blatantly mean-mugging as he passed. He didn't respond.

"Like, a ten-hour day doesn't mean ten hours of nonstop work."

Still nothing.

"Like dude," I continued, self-righteous now, "I'm not about that panoptic mode of grinding nonstop like a fkng peasant for fear the master'll catch you taking a fiver. That shit is basic. Not to mention extra."

"Alright, man. What are you saying?" he said. "I called you because I thought you were up for the gig. If you're not now just lemme know and I'll call someone else."

"Bro do you have a deeper purpose? Like *besides* work?" I was sneering. Tossed the cig I'd just killed out the window and immediately started rolling another. "Besides fkng *labor*? How you're talking reminds me of the basic wooks in Humboldt who'd pull up to the trim scene so desperate for work they'd get played by the property owners. You have to *not need* the work. You have to work on *your* terms. You're not a fkng mule, bruh. But you act like one you'll get treated like — "

"Look dude. S isn't some faceless corporate master. He's my guy. I negotiated the day rate to what it is with the understanding that we'll have the job done in four days. So that's what we're gonna do."

"OK. Sure. But that was before the storm. We all got our plans to keep the water out. But when that shit hits it hits. Nature don't give no fucks about no mfkn expedited day rate bruh."

All our shit was drenched.

We'd been pounding metal beams into the ground, in place of the temporary stakes, with these beam-pounders that resembled like civil war–era artillery.

IN A NONSTOP FULL-ON DOWNPOUR.

ALL MFKN MORNING.

Removing the beams, digging out big-ass rocks and starting over whenever a beam got stopped by one and didn't sink deep enough.

———

The third day, Sunday, it stopped raining and got blasted out again.

We'd finished the beams right at sundown the night before.

S and K had moved me from the couch to their guest/computer room.

Legs and arms doing this wild thing where, when I scratched them, a goddamn blizzard of skin flakes flaked off.

The floor was covered with them.

Like cherry blossoms on sidewalks in spring.

Like shed snake scales.

Skin's external barrier utterly compromised.

We were laying out and assembling the curved-V crossbeams.

Carrying them out into the mud-field, to where they'd be erected tomorrow, with the help of S's tractor's crane-type attachment, and drilling them together.

The moment I awoke, in a beach of my own skin, I knew it was all over.

But had heard E and heeded what he'd said on the way to Walmart.

Plus felt like shit for spraying out skin flakes like I had in S and K's guest room, lodging a good couple thousand irrevocably into the cracks of their hardwood floor probably.

So lathered, gauzed up, railed some Advils, and hit it.

Worked silently, efficiently, and angrily.

Got about four-fifths of the day's work done by midday, before wobbling, realizing I was done, and, without a word, beelining it for the house.

Took an ice-cold shower before passing tf out in the guest bed.

———

Awoke around 8 p.m. to E shaking me.

I was lying on my back, just boxers on, no sheet covering me.

"Dude," he said. "You alright?"

"I mean," I said.

"Didn't realize it was that bad." He looked at my ankles/feet. They were so fkng swollen and cracked, they looked unnatural. Like elephantiasis combined with some infection.

I heard laughter and clinking from the living/dining room. Y, E's fiancée, had arrived.

"Got you some extra-strength Tylenol," E said. "Here."

I swallowed two.

"And a Greyhound back to Philly, first thing tomorrow."

"What about the greenhouse?" I said, sitting up.

"It's cool, Y's here. We can handle it. You need to go see a doctor."

3

HETERO BRO

August 2018: Week Two

The ma still wasn't back from Japan when I got back from Vermont.

New roomie bae's pops was though.

Visiting from the ATL burbs.

Scoping his lil girl's new digs.

Like Bruh—this spot is pretty sketch.

Roomie bae was committed to it though.

To that Hood Life.

Took her pops to the bodega a block north I never even went to.

On the intersection of 41st and Lancaster that always had mad people posted in it, straight lounging.

Merking tall cans no matter the time o' day.

They came back with saltines, a generic-brand block of cheese, some type of 'cured meats' that were more cold cuts.

'Hors d'oeuvres.'

Lol.

Bro I was so flared up when I got back they were actually shook.

I was posted upside down, on my back, on the downstairs futon, with icepacks on my ankles elevated up on the wall.

They were like Bruh—*you good?*

Your ankles look pretty fucked bruh.

Yo you *hella red tho.*

Yeeeah man, I said.

Pretty inflamed bro! I said, scaring roomie bae's dad I think.

Like Yo—*who tf is this dude you decided to move in with?*

Naaah I heard cold showers are supposed to help though! I said.

Gonna take one now.

I think big cuz E musta group-texted my sisters, bc both called within the next 48, acting like they hadn't known how fucked I was but asking about it directly.

Lil sis called and asked how I was.

I remember she called me right when I'd awoken, just after the sun had set.

On my way downstairs to make coffee.

Feeling so fucked.

So swollen.

Lump in my throat.

My voice, as I tried to feign okayness, sounded so foreign.

"I'm...you know...still here."

She was like I think you should come home.

To LA.

To Mama's till you're better.

"I mean," I said.

"I fkng would bruh!" I said.

"But I'm broke af yo," I said.

She said she knew this.

"And that's why I wanna buy you a plane ticket out here, Seanie," she said.

Fuuuck bruh.

This fucked me up.

"What?!" I said.

"You don't need to do that," I said.

"I'm a piece of shit, I don't deserve that," I said.

"Seanie," she said. "Don't even worry about it."

All the massage clients she'd gotten through a company she recently left left with her, so now she was working the same but without the company taking their 70% cut.

"I just want you to be OK," she said.

The lump in my throat was so thick, I was choking.

But I reduced my responses to masculine grunts and Unhs, sounding like the nonverbal Japanese animated boys in early Miyazaki movies.

In short: I held it together.

The minute I hung up, though.

Crumpled into a heap on the kitchen floor.

Flood gates fkng busted wide open.

Type of bawling with a baseline moan that sounded mewly, vaguely goat-like I wanna say.

Like a baby goat.

An abandoned baby goat, stranded in the cold, bleating for his mama.

But mama ain't coming back.

She long gone.

Shiiit, she done died, bruh.

Gotta face up to facts!

"She done dipped on you, lil goat!" I said aloud as I shuffled — squirmed — in the fetal position, to behind the dirty-ass kitchen trash can so no one would see me even though I was home alone, leaving a trail of cry-snot behind me.

———

The minute I started full-on wailing my phone rang.

It was lil sis. Again.

"Hello?" I said all surprised, wiping my face.

She'd known, somehow, that I'd started crying, and had called me right back.

No idea how she knew.

This time I didn't try to hide it.

•

Went to my Medicaid 'primary care doctor' that week.

It was just down the street, three blocks west.

Straight up shitshow in there.

Only white-adjacent person except an ESL, fifty-something Chinese dude.

Just leaking stench out of my soles, through my socks, into my shoes—old scuffed Retro 4's, the only ones my swollen feet fit into.

After waiting in three lines, got called in to see the nurse.

She—blond, busty, resembling a grown-up version of the 'hot/popular' volleyball girls from high school—walked in, stopped short, and went—no joke—OMG!

Are you OK?!

You really don't look good.

The side of your face is swollen!

I was in shock.

The lack of professionalism.

The guise of medicine having any sort of authority utterly puncturing.

Yea no shit bitch!

Why tf you think I'm here!

Tell me what to do! How to get better.

"We'll see what the doc says," she said. "But I think you need to see a specialist."

The doc said: I needed to see a specialist.

Gave me a list of phone numbers.

I called a half dozen of them, same response across the board.

Yes, we can schedule an intake.

Oh...you have Medicaid?

Yeah, no, you know what? Looking at the schedule here, we're actually all booked up. What you're gonna wanna do is, call back in two months.

Two months?!

Bitch I'm dying over here!

I ain't got two mfkn months.

Just sorta gutted it out that week.

Crashed out all day every day.

Paper towels laid out on my pillow, my sheets, to absorb the ooze leaking outta my face.

Forced myself to get up once a night, in the wee hours, to walk somewhere for snacks.

CVS, Fresh Grocer, or, if feeling ambitious, the Wawa way out on 34th and Chestnut.

Still tryna get fired up once per waking cycle—get lit off coffee, sugar, cigs—to 'go in'—achieve that level of litness I associated with 'thinking hard and writing fast'—unable to accept that I was dunzo.

That I done broke.

It wasn't leading to any fast writing, or for that matter any hard thinking.

To any thinking whatsoever.

Just profuse sweating, followed by shivers/chills, followed by profuse sweating, followed by shivers/chills, followed by fetal-positioned stasis in a sheet-swamp of my own fluids / skin flakes.

•

The night before my dawn flight to LAX, I woke up, at night, and went on one final snack mish.

I'd trained my tummy to rail caffeine and a tin of mixed nuts each night at midnight; it was almost midnight, and my tummy was like Yo where tf are my snacks yo.

Settle bud, I got you, I told my tummy while laying down a base layer of paper towels in the soles of my Birkenstocks.

Got the latest Joe Rogan pod going, ffwd-ing through 7 minutes of ads, and hit it.

It was with this dude Steve Rinella, outdoor hunter dude I hadn't heard of.

I was feeling adventurous today — I had a place to go finally! had something new on the horizon! lil sis was rescuing me! — so mustered up the courage to hit the Wawa, even though it was a longer walk and was due east of my spot, meaning in the direction of ex bae's I generally avoided walking towards.

We weren't totally broken up when I moved into my current spot, a half mile away.

Well we were, she was already seeing Z, but wasn't moved in with her yet.

Was still describing her as a 'funny experiment.'

As 'sorta romantic,' but more a 'close friend' — *obvs in a different category than u.*

And a thing we'd always talked about, late in the year we lived together, was how the move would be to live in the same neighborhood, in walking distance from each other, so we could cultivate our own spaces, our own grinds, while being able to visit each other whenever.

So when roomie bro's spot opened up, half a mile NW of ex bae's, I jumped on it.

Only, the minute I did, Z moved in.

Now I couldn't walk in her direction without feeling sus af.

Without feeling like Chris Brown.

And there wasn't shit straight north in walking distance, just more hood houses and no relevant businesses.

I was trapped!

Boxed in.

Could only walk in two of four possible directions.

About once a fortnight for a while there, I'd snap and be like what is this bullshit. We live so close together. Why not just mish it over, say what's up.

Like in the olden days.

Holler at your neighbor right quick.

Tf was with all this texting before knocking.

This some hogwash yo.

We woke!

Shit, why don't Z and I become homies.

Like: I love you; you love her; by that one math concept, I should also love her.

She and I should love each other.

This would always happen mornings.

After the gnarly all-nighter, after later and later consecutive all-nighters, that went so late I tried to stay up the next day.

To 'reset.'

This, above all, was where the root of my neediness towards ex bae lay: when the mania of consecutive all-nighters ran its course, and suddenly I felt like a crazy person, and direly needed someone to tell me I wasn't a crazy person.

To tell me I was on the right path.

To console me.

So, on this particular day, midsummer a summer ago, I waited, waited, waited. For as long as possible.

Till it wasn't *totally* psycho/stalker-y for me to pull up.

Like 8:30 a.m.

Almost turned back like three times.

Walked up the front steps I knew so well, that we'd kicked it on all night while on drugs, that we'd fought on once the drugs wore off, before actually turning back a fourth time.

Like Yooo what am I DOing.

Like I'm fkng WILDING yo.

I need to settle tf down — this some stalker behavior!

I'm actually Chris Brown!

Flipped a hard U, bounded down the steps, and started booking it south.

But this led me past the side entrance gate, past the side/back patio area separated from the street by a hedge-covered fence.

Probably a paranoiac, sleep-deprivation-induced theory, but I swear to god Winnie smelled/sensed me, bc she came scampering down the side steps, to the side gate.

Poked her head through the bars like a prisoner.

Looked at me longingly, like...Dad?

Like I miss u daddy!

131

Like Why'd u leave me poppa!

I involuntarily went Ooooof! Win-win! kneeling and going eye-level with her.

Before our reunion was interrupted by a jarringly unfamiliar singsong voice.

"Win-nie, don't go over there, come ba —"

We were face-to-face.

Locked eyes.

I stood.

We scrutinized each other.

She looked so plain.

Not like how I expected somehow; although also exactly like I expected.

"You're Z," I said.

She nodded.

"And you're…?" she said.

But she knew.

She fkng knew, bro.

Immediately.

The tension was palpable.

I smirked.

"Who am I?" I said, sneering.

"Sean," I said.

"I am Sean," I said.

Then everything went hilarious.

I laughed.

I was filled with warmth, and went nice.

Winnie did a weird, gallop-y 180 and jetted under a hedge, before spastically one-eightying again and jetting back.

"This is Winnie," Z said. "We've been letting her out some, but she's used to staying inside."

All that niceness went poof. A chill of hatred ran through me.

I stared at her, incredulous, trying to figure out if she was serious.

To see if she was fucking with me.

Omg.

Bro—she was serious.

THIS. FKNG. CUNT, went through my brain in all caps.

Bitch do you know who tf I am??

Were you there when Winnie was so small she fit in the palm of your hand, like a goddamn beanie baby?!

Were you there before she had hair? When her eyes were still sealed shut? When she was a hyper lil kitty keeping ex bae up all night racing back and forth skidding out fucking up our studio carpet—tryna play goddamn *tether ball* with the studio blinds—ALL FKNG NIGHT—till I, the stern but necessary father, grabbed her by the scruff of the neck, held her out the front door, and told her "Winnie. See this? This is OUTSIDE. See over that fence there? That's where BIG SCARY DOGS live. Over there? That's the fkng road, bruh. Mad cars. And all of this? No cat food out here. You're on your own out here, girl. OK now see inside? This the safe zone we've created for you BC WE LOVE U.

"Now settle TF DOWN!

"Mama's gotta catch those zzzs bc Papa's a lowlife fuck who just quit both his jobs in order to nurse his drug habits and work on a 'book' no one will ever publish. Mama's gotta get that bacon!

"You're fucking up her shit rn!"

And then play-sparred with her till she got tired and finally chilled out?

Till that catnip hitter wore off?

DID YOU DO ALL THAT?!

No bitch.

I took a breath.

"Ah," I said, smiling. "She's used to staying inside, huh? Her name's Winnie, you said?"

We small-talked uncomfortably a sec.

Ex bae was outta town, Z said.

Oh, I was just passing through, I said. Thought I'd swing by.

Things calibrated.

And I coulda left em like that.

Shoulda.

But did I?

The answer is…No.

No, I did not.

"Hey," I started, with a sense of urgency—of something I had to *get off my chest.*

I sensed her tense up.

Prepare for the impending discomfort blow.

"Before I go," I said.

"I know you have your ideas about me," I said.

"I've heard them," I said. "And maybe they're correct. Maybe I am a sus hetero bro who's been subtly abusive and deserves to be blocked out entirely. To be cancelled. For my basic ways…"

I was seeing red. Blacking out. Blood rushing to the dome making everything go wonky.

I took a step back.

Did my best to calibrate the heart rate.

Like that rant you go on in philosophy class after the all-nighter reading Heidegger that, midway through, you feel slipping out of your control—that you suddenly, midway through, realize you forgot the initial point of.

"Look. You don't know me. Shit, *I* don't know me. Know who I am now, or who I'll be tomorrow…"

She retreated, like this was veering into precisely the sort of abuse she'd convinced ex bae that I, by default, had been guilty of — that had warranted her abruptly ejecting herself from.

"All I'm saying is, I don't appreciate — I think it's unfair — for you to make character judgments about me based solely on my outwardly perceived, categorical identity. Without knowing a damn thing about me.

"OK?"

O-fucking-K?!

I had no idea whether she had any idea what I was talking about.

She musta.

But ultimately, I had no clue.

She bowed her head slightly, but without breaking eye contact. Nodded.

Said OK.

I said OK.

Then knelt, gave Winnie one final, gruffly fraternal head-pat — she'd been hovering between my legs — and sent her back under the gate like a dove I was sending off to find land. Stood, turned, and shuffled off. Heart pounding. Like a crazy person.

I hadn't, since, ever walked back in that direction.

•

But tonight I was.

East on Haverford, slight right onto Powelton, which ran diagonally SE to Center City.

This was the most efficient way into the city proper, but I never used it unless on my bike, when I could whizz past the site of all that trauma, three intersections down.

Or else only in the early a.m.s, when I knew I wouldn't run into either of them.

Steve Rinella was going in about how explorers during Lewis & Clark times were distinct from their contemporaneous natives since they didn't cultivate crops; they moved constantly, so couldn't; they relied on lean meats — those that were most readily available — along with fats their mode of travel — constant motion — made them crave.

Jaywalking across 38th equidistant from Wal- and Chestnut, waiting on the middle island for a semi to pass, something clicked.

A hitherto hidden truth, revealed.

Concealment-unconcealment.

Wheels turning, connections connecting, heart rate spiking.

Euphoric suddenly as I picked up the pace, cutting instinctively down dimly lit, barely trafficked, warehouse-y Ludlow.

Sweating now, rubbing my face like I was tryna tear it off.

Like Fuck it mask off.

Took some deep breaths, sat on a curb, and started to roll a cig. To see what I had...

The major evolutionary shift that led humans from Motion (hunt/gather) to Stasis (cultivate crops) was, as is widely acknowledged, the advent of agriculture.

Was what led to the spike in birth rate, life expectancy — more food and more efficient means of growing it meant more people survived winters.

Before that, muhfuckers had to stock up on whatever they could merk or gather with their hands or rudimentary tools to get em through the cold months.

Was how Japan, despite being a tiny island, managed to

imperialize damn near the rest of Asia: by learning how to grow rice before and more efficiently than the rest, and control them by being their food source.

But here Steve Rinella was saying dudes like this—hunters who subsisted off of what they killed, gathered—existed well into the advent of agriculture.

Suggested that the succession between epochal stages wasn't necessarily linear.

The necessity of this lifestyle didn't depend entirely on the evolutionary era; it depended also on things like individual temperament, terrain, and circumstance.

This made me think of this passage from Tao Lin's *Trip* (2017), about the historical roots of what we today call 'patriarchal society':

Around 7,000 years ago... various groups of dominator-style people from the north... began to invade the Goddess-worshipping civilizations in the south, first in the Near East, then in Anatolia, and, spreading west over millennia, throughout Europe. They worshipped male deities, rode horses and war chariots, were hierarchic, patrilineal, patrilocal, and pastoral, and had lighter skin and were bigger than those in the south. They associated black with death, unlike the preexisting people in Europe and Anatolia — Old Europeans — who viewed black, wrote Gimbutas in The Language of the Goddess *(1989), as "the color of fertility, the color of damp caves and rich soil, of the womb of the Goddess where life begins."*

It only made sense that those who, at some point, developed the most advanced tools survived.

Tools employed, firstly, against Nature; later, once tools of transportation were developed, against each other.

Before the steam engine and cars, horses were the first land transport.

Just think about that a sec: muhfuckers hoofing it around, hunting for berries and shit, tryna hit that watering hole or whatever; then one day some savage wrangles tf out of a horse and, suddenly—boom! That watering hole mish ain't shit! Pull up on a bison right quick with that drive-by spear shot.

This an inevitable, Promethean shift.

But Tao was pointing out the flipside of it: Northern, fairer-skinned folk, dealing with harsher conditions only the most savage didn't die in, naturally, became savager. Those who survived at least, which was sorta case in point.

Had to deal with gnarlier conditions, and so were pushed, by the survival instinct, to develop the necessary means.

And Necessity, above all, for better or worse, was what pushed people into new patterns of Action.

Made sense these distinctions would reflect deifically: when Father Sun was present most of the year (Southern, equatorial peoples), people worshipped the Mother; when Mother Nature was wilding out most of the year (Northern/Nordic peoples), people had to fight back. In order to survive. And so worshipped the savage, masculine, paternal forces. To get em through!

I loved reading this from Tao, fucking with all these classic, esoteric, female-worship-type historical texts.

Bc we did, culturally, associate black with death, with the unknown, with *night.*

And that quote, framed how it was, forced you to consider *why.*

Although my shit was, wasn't the next step to keep it 100 about how we, as Americans, were *the products of these northern, father-god*-type impulses, and so own up to that; there was an inevitable, Pandora's box element to these evolutionary shifts; and so, wasn't it the move to, rather than nostalgically try to re-create the time before someone figured out how to ride a horse, or lay claim to and cultivate land, to instead *use* the power these developments grant, but ethically?

To challenge ourselves to wield that power empathically, with integrity, with the care that much responsibility entailed?

Was this not the *most urgent* task?

With the insinuation of course being that I was one of the chosen ones doing that difficult work. Of applying the integrity of the old, matriarchal ways to this savage, patriarchal new world.

I was a modern-day hunter, riding my horse-bike around, delivering food to these basic fucks unable not only to make it themselves but even pick it up; hunting for food — foraging for nuts — at night, when safe from emotional predators; loving all my baes equally, according to the non-ownership-based polyamory of matriarchal yore.

Only — my mfkn ankles were so swollen I couldn't bike anymore; and, on my way back from Wawa to pack final things before hitting that 5 a.m. flight — while having these very revelations — I chomped tf out of a honey roasted pecan and cracked my left molar in half.

•

Back at the spot, roomie bae was in the living room, in her nighties. Sweeping.

At this time?

It was almost 1 a.m.

She stopped abruptly when she saw me.

139

"Oh," she said. "Thought you left already!"

"Flight's at five," I said, massaging my cheek.

I looked at the pile of debris she'd accumulated.

"Oh jeez," I said. "I'm sorry. Here, lemme —" I took the broom from her and swept up the rest of my skin. Dumped it into the trash can.

I was so embarrassed, and she could tell, so she started to apologize. But I told her not to. It wasn't on her to feel bad — if I had a roomie who was spraying out skin like that everywhere, I'd be tryna clean it up too.

"It was just getting on my socks!" she said. "Didn't mean to be weird about it."

Roomie bae asked how I was getting to the airport.

I told her I was gonna walk to 30th Street — about a mile and a half.

"With all your bags? Is the airport train even running at this time?"

"Shoot, I think... There was an exclamation advisory on the map, had me sorta worried."

"What about Uber?" she said.

"You know I don't fuck with Uber," I said. "I don't even have the app."

I was a walker / horse rider. I didn't fuck with the luxuries my overprivileged, fkng CLUELESSY HYPOCRITICAL twenty-something peers did.

"I mean, Uber Pool should only be like seven bucks. And... look at you! You can't be walking with two backpacks and a suitcase in your state!"

"Shiiit," I said.

But she was right.

I downloaded the app.

Had a swell time listening to slow jamz while other passengers were in the car, and having a heart-to-heart with my driver once the other passengers, tired from partying all night, got dropped off at their respective homes.

That shit was only like $7.50.

Plus tip!

4

LIL BRO

August 2018: Week Three

When the ma picked me up at LAX in her Prius.

Man.

Soon as I exited those auto doors outta bag-claim.

Man!

That Pac Ocean air!

Nothin like it. Straight up. Frfr.

She looked so little and funny, older but more compact, features more refined and crystallized, than when I'd last seen her.

Or maybe more defined since her brow was so furrowed with worry, seeing me.

I don't know how I looked, at the time at least, since we never really see ourselves in the moment. We only see how others see us, although not even that second thing fully.

If we don't wanna.

If we set our minds to refusing to.

Based on the IG stories I was for some reason still taking that week, though.

Face puffed, ears cauliflowered.

Diabetes socks soaked through.

Feet leaking out, all flight.

Walking was like walking on bubble wrap, except the bubbles were the cysts on my soles.

Cysts that on God sprouted up, tripling in number, the night before.

Something about the stress of the sitch making em multiply.

Like I realized I'd gotten so stagnant over the past month since I'd stopped Postmating, just lying half-fetal on my side all nocturnal hours, staring at my phone or a book, save for the nightly snack mish.

Suddenly having to gather my things and hit it, with an actual time constraint…

You know what it was was that moment of finding myself unable to, and so railing additional coffee, and my body not knowing what to do with that additional stimulation.

My body being like Bruh. Tf.

Tf bruh.

Yo—railing coffee at the bitter end of your waking cycle? Not a good look.

Started sweating bullets and scratching my face above my eyes and on my palms and soles.

Then tryna shower to cool down but unable to bc the water was stinging all the tiny, self-inflicted cuts.

Then, like clockwork, 15–20 minutes later, having all those cuts become pus-filled bumps.

Shitty!

And the altitude didn't help.

Posted in the middle seat, reeking, unable to change out the paper towels lining my shoes, my forearms, since I was crammed between two professional-looking bro-passengers I wasn't tryna do like that.

Soon as the ma started asking how I was I felt that stress reaction reacting.

Started digging fingernails into my skin, spraying out flakes everywhere. Onto the dash, the floor, into the middle-console drink holders.

When we got back to her spot, behind a Whole Foods on Wilshire, she had the pullout couch set up in the living room.

AC humming.

Impeccably clean.

I'd forgotten what rooms like this felt like.

That rooms like this were even a thing.

I plunked down my stuff and wanted to pass tf out. But my mom was like Hell no.

Not in this state.

We're going to get you some sustenance. Then take you to Urgent Care.

"C'mon, there's one around the corner," she said, urging me back onto my feet.

It was honestly so nasty removing my 4's in the examination room.

Fkng putrid.

It wasn't even bumps anymore; there were heel-to-toe bubbles that had busted open.

Huge gashes down the middle.

Dead skin dangling.

The nurse, he was such a champ. Made me feel like not a leper. Grabbed a bucket and carefully cleaned my feet with saline solution.

I felt like Jesus.

Then he flipped me over and shot my right butt cheek full of some anti-inflammation antibiotic.

———

Went to a dermatologist out in Fullerton the next day, that the app Zocdoc—which linked you with doctors according to your insurance, but which showed no results for Medicaid in Philly, closest one was in Delaware, with the first available appointment months away—set me up with.

More a Botox-type rather than medical dermatologist, which made sense, given this was LA.

Had to take what I could get.

Homie took one look at me and said: roids.

Topical (triamcinolone), to lather all over the bod; internal (prednisone), to take at a high dose (60 mg/day) for one week, before tapering down over the next.

Plus an antibio to prevent further infection.

I started to say "Is that OK to do? Given the side effects?"

But it wasn't a discussion.

Just look at you bro.

Sorta outta options here.

You a fkng dumbass for not dealing with this earlier.

Touché, I said.

"Just don't make any life-changing decisions rn," he added. "The roids will make you energized/manic initially, emotional/sad later."

•

Lil sis actually left for a weeklong yoga teaching conference at Esalen the day before I arrived, but texted me that M, her new boo, whom I had yet to meet, would be hitting me up about bringing by some cannabis meds.

Lil sis had me text M pics of my bod, to give her a sense of what she was dealing with.

"This is what M does," lil sis added. "And she really wants to help. You're in good hands."

The next day, M pulled up with the weed.

She treated cancer patients, leukemia patients, and others with chronic conditions. Using cannabis.

Before handing over the goods, she explained what we were dealing with.

A toke, or standard hit, was ~5–10 mg.

A blunt to the face was ~200 mg.

"This syringe," she explained, brandishing it, "is 2 g. Or *2,000* mg."

"Yeah," she said, smiling. "This is no joke."

It looked like a medical instrument. It was filled with a black, viscous, tar-like substance.

"Now we talking topical? Or internal?" I said, unable to hide my excitement at the prospect of getting blasted to another realm.

To a realm that didn't involve any of this.

That didn't involve any of my current body.

"Seanie! No!" my mama interjected in Stern Japanese Mom Reprimand. Like Down, dog! Yelling slightly since she was mildly lit off the wine bottle she and M were splitting. They'd poured me a coconut water, in a wineglass, so I wouldn't feel excluded.

"Well actually," M said, smiling cheekily. "It is primarily used topically. To reduce inflammation and fight infection. But it's also very CBD-heavy, and can, in moderation, be taken internally. Talking a grain of rice amount."

"OK we talking sushi-? Or we talking…nah'm sayin…that *long-grain basmati*?"

M smirked.

"*Standard*-grain basmati, maybe—"

"OK!"

"Just to help you rest."

Then she told us about how lil sis once scooped up and railed a fingerful of this stuff that had spilled onto the counter at a patient's house, and within an hour didn't know where, or who, she was.

"Goddamn," I said, grinning, cauliflowered ear to cauliflowered ear.

After she showed me how to apply it, mixing some in a turmeric-infused, aloe-based gel she provided, and getting it into the cracked, open wounds on my soles and palms, I walked — shuffled — her out.

Once down the stairs, she handed me a "strong, indica-heavy" J. "For later. To rest."

I was so grateful I was crying.

We split a pre-rolled American Spirit — that I was smoking, rather than rollies, since my hands were too fucked to roll cigs, the loose tobacco getting stuck in, and stinging, my cuts — in the alley out back Whole Foods.

Unable to roll cigs with my Minnie Mouse glove hands.

Her energy felt different than lil sis's previous partners. Calm, stable. Masculine, but un-performatively. With nothing to prove.

She was 30, I learned. Had a younger brother my age, who she said was going through something similar: dealing with the aftermath of a seven-year relationship, trying to get his shit together.

She said she was confident that I was going to bounce back from this, and that, once I did, things would be different.

That 27–28 was the year she stopped fucking around.

Started really making her own money.

"Yeah, I feel like I'm just now figuring out how the world works," I said. "It's like, my relationship, the affirmation I got from it, enabled me to retain all my infantile delusions."

"Yup," M said, nodding.

She was an encouraging, if uncompromising listener. I understood why my lil sis fucked with her so heavy.

I honestly woulda gone pinto bean that night had the ma not been watching me apply it. I stuck to the program and went maybe 3/4-long-grain basmati, rubbing the black oil into my gums like in some ancient ritual.

After washing my feet, I shuffled, on my heels, to the bed my mama had vacuumed around and tidied and made with hotel-room precision.

M had been adamant that I, once I applied the oil-filled-aloe gel topically — into my cuts — just lie down and not move around.

Which I stuck to, save once, around 9:30, to shuffle down to the alley and merk about a quarter of the J I'd almost forgotten I had.

On my way back up, I got a surprise text from V, saying he heard from lil sis that I was in LA. That he was rolling through — he was at the terminus of a family road trip, was seeing his mom and lil bro off at LAX the next day — and was I down to hang.

Yuh hmu! I texted back.

I was KO'd by 10 p.m.

148

•

I awoke at 1 p.m.

Fifteen hours.

Feeling calm and unfrantic in a way I didn't trust.

In a way I'd forgotten was a possible way.

The ma was at the Waldorf School, teaching. But had left a note on the kitchen counter directing me to a plate of greens, chicken, beet sauerkraut, Japanese sweet potatoes, and miso dressing. Saran wrapped. In the fridge.

Unreal.

I had a text from V from 30 minutes earlier saying *Wya? Lil bro's flight's at 5, heading out to Santa Monica now lmk where to meet.*

Texted back *Wilshire Whole Foods food court.*

When they pulled up they were initially stoked.

Then they were still stoked but looked worried also.

Like Yooo…you look…different.

I was posted at a patio table, in the sun, stuffing the wrapper from the 'vegan' maple cake donut I'd covertly railed — that I'd copped with my Philly EBT card to go with my coffee and 60 mg roid dose — into the revolving trash can lid that wouldn't stay open.

Wiping my face of crumbs.

Their arrival adding to the activation of the roids the sugar, the caffeine, were already enacting.

Lil bro was keyed up. Like Yo so we tryna shoot this vid or what?

They'd texted about shooting a music video for one of the songs off the tape V and I had put out just over a year ago, when V was still in Philly. I'd been KO'd so hadn't seen it till this morning.

"Ha," I said. "Nahhh," thinking how crazy it was how far back we actually went how *V that summer we met summer before senior year in V's tree house rapping sorta half-rapping half-Jack-Johnson-singing how legendary the bond off the rip how V not only accepting of but encouraging both sides of then-me the ratchet Jordan-wearing tall tee-copping fitted cap-rocking vato wigger boy on the one and the cello-playing reader writer philosophy bro sensitive boy on the other how before V these sides kept discrete only performed when audience appropriate* "Yeah that ain't happening," I said, with a finality lil bro was visibly disappointed by.

"But fkn dude," I said, turning to V and going in for the hug. "It's actually been…a year?"

V looking wooked out hair dangling vine-like down his angular-ass face.

"Well August 1," he said. "I peeled outta Philly August 1."

"So yeah. A year and" — checking my phone — "a fortnight."

"Since those dishes," said V.

"That diss track," I said, laughing, thinking *how late that summer start of that school year V and lil sis started how weird it got but how it also made sense how lil sis initiated it did that repeatedly even before V repeatedly homed in on the bestie the main homie how this had to be bc how close we were growing up moving so much how it was almost like whenever I got attached to another bro lil sis going in for the swoop was her saying Wait where ya goin?! just wanting to be included* —

"*Too* fkn wild," I said, grinning. "Cycles."

"Fkn cycles," V said.

And us just standing there, in the corridor between the tables, Whole Foods fucks chattering all around, oblivious to the scope of this bromance reunion. Till lil bro cut in like,

"Yo so we tryna hit this juice bar or what?"

"Yeah. Let's nab a mate," V said. "Sit tight," leading lil bro into the Whole Foods.

I sat back down.

Realizing I'd killed my last pre-rolled cig so starting to roll one *bc that shit that year definitely got weird got sus like V suddenly over to hang with lil sis like walking past my room to use the bathroom like occupying a different sphere was honestly highkey sus* licking the cig closed, tearing off the tip strands, starting to light it before realizing the patio rules and getting up, slipping into the 'stocks, making sure the paper towels were set right, shuffling out to the sidewalk to the bus stop bench where the rules didn't apply *bc OK maybe it was me maybe I made it sus but there were rules there were codes to this shit V never got* sitting down in the direct sun, looking back one time to check the table before going Eh it'll be fine and sparking up *like sure V was a rapper bro insofar as he rapped sometimes but not like actually not like affectionately called My nigga by fools at school who could say My nigga or hostilely called Wigger by fools who couldn't V isolated in his theatre kid world then abroad in Brazil so not there for everything that led to the excommunication the mass blackball the fight at every party I pulled up to for being a Valley Wigger Kook just bc, what, I couldn't ball tf out present how I did and also be valedictorian like I didn't mean to fuck all their bitches those white girls were the ones fucking me fetishizing me fkn haters bruh —*

Looking back to check the table, V and lil bro still inside, so stubbing out the butt and rolling another *but nah V never attuned to the implications of that how V's with your sissster became the new hater ammo like I was supposed to be mad but how them expecting me to be somehow making me as if lil sis couldn't handle herself didn't know what was best for her was susceptible to fuckboy advances but also how cute V when he approached me like he did like a young suitor asking a father for his daughter's hand in marriage like I really love her! me being like Bruh that shit neither matters nor is up to me! although sus as it sounds that also sorta was the position placed on me ever since the actual ole man dipped to Germany to marry live with his 24 y/o new wife* as I looked back and stood and saw them, V with a mate, lil bro a green juice, and so starting to make my way back when remembering suddenly *that fight we got into late that school year out front that party us both near blackout one of those FUCK. YOU. DUDE Cain and Abel fights to the death spilling out into the street rolling around wrestling on speed bumps in potholes and shit but how that got out whatever pent up subconsciously held disrespect I mighta felt how after we finished fighting that was it, we were done with it, were good again* stalling a sec to kill the cig before reentering the patio, to let the heart rate calibrate, thinking *Sheesh these roids are no joke.*

•

It only took a couple sips to realize the Whole Foods patio was blown.

V was like Fuck this, let's hit the beach.

So we mished it, in their rental car, down Wilshire.

Along the ocean.

To the beach.

Letting lil bro get shotty and us all going quiet, looking out windows, turning up that new Young Nudy, V commenting on the subtle genius of the understated, whisper flow, how Nudy was the best at it since 21 pioneered it, me looking out at the waves, feeling the body thaw, not till that moment realizing how tensed I'd been or that I'd even been tensed *how when at the end of that school year they split I dipped for college and V for his gap year bike mish all over the east coast from Florida up to the ATL to Philly basically ghosting going Chris McCandless sleeping out in highway dividers and shit Into the Wilding out till that spring he pulled up unannounced to campus like he did looking all scraggly harassing randos for where I might be before finally finding me in the library how lit that reunion but then that next summer things different with V and lil sis how I tried to keep my distance let em do them living with the ole man who'd outta nowhere abruptly returned from Germany where he'd lived all high school years with the new wife only they'd divorced and this was supposed to be our reunion since he was on the eastside and the kids' camp I was working at sorta was too till that once I went back to the ma's for dinner and heard yelling out front and lil sis going Go away! and going up-stairs to see what was good and seeing V out there spazzing yelling up at the window John Cusack boombox-on-shoulder-like except angry-crying and having to be the one to go out there and go You gotta make moves bud, leave it be, and not until later asking lil sis what happened what changed and she saying I love him, he'll always be my first love but he left when things were good and then wanted things to suddenly go back to being how they were when he returned Wouldn't accept it when they didn't Couldn't handle that they wouldn't* before, as we pulled into the beach parking lot, dropping all pretense of being like rap historians and turning up to "Sicko Mode," which had just dropped.

V catching my eye in the rearview like This shit, huh.

Fkn *slaps.*

Then blasting the Drake part in the rental car speakers so loud I felt like I was picking up on aspects of the bass line as if for the first time.

Like it almost became a different song, when amplified that high.

•

"Nah it's like. Like *listening*," lil bro was saying. "Like *openness*. Or like, *participation*. With *open listening*," toking from the bowl one time in the wind-protected open front passenger nook. "*That's* what I'm tryna study."

He'd just started school at Naropa, in Colorado, and was explaining his Special Major.

"So you're studying...openness and...listening?" V said, straight-faced. "Fkn hell ya," turning his body towards the ocean, to lead the way.

"Nah, not just that though," lil bro said, tapping the cashed bowl out and slamming the door closed. "Like, there's a *method* to this shit..." running to catch up to V.

I made sure I had all my shit on me.

Cigs. Water.

Before letting them walk ahead *bc the thing about that summer was despite everything that had happened with lil sis how wild things got V and I kept going in hitting the bars still over guitars but now layering 808s hi hats over them on GarageBand V all fucked up about lil sis me about that camp counselor bae I'd been tryna get at all summer who for sure wanted it but had that bitch-ass boyfriend she wasn't tryna leave* this part of the beach a vast flat expanse unlike higher up the coast where the cliffs jutted down to narrow, hidden, nook-like sand patches down here there was plenty room to park, roller-bladers and cruiser-bikers and Bird scooterers scooting along this bike path I paused at to let one pass *but us over here doing diss tracks at camp counselor bae's mans I barely knew and V didn't know at all lol* the paper towels lining my 'stocks just pus-soaked smelly yellowish wet, seeing how far ahead they'd gotten, lil bro gesticulating tryna convince V of his Special Major's central point *till the summer*

ended the season shifted we both went east into the cold V to
college to start his rap group the Feminists with the homie A how
well-intentioned and funny the Feminists' mission initially You
know tryna ramp up the misogyny of the bars to an absurd degree
to make us aware of the more subtle and so accepted elements of
misogyny that pervaded rap or popular music generally like we
hear the misogyny but it no longer affects us we don't even realize
it the Feminists were here to make *it affect you* make *you realize it*
realizing they were gonna try to walk out to the water so picking
up the pace to catch up to tell em I couldn't that the cuts were
open and would get sand in em if I did *like OK their mission was*
a lil silly lil condescending maybe but harmless till it stopped being
harmless till the school took it as real and spazzed out doing the
roundtable discussions the protests the op-eds students venting
to the admins their concerns till they got blackballed pushed out
V dropping out with a year to go, right after that Lil B show —

"Yo," I called out. "Hold up!"

V and lil bro stopped at the edge of the sand pier and turned
back, hand-visoring their eyes.

"I can't go that far!"

"Why not?" said V.

"My feet," I muttered, getting hit with a gust of sand-breeze,
before realizing it was too much to explain, so sorta gesturing
back, away from the water, and moving in that direction, trusting they'd follow *bc while I knew V's intentions were if not good*
weren't bad that he wasn't hateful or evil *like how some of those*
fucks made him out to be at the same time unable to help but a
tiny part of me think that some a fraction of V's impulse to rap
so irreverent stemmed from the pain lil sis dipping caused like
it's even hard to think to say nothing of saying so I didn't ever
think it the minute I started to I'd get alarmed shook confused
immediately repressing it especially so when lil sis started seeing

155

women me always making light of this outwardly but inwardly sorta pitying feeling superior to V like that would never happen to me submitting to that socially encouraged idea of Oh, you flipped her! You were the one who made her stop fucking with your entire gender. Until, of course, years later...

V and lil bro eventually got the message, and turned back.

We sat on a berm overlooking a roller hockey game on a cordoned-off part of the parking lot; beyond that, a wooden path extended out into the sand, like a pier; and beyond that, the ocean, looking slab-like, shimmered.

Less rugged than the cliffs we used to hang on up in Santa Cruz. But comparable, considering.

We got to talking money- vs. art-making.

I felt the need to articulate my recent epiphanies, especially those with effectual outlooks that deviated from my previously held stances.

This was central to our relationship: reporting our changing stances to each other; and, by listening, recording them. Like we were each other's scribes. Logging this info for a hypothetical, eventual posterity.

Or maybe not for that.

Maybe we were just interested in, and stimulated by, each other's evolving ideas.

I went on this whole rant about how I'd made a LinkedIn profile and was trolling Indeed.com for jobs — in Philly, in LA, in NYC. Writing-related jobs at reputable media outlets like *Vice* and ESPN and *VladTV*.

Nothing would ever come of these apps. But this was a major deviation from the DIY-till-death ethic I'd preached till then.

V was officializing himself also: living in Monterey, about

to start school for body massage—taking a page out of lil sis's book; she'd told him what schools were best. Plus doing contract building work for his landlord.

V hadn't needed a complete breakdown of his body to come to this; and, unlike me, who was merely humoring the idea of legitimate application of self, academically and employment-wise, he was actually doing it.

At some point, lil bro cut in like "Yo—you *sure* you not tryna shoot this vid? Freed up space on my phone and everything."

"What song were you even tryna shoot?" I said, humoring him.

"The best one. 'Moves.'"

"Moves" was about Making moves.

About Having all the tools / Cooking up all the foods.

"That one's the best?"

"Yeah dude," he said. "Hands down."

"Moves" was the one track I'd removed from SoundCloud. Had made 'private.'

It was still on the YouTube version of the album, which we'd uploaded as a single, full-album track, probably precisely so we wouldn't be able to do what I ended up doing: losing sight of the vision and nixing the more aggressive tracks. Pulling out after the fact.

Going all the way in, planting the thing, and then not following through with the watering / tending to.

But I'd deleted it because it was on some 'I need this / I need that' 'I do this / I do that' braggy flow I cringed at whenever I imagined specific people entirely outside of my target audience, like distant family members, potential employers, or reviewers of my literary submissions, hearing it.

157

"Yeah I was looking for that one on SoundCloud, on the drive over," lil bro said. "Couldn't find it. You change the name?"

"I didn't change the name," I said. "I took it down."

Lil bro looked at me like Tf is wrong with you. Like Why would you.

"I don't know dude," I said. "I just. Thought it sounded sus. Thought people would judge me."

He stayed silent, listening face on. To see if I was done. Then said,

"You should put it back up."

I thought about this.

"You're right," I said. "I'll put it back up."

5

LIL SIS

August 2018: Week Four

Lil sis got back from her yoga teacher training and we had some killer hangs at the spot she'd just moved into with M in the Canyon.

Hitting the medical trees, kicking it on her back porch, shooting the shit.

Dr. Botox's roid regimen, combined with M's edible-induced sedation and my mama's immaculately clean living quarters had me looking pretty again.

Ankle bones and foot veins visible.

Greeting the world with a brand-new, hyper-sensitive, infant-like layer of skin.

But there was still something wrong with me.

Still not eating, or for that matter sleeping right.

Every third or so night I'd get overwhelmed by what a piece of shit I'd become for, at 27, living on the ma's pullout futon, utterly unable to support myself.

At which point I'd slam shut Knausgaard's *My Struggle: Book Five* (2017), don the Birks, and walk somewhere that was open in the wee hours.

CVS, Rite Aid, or this 24-hour donut shop with all sorts of wild flavors like green tea and Oreo and Cinnamon Toast Crunch.

Right molar straight cracked, root nerve exposed, but none-theless out here mishing it to get that 2 a.m. donut hitter, chowing down on one side only.

Railing through pods, pit-stopping in parks, bundled up stumbling past muhfuckers KO'd on benches, on lawns, in the awning-ed storefronts on Wilshire.

And then, on the last night of my month of rest and relaxation.

The plan had been Go somewhere for a final fam meal, that served shit without the stuff the internet said to lay off of. Namely, processed carbs.

The ma and lil sis didn't know about my nightly donut mishes.

That I was out here like a goddamn possum, scavenging for scraps while everyone else was shleep.

But the three of us mished it, down Wilshire, to this like raw-food-type Mexican spot, outskirts of downtown Santa Monica.

So we went to order, and they already had my meal decided for me. They were like Here, you're gonna order the chicken asiago leafy goodness salad or whatever K?

I was like Yooooo — *am* I?

They were like Yeah. You are.

And look I was over here thinking, I got this night flight coming up, this finna be my last solid meal in a minute, I'm not about to order a bowl of leaves and then have to hit the Whole Foods bakery later, in secret, to merk an entire EBT-copped sourdough boule with a block of Kerrygold butter. Like I'd done, right before they closed, maybe three times this past week.

"I'm tryna fuck up this torta rn; so what I'm finna do, bruh, is fuck up this torta!"

———

All lil sis saw was me acting directly counter to how the reasonable consensus said I should.

Like I was so over it all that I was deliberately harming myself. This bummed her out.

After a tense, silent meal, during which I indignantly ate my torta like I was enjoying it, like an asshole, lil sis couldn't take it anymore and started crying.

"I just don't understand why you won't let us help you," she said. "We just wanna help you get better, we don't like seeing you like this. Why won't you let us?"

Once, back in high school. Me a junior and lil sis a freshman. Back in the birth-city for my *jiji*'s funeral memorial weekend.

It was a Buddhist thing, you held the funeral, which was two-hours, chant-filled, open-casket — such a different, jarring sense of death's *physicality* — followed by the cremation, the picking through of the bones, lined up on either side of the baking tray, with chopsticks, to be transferred — two sets of sticks to a bone, a move that, besides in this context, was completely taboo — into some Buddhist bone receptacle; and then, two years later, you had the memorial.

But we were back for this two-year anniversary of his death, with all of Jiji's relatives, the kids of his one sister who survived the firebombings.

We were late in the trip, staying in this economy hotel in Nakameguro that had these dank croissants at their continental breakfast with these wild and wildly-Japanese-somehow butter/ jam combo squeeze packets, the butter and jam came out simultaneously when you squeezed em, like the squeezing of them did the mixing for you...

But we were at the stage when prolonged travel time together was wearing on us.

We'd gotten into some tiff, can't remember what about exactly, but it was a reenactment of our fights growing up, where we'd be playing and everything would be good so long as I was winning; but if I ever lost, I would, if we were younger, hit her, or, if older, go ruthlessly mean. Shut down. Non-physically bully her into tears.

Something along those lines had happened that day, during a long, exhausting, blasted Tokyo day mishing it around Harajuku, she looking for Gwen Stefani–type drip, me for rare but fake and so even more rare Jordans Nigerians would slang at wild over-prices to unsuspecting, American-wannabe Japanese kids.

But that night. We'd conked out, I think we were splitting a king bed, and she woke up in the middle of the night and started yelling and hitting me.

Except she hadn't woken up.

She was sleep talking.

"You never *lis*-ten to me! Why don't you ever *lis*-ten to me!" she was saying, in an eerily indignant, urgent, but also distant way, hitting me on the *lis*-es.

"Hey, hey, what? What's going on?" I said, sitting up and prodding her.

It went on for a minute, and progressively fucked me up.

But then she woke up.

And when I told her what happened, she made light of the whole thing.

Laughed, and said "Seanie, that was nothing. I was dreaming!"

But that always stuck with me.

Like she had to be in that half-sentient state to tell me how she really felt.

———

"You're right," I said. "I'm sorry."

I stared at the last bite of my torta.

Couldn't do it. It looked so unappetizing.

"I just feel so helpless right now!" I said, breaking down.

Once, not long after the ole man dipped.

Dipped, but only across town with F *not to Germany with her to live near her same-age dad yet, me 11 or 12, lil sis 9 or 10, playing the game we played upstairs where one ball, one of those poof-y dodgeball type balls, and two goals, the doorframe end of the hallway to downstairs one goal, and the door opposite, to Mom and Dad's now just Mom's room the other, the rules Get the ball into one doorway, one point, and into the other hallway, for the other, also one point, first to ten or whatever. Throw it if ya wanted but if blocked/deflected the other had it, so mostly us running it bulldozing past running-back style, laughing our asses off hysterical bc how dumb the game but also how fun.*

Lil sis lately doing a cheating thing since I always won, was getting stronger getting first sprouts of hair down there my body doing new things it hadn't before, hers not doing different things yet I didn't think, but she'd just corral the ball lay atop it not even trying to get it past since even if she wouldn't get it past me, wouldn't win, if I never got it I wouldn't either, laughing in stitches sitting on it squishing it like an egg protecting warming it so it'd one day hatch, prolonging the game in a stalemate she dictated the length of, only I didn't have time to waste, I had free throws to shoot the NBA to make balling to ball out on to show Dad he done fucked up played hisself dipping like he did.

Funny at first, lil sis splayed like a turtle on the ball goin

163

You can't get it you can't get it, how it pivoted the whole logic of how games worked, how they only worked if ya tried to win, only I still wanted to win wanted to play the game so once it got un-funny I dug my claws all up in there tryna pry it out only she'd turn block me from whatever side I entered, laughing more going Nope, nope, you can't get it, till next thing I'm on top of her tryna pin her down hold her still tryna pry it while smushing her, all of me smushing against her so focused on the ball on the goal not even realizing the change till finally she musta noticed bc she went Ow ow, Seanie, I can't breathe you're hurting me, I give up, releasing the ball.

Coming up outta that lizard brain feral mode like out of a half-sleep dream both of us panting red-faced only then realizing my body had done the thing it had been doing, smushing directly into her, she getting up straightening out her hair her clothes looking at me strange unfamiliarly like I had changed like something in me had bc something had.

•

When I got off the airport train at 30th Street, post–red-eye.

Sweltering.

Shirt sweatsoaked, sopping, within seconds.

I was like Fuuuuuuuuh.

Like I'm fucked bruh.

Came back too soon.

Dr. Botox had thrown me two more weeks of roids, when I relapsed after the first stint and came back fiending for more.

But only five doses left.

Still addicted to everything I was addicted to before, only now addicted to roids too.

——

I started walking back to my spot before, after a block, getting overwhelmed and going Fuck this.

Swiveled around on the blown intersection of 30th and Market, staring at my phone, not knowing where to go.

There was a cop merking a deli sammie, standing on the corner.

I had a backpacking backpack on my back, a Jansport on my front, pulling a roller suitcase.

"Hey you know where the entrance to the ten trolley is?" I asked the cop.

"The ten? Trolley?" he said, squinting.

"The ten trolley, yeah."

"Well where ya tryna get?" He railed the last bite, patted his hands clean.

"Forty-first and Haverford?"

"Why don't you just take the El to fortieth?"

"The El? To fortieth?"

"The El. To fortieth," he said.

"Walk down these steps here. Follow signs for the El, or Elevated Rail, or Market-Frankford Line. Take it to Fortieth Street."

I repeated back what he'd said to him, then did what he said.

6

BIG LEAF

September 2018

First roomie bae approached me about moving in with me I was so flattered.

Me? You wanna live with me?!

This was a novel concept: a woman who wanted something from me that wasn't my undivided and exclusive sexual attention.

Ha.

Nahh.

But it was on some different shit.

And had side-effect benefits.

For one, it immediately established me as non-predatory.

Like Fuck outta here—I *live* with a woman!

This was good.

Second, my relationship with roomie bae was different than my relationship with roomie bro: I couldn't even imagine pulling some of the shit I'd pulled with roomie bro—like allowing my room to become an untraversable cesspit of unlaundered clothes, or stealing drugs from him, or becoming a full-blown, nocturnal gremlin—with roomie bae.

This was definitely good.

And lastly, there was always the possibility that we, with the forced intimacy of cohabitation, would hit it off.

I honestly didn't think this.

But when V first arrived in Philly, I'd told him about side bae, and at the first House Gathering at the old spot, upon seeing me and roomie bae interact, he'd said Her? Like Is she side bae? To which I'd said Her?! Nooo. To which he'd said Oh, well y'all are definitely gonna hit it off at some point. Mark my words.

So that stuck with me.

But same time what tf did V know.

One evening roomie bae came back from her nannying job all energetic, like "ex-roomie bae is having people over — wanna go?!"

Ex-roomie bae was technically both our ex roomie, since roomie bae moved into the house I used to live in, with her, after I moved out. For the summer. Right before moving in with me.

"I mean..." I said. "What about this storm though?" peeking through the blinds at the cloud cover.

I hadn't left the house all day, save for out onto the covered stoop every hour or so, to smoke. Roided up on the last of my roids, doing job apps.

"Well I was thinking," she said. "Wanna drive over? In your truck? Haven't driven in your truck yet I wanna drive in your truck."

"Shooot," I said, first getting stressed about this idea, before going Hey, why tf not.

While roomie bae bustled around the downstairs living/kitchen area, I tried to do what I used to to ex bae.

What I did to all my female friends/lovers.

167

That is, ramble my unformed thoughts about some new idea, treat her like my sounding board, and then, once I'd finished, had nutted (intellectually), sit there and wait for her to tell me my ideas were in fact fully formed.

My most recent idea had to do with an idea I'd stumbled upon revisiting Terence McKenna.

About how I'd been weeded almost my entire time in LA, but was now out of trees, was roided, and only had tobacco to smoke.

Thinking about how keyed up I was.

How this of course had negative aspects, re stress levels, etc.

But how the 'bacc-y, the lack of weed, also had me reading faster, thinking clearer.

I was more myopic and more aggro, but this also allowed me to bang shit out.

To home in on what had to be done and do it.

It made me think of this McKenna quote, from *Food of the Gods* (1993), which stated that, while

Cannabis occurs in both a male and a female form...it is the identification, care, and propagation of the female of the species that is the total concern of the grower interested in the narcotic power of the plant...

The resin is the exclusive product of the female plant...

Not only do males not produce a usable drug, but if the pollen from male plants reaches females, the females will begin to "set" seed...will cease their production of resin.

A task V and I did a lot the season we worked up in Humboldt was Big Leafing. Throughout the growing cycle, but especially late, nearing harvest.

The goal was to maximize the buds/flowers, or female components. The parts one trimmed, smoked, and sold.

The nugs.

But there were also the leaves.

The infamous pot leaf.

Dre's *2001* (1999) cover.

These, like McKenna said, were the 'male' components.

While they didn't have pharmacological value, they did have implications for the bud during the growing process.

Protruding out of the stalk right beneath the bud, they served essentially as satellite dishes, to absorb sunlight and send energy to their flower.

They weren't totally useless.

But when they got to be too big, or there got to be too many of them, they began to either:

Suck up too much water from the roots, not allowing enough to get to the buds.

Or: block the sun from flowers lower down the stalk.

Become overbearing.

Stifle.

Suffocate.

Deprive the flowers of sunlight and clean air. Invite mold.

And once your buds got moldy bro? You were fkng done.

So V and I, the last fortnight pre-harvest of each hoop house's grow, would be those hired-hand Big Leaf Assassins.

Spend all day in there, railing through albums and playlists and pods, working our way down the rows. Letting the support-ive leaves be *just up to the point they were still supportive,* and then fkng nixing em.

Taking em out.

Population control.

Offing all the non-productive, destructive male leaves no longer serving the female flowers.

―――

I touched on some of this in my rant to roomie bae.

But the main, the new, epiphany was that, in tobacco, it was the opposite: tobacco *flowers* (female) had no pharmacological value; the *leaves* (male) were what you smoked.

I didn't get wind of this till, late last summer, early fall, when first facing up to the reality that ex bae might really be done, and that I likely wouldn't make it out of Philly by winter, I'd ordered tobacco seeds online, started watching tutorials, and had this idea of—*I don't need you bae! I'ma give all my love to these 'bacc-y plants here.*

Of course, them shits didn't even make it out of the sprouting phase by the time the snow hit.

But I remembered that. That with tobacco, it was the *leaves* that you harvested, hung to dry, and sliced into strips.

"And isn't that so interesting?" I asked roomie bae, having finally got to this part in my spiel. Waiting for the light to go green at 46th and Market.

"Bc, if you think about it," I continued, "the respective effects of tobacco and cannabis sorta reflect those aspects.

"Of masculine and feminine.

"Solitary, self-concerned focus, on the one; and somatic, empathetic concern for others/the group, on the other.

"Y'know?"

Roomie bae went "Yeeeah that's all complete BS."

I looked over at her and just stared, thinking she was fucking with me.

She wasn't.

Someone behind me honked to go.

I looked up. Green. I eased the box forward.

"What do you mean? Which part is BS?"

Roomie bae said she disagreed with the notion of masculine and feminine in the first place. That they were social constructs made up by dead white men to assign negative traits to women. To keep em down.

"Oh, I'm not saying everyone born a 'man' or 'woman' *necessarily* adheres to all supposed 'masculine' or 'feminine' traits," I said. "Or even that they do at all. Alls I'm saying is, our bodies—both hormonal makeup and social nurturing—*encourage* us a certain way, temperamentally. And only through *awareness* of these tendencies can we subvert em.

"But in terms of self-representation and -understanding? We're capable of occupying either side, either archetype, for sure."

"No I'm saying that whole binary is a lie," she said.

"What about nature? Pollination? Mating?" I asked, turning onto Baltimore. It was way more lit than the tree streets—Pine, Spruce, Osage—we'd been passing, and I felt suddenly exposed in my U.S. Air Force box van with stickers repping my blog in reflective 'mailbox' alphabet all over it.

"Well no. Not all of nature reproduces that way. Some things reproduce on their own," she said.

"Examples?!" I damn near yelled.

She typed frantically into her phone, into Wikipedia. Like we were on a game show and there was a countdown timer.

"Some rare, single-celled bacteria—"

"Oh c'mon!" I smacked the steering wheel.

"—and fungi, like mushrooms—"

"Oh word?" I said, curious suddenly.

"—don't reproduce by mating female and male parts, but instead do so on their own."

I pulled onto ex-roomie bae's street. Into a corner spot, by a stop sign. Killed the engine.

"Well that," I said. "That's interesting. Fungi and mushrooms, huh?"

She nodded.

"The ole shroomies, huh?"

She smiled. Smirked. Like See?

"Nah girl," I said, laughing. "This ain't over. That's still an outlier!"

●

Over the six months after I agreed to work on my Walk Book with editor bae, I cut—nixed, snipped—every savage, ugly, testosterone-fueled, shameful thing it had been the most difficult to write.

I re-buried all the parts I wrote the thing precisely to force myself, and the reader, to look at.

Everything I wrote so others might be more aware of such flagrant tendencies in themselves.

When editor bae ghosted I honestly didn't know why.

I thought maybe she didn't want our correspondence to end, and was stalling, since once the book was submitted, we wouldn't have a professional reason to stay connected.

I thought maybe she felt like I was using her.

Thing was, I wouldn't have given two fucks if she shared the script and the agent said No, this isn't for me.

I was just not about *not* sending it.

You gotta *send that shit*!

I almost wanted it to get sent and get rejected, so that way we'd no longer have this veneer of professionalism preventing me from doing what I actually wanted to, which was turn on all that fuccboi charm and get back inside.

Or whatever, just kick it as homies.

I tried to communicate this.

It was the first week of summer, and I was on a one-day

job on Randall's Island, building a Nike set for Governors Ball that would sell custom-stitched NBA attire to festival goers — a two-story, full-size court we assembled on a slant, that it took forever to shim level, with sewing machines, stacks of every team's jerseys, except just blank canvases, no numbers or team names on em.

During lunch I shot her a text like *Hey, in town for a job. Drink later?*

She responded immediately.

No. And I changed my mind about the manuscript, I don't wanna submit it anymore. And tbh I don't wanna spend time with you in any other capacity. I'm too busy with work and wanna spend the free time I do have with people I'm actually close with. Have a good summer!

IV

Fall

1

X

This new drug cyclosporine Dr. Botox was switching me over to, now that I'd run out of roid re-ups.

How it worked was, it suppressed the system's immune response — something one generally wouldn't want to do; only, in my case, my immune system was *over*-responding.

Was confused about what was happening and so was going full tilt, tryna fight off whatever was attacking. But incorrectly.

It was still unclear whether anything — and, if so, what — was attacking. Diet, airborne allergens, psychic trauma, or some endocrinological anomaly there weren't yet tests for — all possibilities.

But regardless. The *response*, whether warranted or nah, was causing issues.

Immune system too keyed up, reacting gratuitously, dispro-portionately to the purported attacks.

Inflaming things.

The theory went, if we just shut this bitch down completely, maybe my bod would chill out.

This of course left the door open to risks the unsuppressed immune system generally protected against. Liver problems, lymphoma, viral infections.

It was sorta like: I was out at sea, getting fucked by the waves, skin tore up, and now I was nixing my life vest — the one thing designed to keep me afloat—since the life vest had malfunctioned.

Had started weighing me down.

I mean, chances were I'd get fucked if I went ahead and started taking the stuff since...I was out at sea! Nixing my life vest! But would *for sure* be fucked if I did nothing, how fucked shit was already—was the case Dr. Botox made, over FaceTime.

Other side effects included confusion, gum enlargement, trouble breathing, increased hair growth, nausea.

Generally used for transplant patients, to prevent their immune systems from spazzing on the new organ that had set up shop in their bod.

To help em adjust to the new, foreign heart they were learning to live with.

I sat on the stoop, reading all this.

Confused. Breath short.

Feeling, vaguely, like I was about to puke.

Scanning the Wiki page for anything even remotely reassuring.

Cyclosporine, cyclosporine...

Cycles. Spores.

Was there a shroom connection?

In 1970, new strains of fungi were isolated from soil samples taken from Norway and from Wisconsin...components that had antifungal activity were isolated from extracts from these fungi. The Norwegian strain, Tolypocladium inflatum *Gams, was later used for the large-scale fermentation of cyclosporin.*

Oh so we talkin...*shroomies*?

You *know* I fuck with my shroomies, bro.

And you know what else I fuck with?

Fkn cycles.

Aw man.

OK.

Time to ride that shroom-cycle.

•

I couldn't work and I couldn't write.

I mean I could, technically.

In theory.

But the confusion was real.

The roid withdrawals.

Feeling these manic spurts, followed by deep dips.

Moments of illumination that faded into disorientation before I could even identify, let alone capture them.

Reading anything beyond the quickest hitter impossible.

Turning to song; gravitating towards brevity.

One-minute, single-verse, no-chorus tracks; single-taken, long-shot music vids.

Them Florida rappers were popping recently, specifically bc of this. Lil Pump, Ski Mask. XXXTENTACION, before he got merked last June.

How X popped off outta nowhere like he did, on SoundCloud, bc of this.

He started his verses the second the song started. No dilly-dallying doing eight bars of Woah and Yuh ad libs to gear up. No hooks. Just ripping it off the rip, then cutting the verse/song off before the listener knew what hit em. And even when he did ad-lib-stall, like on "RIP Roach," the beat/verse came in so hard when it did it slapped you. Like it started its own song.

The immediacy.

179

There was no time.

And then Valee. Chi-town-based, 'Ye understudy.

Initially feeling his bars to be lackluster, low-energy.

Confusingly simple.

Rudimentary, almost.

It took some listens to figure out their nuance.

What was esoterically next-level about em.

His feature verse on "Two 16s" by Z Money—the second 16 of the song's two. He doesn't take a single breath between bars, just keeps flowing in this eerie triplet flow that's syncopated in a way that he doesn't stop when a bar ends. He rides right over it.

No call-and-response between establishing and echoed rhyme.

The entire verse a single, uninterrupted stream.

And visually.

Young M.A's "Petty Wap" video. She starts out with six quick cuts—of her inhaling blunt smoke; of her exhaling; of a girl twerking; of a dude getting thrown into a pool; of a pool queue shooting a pool ball; of another girl twerking—almost just to show she was capable of cuts, it seemed. But then, subsequently, holding the camera on her for the rest of the song—also a single verse, no choruses—as she moves gradually towards the camera, poolside at a pool party.

A single, unbroken shot.

Like relying fully on her swag, her charisma, to hold your attention.

And once she'd gotten it, not letting go.

These became the daily mode-setters.

Became more important than reading, writing.

Or, became the only art forms I was able to ingest, how scattered I was.

That New Art.

That generous, considerate sharing.

That quick hit.

I wanted to partake.

To encourage its continuation.

Contribute.

So I got to jotting. Writing bars to the instrumentals that spawned em.

I couldn't write a book but I could a bar.

And then another bar.

A bar at a time.

About all the drugs I was on.

Switching from illegal to legal ones, but no less sketch.

About how, even still, despite everything, I was *still* the prettiest bitch out.

About how Yes I *still* loved ex, had love for editor bae; but also, they could get fucked.

Yes; and but also.

Both/neither.

Once I recorded them — each under a minute, done in a single take — into my voice recorder.

I wanted to represent them, visually.

I didn't have V around to shoot em for me, but I did have other homies.

I turned to the homies I had.

Ex-roomie bae shot the first video. In an alley, around the corner from my spot.

Single-take, mid-hang.

And roomie bae, the second. On a Lowe's mish, for light bulbs, in the parking lot.

Ended up shooting a couple more with roomie bro at the spot he'd moved to, around the corner. Although those turned out less good.

Less interesting.

Maybe bc they weren't shot out in the world.

Or maybe bc they reverted to the all-male, rapper-boy zone, like from before. From college.

Felt less giddy. Less *light*.

Weighed down by the seriousness of the boy-flex.

More interesting when I held the bars up to the bae-light.

2

THE OLE MAN

Feast of St. Michael & All Saints 2018

Walking back from my Medicaid-covered dental school appointment, where I'd gotten that new grill fitted.

Rubbing my tongue over my new, temporary molars, grinning like What's good bruh! to everyone I passed.

Finally able to chew again since, a week ago, not wanting to waste the last of a week-old baguette roomie bae bought.

Captain save-a-loaf.

Since torching that shit in the toaster, lathering it with grass-fed butter, and chomping tf out of it, before...

You already know.

Other molar straight snapped.

Like Fuck the other side.

Had been merking smoothies and smoothies only all week.

Hitting my tooth chasms with one of those lil toothpicks with a pointy side and a brush side.

The pointy side too pointy.

Like a goddamn lil dagger.

So every now and then just blasting my gums.

Fkng bleeding out...

But now.

Feeling hype about the new chompers.

Too hype!

So damn hype that I went Know what? I'm finna call the ole man.

Then I FaceTime called the ole man.

I hadn't spoken to him in some months.

It was midmorning my time, evening his.

I hadn't heard from him since, right when my skin had started spazzing, he'd emailed me about this thing Urinary Therapy:

Westerners don't get it but it's been an accepted medical practice in India for centuries. Madonna even used it.

But basically, what you do is:

Rub your own pee onto your skin. Piss into your cupped hands, blast all infected parts with it. It will cure virtually every affliction. It's cured eczema like yours. It cured my cataracts.

No seriously: I went to the mainstream doc here in Sapporo and he told me my condition was incurable. But then, each night the next fortnight, I started saving em bladder dregs. Setting em aside. To douse my eyelids with.

And now. You won't even believe—

I had yet to respond.

The thing with the ole man was, if I never hit him up, we'd never talk.

Had it always been like this.

There maybe had been a time when we did.

Musta been that six-month stretch, in 2011, so seven years ago, during my junior year back at school, after he dropped out of the priest training program in England, before he got a job teaching English in Hokkaido—where he lived now and 'will

184

till he dies,' he'd said recently—when posted up jobless in a rental his lil bro, my uncle, owned but hadn't rented out yet.

Maybe then. Maybe we spoke with some consistency then.

Although maybe not since that was around the time ex bae became main.

When ex bae and I became each other's fathers, mothers, brothers, and sisters too.

When the extreme codependency enabling shutting out / ignoring our respective families began.

I told him where I was at.

That I'd been roided for a second stint, but was now on this immunosuppressant.

Could feel the unease in the silence after I finished speaking, before he even spoke.

"That doesn't seem good," he said.

"It's not about good or bad rn, bro. Pretty out of options here...

"If you could only see...

"If you happened to be around..."

"Well did you try what I told you to?"

"Dude—"

"I know you're not used to hearing stuff like this, bc you've been raised in the Western system—"

"Bro—"

"But tellin ya, son. My cataracts—"

"BITCH don't call me son I ain't your son."

"Well you are. Technically."

"Relationships aren't relationships de facto. They only are if you make em. Like plants; you gotta water em. Maybe if you had the balls to ever talk to your own dad, you'd—"

185

"Whether you like it or not, you *chose* me. Your soul did. Chose *me,* as a parent. So—"

"You're still telling yourself that? To justify your fuckshit? That's weak, bro."

"Whatever you say—"

"That doesn't even make sense. What about abortions?"

"Well yeah. Abortions. Abortions are wrong. Unnatural."

"So, what. You have an abortion. Then…what?"

"Well your soul is gonna have to pay for that. At some point. The soul of the child—"

"Dude, you fuckin serious?"

"What? Yeah. Snowflake liberals want you to think—"

"You're saying that. To me. Now." I was losing my shit. "Knowing what I went through. What happened with—

"Why I can't get over—"

He said he hadn't known about that…

So yeah.

The ole man convo wudn't too productive.

Worse, it set me back; I rage-scratched another layer of roid-weakened skin off my forehead and -arms, restarting the whole cycle.

3

SCHOOLBOY

October 2018

N was a bestie from way back, from abroad in London, when we were flatmates our junior undergrad years.

A year after I quit sports and committed whole hog to that Art Life.

Right after I'd met, but before I in-earnest fell in with, ex bae.

Not in-earnest falling in with ex bae till I'd gone abroad, fucked around, then returned.

London marked that first Young Death; that first Fall.

N, that year, had been integral to easing my way into this transition.

That no-sex bf I could talk to the same as I could a bae. About whatever tf.

His ole man also dipped when he was ten or eleven, remarried; while his ma, like mine, stayed and stayed single.

And although we'd never lived in the same place since that semester — he'd gone to a different college stateside, then straight into grad school for a poetry PhD — we'd kept up a consistent and thorough email thread over the seven-or-so years.

But he was moving to Philly this month! he told me, over email, last month.

———

Philly, by foot, over the two years since I'd returned, had been reduced to like three places.

Three routes.

Especially so lately, now that I could no longer bike.

Everywhere with even the faintest whiff of a pre-walk ex bae memory too treacherous, unless whizzing past.

Philly had become: along 41st to the Sunoco on Baltimore (cheapest tobacco in town), to pit-stop at Clark Park there for a bench cig, and back—detours off of which included the Fresh Grocer, CVS, roomie bro's and, now, the dental school.

To the Wawa SE of my spot, that I rarely walked to since it was ex bae's way.

And…

Wait yeah.

That was basically it.

That was Philly.

But then N pulled up.

And with him, the vicarious newness with which he saw the city.

We recorded a pod in the graveyard south of Baltimore, that I hadn't been back to since getting locked inside with ex bae, way back when, and having to circle its perimeter, as twilight became night, till we finally found a traversable wall.

We went to a reading at the Kelly Writers House, that I'd never been to since it was on UPenn's campus and UPenn meant ex bae meant I steered clear at all costs, unless forced, by Postmates, to deliver something there.

And he'd moved onto 43rd and Pine, so right on my sole walking route; only, once I linked with him, he'd lead me elsewhere.

Along routes I'd deemed beyond my range.

Un-triggering all the spots.

Re-instilling multiplicity to all the places I'd decided were, and could only be, a single thing.

I texted him What's good around 5 one day.

He said he was going to an Eileen Myles reading at the Penn Book Center, a bookstore on 34th and Walnut, if I was tryna join.

"You'd just be going solo otherwise?"

"Yeah!" he said.

I'd been peripherally aware of this spot, but had never been inside, I realized, upon setting foot inside.

The reading was lit.

Poems that didn't sound poem-y in the way I hated that most poems sounded.

More like rambly yet deliberate bars that loosely adhered to poetic form.

And Eileen Myles didn't do the thing poets be doing at poetry readings where they make everyone uncomfortable at their self-seriousness, and by the end feel (the audience, or at least I, would) like the poet just jerked it, straddling them so they were trapped, and then busting prematurely onto their chest.

No; Eileen was charming, charismatic, self-aware.

Honestly hilarious.

Lubed everyone up with killer banter before plunging into the bars.

Which themselves didn't sound all that different than the banter. Just more ordered.

189

It all sounded natural.
I was wetter than I'd ever been at a poetry reading.

So many young, attractive, femme women in there with their bla-tantly, almost parodically masculine-presenting female partners.
Like the divide was so distinct.
Hi-top fades, fuccboi haircuts, blazers, vests.
Cowboy belts.
A lotta Carhartt.
And I mean, I was wittit.
Eileen Myles, even, had just changed their pronoun from she to they, they mentioned.
And I fucked with—roundabout-related to—how wild/tricky some of their bars. From *Evolution* (2018):

I shoot these themes
themes
I mean my
jism
that look on your face
is covered
with my thought

Lol.
I mean damn.

It was out front the bookstore, after the reading, that I recog-nized, across the way, the poet Gina Myers.

Sorta spazzed out and wanted to go up to her, but then didn't.

Then N and I walked to Local 44 on 44th and Pine, for a drink, and who did I see, sitting at the bar, but the poet Gina Myers. Again.

Wanted to approach her again but then didn't.

•

First I encountered the poet Gina Myers was a season after moving back to Philly, late-fall two falls ago.

My first season back in Philly the first season post-Trump.

Spent full nocturnal and focused solely on stimulant intake and banging out the first draft of my weed farm novel, stretching out the weed bands I'd saved.

Come spring though I could sit and write in solitude no longer.

I had to make moves.

To scheme.

And this, at the time, meant proving myself — affirming my worth — to my alma mater.

Wrote my undergrad fiction advisor a thirsty, harass-y email.

About Checking In.

About *could I buy you a drink.* To *catch up.*

He responded after a week or so *Semester's a little crazy rn but did I wanna come out to a faculty reading later this month?*

The reading was at a site that wasn't a site when I went there.

When I went there there had been talk of a hotel to be erected adjacent to campus in the near future; I remember bc there had been much protest-ruckus about the 'ethicality' of this.

But they had, since, gone ahead and built the thing.

I pulled up in the box feeling excited and also ashamed for feeling excited, and also crazy.

Everything surreal, entering the room the reading was in.

I'd been planning for this all week, but was somehow still almost late.

Only one open seat.

Wasn't till I sat in it that I realized who it was next to.

"Professor E!" I said, when I sat.

He looked at me with a sardonic twinkle in his eye— immediately recognizing me.

"I'm sorry, you'll have to excuse me," he said in that dainty, parodically academic, lowkey Asperger's way he spoke. "But I've forgotten your name."

I felt the wheels turning in my head. Felt my School Voice/ Self wash over me like a mask.

Professor E was a savage.

First I had him was fall of senior year which was actually spring since I'd taken what would have been senior fall to move out west with ex bae (she'd graduated), work at a coffee shop, read all of Bolaño, and dwell in the romanticism of having 'dropped out.'

He'd do shit like take a sentence out of everyone's papers and read them aloud, one at a time, smirking after each, to show how shitty everyone's papers were. Only never mine.

I had no qualms about assuming School/Academic Voice back then.

Plus I was grown and actually read the shit—on the Philosophy of Art, 'life as a work of art,' that was his thing—unlike the rest of those spoonfed fucks too sure of themselves, too concerned with pushing their woke agendas, to actually challenge themselves to consider anything they didn't already think.

Things were good with us till the first class of his Philosophy of Language honors seminar, the following semester.

I'd finagled my way into writing a book on *2666* (2004), sexual assault, and the Juárez femicides for two of my final four credits to graduate, and was more shopping the seminar to gauge its relevance.

Like five people. In Professor E's house.

That Wittgenstein was on the syllabus mainly why I signed up.

But the class, as explained by Professor E in a no-joke three-hour, unbroken monologue, was Wittgenstein, and then a whole bunch of fucks responding to/trying to understand Wittgenstein.

Misunderstanding Wittgenstein.

Trying to understand the rules governing what could be said, since they no longer could say what couldn't be said, when Witt's whole point had been that everything that could be said could be said clearly, without knowing any governing rules.

Getting bogged down with nitpicky metaphysical questions entirely unrelated to the real, tangible problems of the world.

Like, say, why raped and murdered corpses of women kept showing up fortnightly in the Sonoran Desert, on the U.S.–Mexico border.

And I wasn't even a dick about it.

Just went Thanks but no thanks is all.

I actually reached out to him to co-edit my Bolaño book-thesis, and he was like Nah.

And our subsequent interactions around campus were sus.

Such a meanie!

Which convinced me that, when my thesis got blocked by some faceless, unnamed member of the administration, he'd been behind it.

But so I was sitting there feeling judged af, barely able to remember how my School/Academic Voice even sounded anymore after all those nightly spliffs to the face during that season growing weed in Humboldt.

After that year of trying to become a rapper in Oakland, before that.

After sleeping outside for a season, before that — a mish/spazz-out his arguable diploma-block directly precipitated; I set out walking, from Philly, after being told I could return to finish out my degree, but at full price — my eight, need-based, full-ride semesters had expired — a month later.

"And so what have you been up to ... Sean, was it?"

"Erm ..."

"I remember you were trying to write a book on ... Borges?"

"Bolaño."

"And so?"

"I mean ... I've been ... shoot ... still tryna write that book!"

But then, thank fuck, the reading started.

Everyone who read was whatever till this girl who seemed not much older than me went up there.

Sleeve-zatted like a muhfucker.

Fkn hella swagged out.

Super sexy but in a way my brain couldn't objectify due to my awe/admiration/fear of her.

How she read, her voice had a quivery quality she overrode with her deliberate and concerted pacing.

Like she knew that what she was reading was Out There, but like she'd thought it through and had decided that she, still, nonetheless, was gonna read it.

The sense of anticipation in the room — heightened for me no doubt given Professor E and I were damn near touching knees — pin-drop-y in a way no other reader — who unanimously created an affect of circle jerk-y formality akin to a story told at a stuffy dinner party — achieved.

Hers was like: Yo, here's a concerted, focused communication of my realest, deepest, fkng feelingest feelings, bro. Take it or leave it.

My heart was beating so fkng hard, so sick.

Needless to say, I fanboy-ed tf out on her after — my advisor was there with his wife and wasn't tryna turn up.

I copped her chapbook, *Philadelphia* (2017), literally about living itinerantly post-college till settling in Philly and coping with the urge, every time new feelings surfaced, to flee again.

But then not fleeing.

But then staying.

I came somatically the entire drive back to Philly.

•

When I got home from the Eileen Myles reading, I started frantically going through my bookshelves, tryna find Gina's chapbook.

But then remembered. I gave it to editor bae, last summer, right before she ghosted. For her birthday.

195

And when I checked online, I learned that they'd only printed 100 copies and…were all sold out!

Editor bae had no clue what I'd given her.

How much.

Would likely never.

Luckily, I took pictures of every page.

All twenty-four of them.

Reading em over that night, I remembered why I fucked with em so heavy.

Philadelphia wasn't a book that tickled my literary sensibilities. That instructed or entertained me.

It did much more.

Each poem a *mantra*, to be read every morning.

Every time I felt I was about to spazz out.

Every poem medicine — calming agents.

For one, the book felt like an obverse, companion piece to my Walk Book.

The Walk Book was 100 page-long anecdotes, each titled the name of a city/town, and dated, spanning *March–June 2014.*

The title of Gina's chapbook was literally *Philadelphia,* and the first page was simply

August–October 2014.

My Walk Book Winter–Spring, her chapbook Summer–Fall, same year.

'Obverse' meaning not only opposite but part of the same thing — rather than opposed — like sides of a coin.

Mine a prolonged manic episode about constantly moving to flee the feelings, the crisis.

Hers about having the same impulse to flee the feelings,

the crisis, but instead staying put. Having the courage to look right at em.

It starts:

New city same shit
Moving through
the streets
pre-fall golden
in late afternoon
sunlight / bright red
crumbling brick
& shoddy graffiti
asks freedom?

She out here, moving through these streets. Walking. Yet she accepts that she can only go so far. Doesn't try to turn her stroll into a neurotic, completionist quest bc she knows she can't. Knows that that impulse is futile.

There is
no breeze
I do not
put myself
forward / I am
just here
walking down
the sidewalk
refusing
to make sense

of things
that can't be
made sense of
& appreciating
my insignificance

It's not like she dulling herself to the feelings. She feels them. Heavy.

We can go
to the coast
It's a short drive
We'll make believe
a getaway vacation
& walk the boardwalk
& in the morning
I'll take you
to the airport
Everything is
fleeting
& it makes life
more interesting
We will have fun
until we won't

And bc it's so full of feelings, it's tempting to write it off as sentimental. As 'different than serious art.'

But this is the statement she's making about supposed 'serious art.' She makes this statement:

I don't want
to hear it
if I can't
dance to it
Stevie sings

That line break, after can't.
How I feel about so much writing.
I...just...
I can't.
Bro cut the fuckshit make me feel something *sing to me*!
Why are your bars any different than your writing?
Why the fuck.
Why indeed.
There should be no difference, what she saying.
What she demonstrates.
She even takes shots at the specific rage-impulse I read her over and over specifically to quell. To calm my way out of.

Hey baby
come sit on
my lap / Why
don't you smile
Oow I could
get me some
of that
You got a
boyfriend

Bitch, you know
you want it
Dumb cunt

But back to *freedom,* and whether it lies in *art* or in *walking across country* or simply here, in *Philadelphia,* meaning wherever you happen to be. Whatever body you find yourself inhabiting:

I thought
I could find
freedom in
a book
but I was wrong
Now it's the dream
of the road
to go & never
stop / Now it's
the moment
at the end of
the work day
when I take off
my dress

Fuck bruh.
    I wanted to talk to her.
    To tell her I done explored this dream, *of the road / to go & never / stop,* and

I don't know...

Ended up back in the same city.

Same shit.

How did she do it?

Manage to stay put?

I wanted to learn.

To tell her / learn.

Be taught what I didn't know / tell her what I did.

We all knew things others could be helped by, it was just about locating what.

About reaching out.

So I reached out and asked if she wanted to record a pod and we met up and recorded a pod.

Hadn't realized you could just do that.

She talked to me about the New York School of poets and writing like you talk and studying under Maggie Nelson during her MFA and how she was from Michigan and loved the Pistons and Tigers and Spartans and about struggles she'd been going through surviving and maintaining her health and working in order to secure her healthcare.

I guess I hadn't realized you could just be all the things you were to anyone whenever and that that was an OK thing and that it was an OK thing to talk and write and correspond directly and clearly rather than cryptically and strategically and manipulatively...

4

RYDEN

November 2018

I picked up Ryden at his new spot, 49th and somewhere south of Baltimore. Warrington maybe.

Near there.

His roomies headed out to campus too but in a different car.

Room in theirs, but Ryden wanted to roll with.

Four-ninety-five five minutes faster but I decided on Baltimore. To retrace the steps.

First time retracing them and first time out there this Philly stint since seeing Gina read—got led some rando route last time, and at night, directly from the 41st spot.

It was Ryden's detour—his decision to roll with, to think of and hire me / my van, and for that matter to even move—that led me back this way.

Past the gated park in I think the 60s that marked western-most West Philly.

Past the Kmart I found my waterproof pants at T–3 days, and had that breakdown in the Kmart parking lot that almost broke the resolve.

Almost quelled the mania.

But then the mania survived; the mania was too strong; the mania doubled down—pushed me all the way to Mountain Time.

Past the Rite Aid on Baltimore I ducked into for bug spray

late Day 1 of 100, wiping ex bae's departure-tears from my memory (and mine from my face), suddenly realizing 'Oh but ticks though' while considering, for the first time tangibly, what sleeping out would *actually be like,* while walking that first day — although probably mostly stalling.

Three days ago, wandering around all night, realizing the LA trip hadn't done shit. The roids, the spores, neither.

Panicking.

Peak mania, again.

Why Ryden hired me partly, probably, witnessing this.

Out of a sort of pity, but one that didn't feel patronizing; out of one that operated within the System — according to a basic logic that was thoughtful and utilitarian.

He needed a thing (pick up furniture; move); I had the thing — could provide the service — he needed.

My mania on that morning was distinctly Scorpion: gritty, stiff-lipped, ready to snap, wield that pincer at any moment.

I remember bc that morning was the Friday morning Lil Durk's *Signed to the Streets 3* (2018) dropped.

Was primed to make the mish out to the old walls bc of the courage that project gave me.

Signed to the Streets (2013), that early Drill rap classic, the anthem, going into the walk.

What helped me stare the savagery of the world head-on, unflinching; what reminded me what the world outside the walls of our safe dwellings looked like.

What unfiltered nighttime sounded like.

Late in the acid trip the February before the March 2014 I set out — the trip I decided to set out walking, after walking all over West Philly, tripping so hard but totally OK somehow — I remember walking back to ex bae's, parka'd up, blasting Durk's "Dis Ain't What U Want," realizing that I, this, me, wasn't, could never be, what she wanted. No matter how much she thought I was.

That song became the intro music to the opening pod that validated and perpetuated the prolonged manic episode that was the walk.

But I was listening to Durk's newest, third iteration of the same project on this morning, the morning Ryden follow-up texted about moving the couches, after turning up with autonomous bae the night before—she'd just returned from Wyoming from a months-long EMT training—for some reason emboldened to mish it to the Penn Bookstore across the street from ex bae's grad school office, where I used to grind at and was posted out front of when I first got that call from her, saying she was fucking with women now.

Saying how all those jokes about *Blue Is the Warmest Color* (2013) had been real.

I was going back to the scene of the crime.

Flying into rather than fleeing the storm.

Or—I was about to. Till Ryden texted.

Accompanying him back to campus, to pick up the couches for him, then, felt like a natural progression.

And possibly saved me from an ex-bae run-in/spazz-out I didn't want. That would have been a bad look. That I wouldn't have been able to handle.

It was the tail end of an all-nighter that I ran into Ryden, three days ago.

Seven-a.m.-folks-commuting tail end.

Ryden himself commuting.

204

Suited up, headed to the El.

Me looking wooked out geared up like a hobo, bundled in jackets on jackets, shivering from sleep deprivation.

From lack of hormone regulation.

Thing was, he knew. Immediately.

I was all: Getting going?

He was all: Winding down? smiling sadly.

Ryden didn't talk much.

Didn't small talk.

He spoke when he had something to say.

We rode in silence, looking out the windows, he unaware of all the shit these spots I hadn't traversed since walking em, almost five years ago, were making me feel.

Ryden used to work with a crew of my ex housemates, at a fancy hotel downtown.

A fancy hotel they were unionizing.

How I met him.

The connections off the rip were too many to fathom.

He hapa—mom Japanese, dad white (Scottish-Norwegian—mine Irish-Swedish). Grew up in California.

His middle name Ryden—'thunder god' in Japanese; mine Thor—'thunder god' in Swedish.

His birthday February 13; mine, February 14. But lowkey the same since Japan was a day ahead of Cali, timewise.

First (Anglo) name same name-root as mine.

Except he went with his Japanese name, was the difference.

My three-years-younger double.

———

Ex-roomie bro—from the old house I used to live in—once asked me about Ryden, early on, when he was first inducted into the fold.

Like we were a cult.

We lowkey were.

With the price of admission being undying dedication to the takedown of the Man.

Of *men*...

But ex-roomie bro went What you think o' Ryden?

I went Bro I fuck with Ryden. Heavy.

He went Yeah? Can't get a read on that guy.

"What's there to get a read on?"

"I don't know. He doesn't...*show* enough.

"Keeps you on your toes.

"Doesn't react immediately to actions in his vicinity."

This always stuck with me.

I thought of my response weeks later:

Well yeah, just bc this fool doesn't *overwhelmingly affirm* every damn thing you do like you woke organizer fucks be doing.

Doesn't *obviously support* every stance you take on this or that endlessly complicated, nuanced, inescapably dual-sided issue we, as Americans—eating off the system, whether explicitly 'supporting' it or not—are complicit in.

That understated, observant, withholding social mode might, could possibly be, some Japanese shit you just don't get.

When I was first running out of weed bands, spring after I came out to Philly, my uncle N, Mama's bro, who lived in Tokyo still with my *baba,* hit me and my sisters with that quick $5K bundle, an advance on whatever inheritance he would throw us when he passed (he unmarried and childless).

It came outta the blue, and we didn't know why, were slightly worried he had some medical condition he wasn't telling us about.

Even my mama, she didn't know.

"Baba won't say what happened. I think they got into some fight."

"What about Uncle N? You talk to him?"

"Ha. Seanie. We don't talk."

This always baffled me. I never understood why they didn't.

"Seanie, you know Baba. She doesn't like to talk about stuff like that. Doesn't like to admit anything is wrong. When she fell and broke her hip, she just lay there. Didn't call anyone. Till N finally got back from work late that night."

"Did she have a phone? You gotta get her a phone."

"We got her a phone," my mama said.

She then diverted from the fact she hadn't, since leaving Japan in her twenties, ever had a conversational relationship with her brother. She told me about a book on World War Two she was reading. How Baba reiterated what the book said when my mama told her that, even after the first bomb dropped, first week of August 1945, the government was rallying the women and children, telling them to get whatever bamboo sticks they could find. To keep fighting.

"Bamboo sticks!" my mama said. "When what they were dealing with was another atomic bomb. No one even knew.

"Till that second week of August, when the second one hit.

"But that's the Japanese way: put your head down, erase your feelings, and keep pushing to the bitter end."

———

Later that week I remember I linked with ex bae.

This weeks before that call in which she told me she was done.

We were at the Green Line on Baltimore, reading together like we used to at that Green Line before I walked.

Sitting across from each other, footsying, maybe splitting earbuds.

Going in on our own, but next to each other.

Content with silence in lieu of each other's presence.

But I couldn't not tell her what I'd been thinking.

I told her what was going down with my uncle and grandma.

What my mom said about the temperamental bent of half of my genetics. How that quality, of suppressing feelings/emotions, was, in her eyes, quintessentially Japanese.

"I mean, don't you think that could explain stuff? Why I can't ever sleep next to you? Why I can't rest until I *do* something? *Finish* the book? Prove my *worth*?

"Like, that's an aspect of my upbringing I can't ignore: it was always pack your shit, nix your friends, keep it moving. That bomb hit but forget about it, we gon' keep pushing. Go out into the yard and find a bamboo stick to keep fighting with.

"And I'm even not saying it's bad," I continued. "It just is. Is why I'm still pushing on this Art Shit. Even though everything is getting bombed to shit.

"I feel like being more aware of my tendencies could help me calibrate them. Prevent me from fucking up my shit, my relationships, *before* they get out of hand.

"Like better understanding Japanese culture/temperament is key to that."

Ex bae mighta just been stressed about how much grad school reading she had to do by nightfall. Been annoyed that I was ranting so unboundaried at her.

But she hit me all scripted like "So you're saying you have specific traits due to your ethnic background?"

"I mean. Well yeah."

"That's racist."

"You tryna tell me there are *no temperamental differences* between your whiteness and anyone else's cultures?"

"Well that's how people justify racism."

"Bro — Japan was a *closed country* until 1865. No one entered or exited. For centuries. Off on this isolated island. When people go to Japan they marvel at how random their customs. How strange, to them, their social quirks. Bae — you ever been to Japan?

"That's what I fkng thought."

And that ended that.

Ended maybe much more.

Didn't occur to me till later that my preoccupation with my hapa-ness distracted me from the deeper issue: I was getting money from my family and was talking about moving in with V, rather than using it towards her, towards us, in the natural next step in our half-decade-long relationship.

Bc of course we were above such basic-ass customs as cohabitation, 'marriage'...

•

We passed the Giant supermarket on Baltimore where I stocked up on final rations for the first leg. The Target I dipped into, as the sun set that first night, for the bug spray Rite Aid didn't end up having. Ryden started telling me about his relationship.

Relationships.

He was dating a lady out in Brooklyn whom he knew from

college; they'd visit each other on alternating weekends, as they were able. As their jobs allowed.

But they were 'open.'

Ryden also seeing his ex, who lived in Philly.

And his BK boo, seeing others also.

"That actually works?" I said, turning off of Baltimore, onto Chester, that led towards roomie bro and my old college house, the Barn—along the stretch I used to walk along for cigs every other night, while writing my Bolaño book-thesis; this stretch that walking along made me feel so calm it gave me the initial idea to keep walking—to keep basking in that calm—all the way to California. "Don't y'all get jealous?"

Ryden thought about this.

"I don't know," he said. "Not so much. Surprisingly.

"We just communicate how we're feeling. We're good about that.

"Like, ultimately, we don't own each other," he said. "I wouldn't wanna limit her intimate experiences outta that impulse."

Things were so damn windy, shit was flying all over the place.

Breaking open.

Sloughing.

Bro straight up we were whizzing down these alma-mater-side, Stepford-wife-ass tree-arched lanes I knew so well—so deeply, like from childhood, or from a past life, or from my subconscious—box momentum propelling us forward like a goddamn pendulum, fkng *coasting*—when a fat gust hit and got the leaves swirling like out of a street-sized blower, or leaf-snow globe.

We looked at each other like Ohhhf!

Like putting hands over mouths incredulous.

Like lil youngins do.

Blowing bits of air out and making choppy, pre-laugh sounds.

The house where Ryden's roomie's boss — Ryden's roomie didn't go to, but worked at, my alma mater — whose couches we were picking up, was across the street from a kids' soccer game.

Pulling up in the box, I had to stall till Ryden's roomies showed. We'd somehow beat em out there.

Woulda felt weird idling out front all those kids, dads swiveling like Tf is this guy.

Except I had Ryden by my side.

Ryden stayed calm.

So I stayed calm.

All you gotta do to fit in is stay calm, I wanted to jot down.

Back at his spot in West, we took a paid lunch break, per union standards.

He copped me a banh mi at the corner store there, with his two roomies.

We were shot from carrying those big-ass couches up the three spiral flights of the Victorian he'd just moved into, that I kept having to convince em would fit.

That we just had to find the right angle.

"Dude — couldn'ta done this without you. Honestly," he said, cheers-ing his still-wrapped sammie with mine.

I wanted to wolf down my sammie then and there, but Ryden was tryna walk back to eat his, so I followed suit.

His two roomies — gals in their early twenties, fresh outta college — trailed ten, twenty steps behind.

"So this some new shit for them, innit. Being in the city," I said to Ryden.

They'd been sorta looking around, all shook, out front the sammie spot. At the homeless folks. At all the activity in the intersection there.

"Lowkey," he said, smiling.

I was telling them about where was good for groceries. Where was cheapest and where had the best produce. Getting reminded of how long it had been since ex bae and I first made our initial move out here — half a decade ago!

How it was lowkey absurd that I was back out here.

That I was *still* out here.

Tf was I still doing out here?!

Ryden, under his breath, looking back at his roomies to ensure they were outta earshot, said, "I didn't wanna tell them, but did you hear about the robbery last week? There was a robbery here last week."

"Where?"

"Here. This intersection," he said, bounding up onto the stoop of his new digs.

"Goddamn," I said.

He raised his eyebrows like I know, right?

"Well that's what you're here for," I said. "To protect em."

My ankles were swelling and peeling and leaking again — I could feel my diabetes socks sticking to them, smell the weird smell they made when they got like this.

The immune suppression not doing shit. If anything, making things worse.

212

I had a feeling things would break down and I'd have to mish it back to Cali again — lil sis had already started looking at flights.

But Ryden asked if we could do one more run. To move the bigger, bulkier stuff he hadn't been able to fit into his roomie's car. "I'll add it to the tab, obviously."

At Ryden's old spot, one of his roomies, flamboyant hapa boy, had all these human-sized plants in the backyard. His babies.

He told Ryden he could pick one out for the new spot.

Ryden asked if I could, too.

"Oh, that's not necessary," I said. "Unless you wanna get rid of one."

I could tell he really loved these guys. And this was, after all, the first time I was meeting this boy.

"Oh. Sure. Yeah that's fine," he said, looking me over all suspicious. Sounding like it clearly wasn't fine.

We went out back.

Ryden picked one.

I picked the smallest, most deformed-looking one.

"These OK?" Ryden asked.

His roomie said they were, biting his nail.

I carried the first one, Ryden's, through the house, down the front steps, and into the box.

When I picked up the second one — the deformed one — Ryden's roomie went Wait wait wait.

I put him down.

I just gotta take a pic, he said, taking one.

After he took the pic, I said We good?

He said we were.

But I didn't even make it to the kitchen before he went "Wait wait wait. I can't. I don't want him to get neglected."

"OK," I said, setting him down. "Of course. No worries."

I moved him back to the backyard. Back amongst his friends.

"I'm sorry, man," he said as I made my way back through the house. "I didn't have a mom—and these are my babies!"

I told Ryden I might be dipping soon.

"Well holler when you back," he said.

We were out front his front steps. It was night.

We dapped each other up.

He backed away, saluting.

I went to close the box's side sliding door.

"Wait—your plant!" I called out.

He turned and went "No, that's all you," doing a prayer gesture and bowing.

•

Three weeks later, in California, autonomous bae called me from Philly and said Did you hear? Did I hear what? I said. About Ryden. Did you hear about Ryden. What about Ryden, I said. She told me he had a brain aneurism in his sleep and was in a coma. It's a year later now, writing this, and he's still in a coma. His parents have been out in Philly for a year. I don't live in Philly anymore. They're gonna take him back to California once his insurance runs out. I need to go visit him, before he goes. I'll let you guys know how he's doing once I know.

5

BALLBOY

December 2018

I couldn't believe shit was getting fucked again.

That I had to go through this all over.

Back to Fullerton in the ma's Prius, to see Dr. Botox.

I mean he was a good dude, like he was doing his best.

But homie had no clue what to do.

Took one look at me and probably thought Jeez, not this dude again, this dude is fucked.

And promptly got me back on the roids.

My uncle J, big cuz E's pops, heard about how fucked I was and was adamant I see this Tibetan doctor who'd cured his friend's breast cancer.

Uncle J a U.S. naval chaplain stationed in Okinawa.

Posted like much of the U.S. military these days, on bases secured by our WWII involvement. To keep tabs on Kim Jong.

Like Bro you make one fkng move we blowing this bitch.

Sending in the boys.

Sitting waiting *wishing* a ninja would.

But Uncle J was the man; he offered to pay for my visit.

I didn't ask how much it was.

———

In order to see the Tibetan doctor Dr. L, I had to not eat sugar or drink caffeine for 48 hours before.

I straight up laughed, thinking it was a joke, when my mama told me this.

I felt so naked, like my brain wasn't able to defend itself with quips and manic rambling.

Honestly didn't know how to function not constantly showing how funny/clever I could be.

At the end of the 48, I had to piss in a jar and present him with it.

Which, I later learned, I think he took a sip of to figure out what was wrong with me.

The office was in a 405-adjacent strip-mall-type spot.

One of those spacious strip malls they have in LA, with like trees surrounding the parking lot.

A vape store, a CrossFit gym down the road a ways.

Dr. L's son the receptionist.

Super Zen, gentle vibes all around.

Smelled like herbs in there.

Dr. L just smiled and told me put my forearms on this throw pillow he had at the ready on his desk. So he could take my pulse.

Felt bad that he didn't have a pillowcase bc I don't think he expected my arms to be as flakey and gnarly and weepy as they were.

But if he felt a way, he didn't show it.

Just breathed through his nose and exuded calm.

The mama sitting in an adjacent chair, brow furrowed, holding her purse on her lap.

———

After feeling my pulse awhile, homie took the pee jar, rubber-banded and wrapped in a Whole Foods produce bag, into a back area. Then came back.

Said "Hot. Too hot. Too much inflamed."

Hit me with some herbs—deer-poop-looking black pellets I was supposed to chew but ended up not being able to bc I had temporary caps on both root-canalled molars, and so had to blend in the mama's NutriBullet and dilute and drink—and an anti-inflammatory diet:

No sugar except maple syrup.

No chocolate except raw cacao.

No processed grains, just basmati rice, corn tortillas, quinoa.

No dairy except grass-fed butter.

No caffeine (!) except green tea (1 cup) before noon.

Even some fruit/veggie stuff like no nightshades, no pine-apple, no avo.

Animal-wise, nitrite-free turkey bacon, salmon, chicken breast, eggs OK.

And a supplement to add to the leafy green–berry–apple–celery–centric juice I was to hit daily.

The best diet, turned out, didn't involve narrowing the number of groups you fucked with.

It was best to fuck with all groups.

To take all groups on their own terms, identify what each had to offer, and fuck with each group's most useful elements.

And never fuck too unanimously with any one group.

Back at the spot, I didn't know where to go.

What to do.

My life since I read *Infinite Jest* (1996) freshman year of college and first tried shrooms and quit basketball to go abroad to study writing, only to cultivate a nicotine addiction, a molly habit, contract herpes the second (or third) day I was there (was never sure which girl it was), and end up engaging in a semester-long flex beef with my creative writing prof (a Scottish novelist of moderate renown who will remain nameless but whose first name might start with A — we were both tryna impress the same undergrad girls) before failing said writing class due to a late submission due to a miscalculation of the California-London time difference —

But my life, since then, had been: get as lit as possible, starting the moment I awoke each day, to either read or write an unnatural amount.

Now I was finna fkng die if I railed another coffee bruh! what it was looking like.

In the kitchen, the mama handed me a shot glass of blasted Tibetan deer-turd-pellet powder, diluted with water, and told me Shoot it.

I shot it.

Then she whipped up this wild like lowkey 100% celery juice (lil apple also) not even in the NutriBullet but in the Cuisinart which made wild pulp waste and was a bitch to clean, that she read on a blog (after printing out and magneting it onto the fridge) was Top Ten Anti-Inflammatory Foods.

Told me rail that shit too.

I railed that shit too.

Then the mama was tired from all that blendering and chauffeuring. She retired to her room to keep plugging away on the newest Murakami, *Killing Commendatore* (2017) — the untranslated version.

———

There was this alley that ran adjacent to Wilshire, from the mama's to this park next to a Starbucks, a few blocks over.

One of those garbage-type alleys I feel are unique to LA.

Where the storefronts facing Wilshire dumped all their trash and like dishwashers would pop out onto to smoke.

But this had become my 'around the block' equivalent, quieter and less exposed than going actually around the block.

Was an extension of 'inside,' where I could smoke and stroll and feel OK in PJ-type attire.

Rocking flippy-floppies.

So long as I didn't get too immersed in whatever I was reading/writing on my phone and watched where I was going, to steer clear of the trash-bile puddles and not step toes/toe-cuts exposed into them, like I didn't more than once.

It took everything in me to not order a coffee.

I needed one bc I was tryna read Guy Debord's *Society of the Spectacle* (1967) since V kept recommending it and quoted it in (or *as*) a letter he wrote me once.

I'd been tryna read it for months now.

Unable to.

Not understanding.

Reading the epigraph and opening paragraphs over and over.

Had that first part down!

But once it started getting into all kindsa Marxist stuff I was like WAIT WHAT?

WHAT IS HAPPENING.

WHO WHERE WHEN.

Like Slow tf down dude how tf does that follow that bro what.

Felt I needed all the fuel I could get.

But didn't cave.

Went with a Passion Fruit Relax Calm tea or whatever.

Sat against a tree in the park across the street, reading the same passage over and over, laughing aloud at myself for how badly my brain was working.

White woman pulled up in a minivan, rolled down the window, leaned over.

"Dinner?"

Her daughter held out a greasy fast-food bag.

"Go ahead, hon," she urged. "Feed the man dinner!"

"Oh no," I said, semaphoring a hard redirect. "On a diet."

Something about that confused her.

"Wait —" she said. "Are you not —," looking around for some reason, checking that no one would hear maybe. "Are you *not…* *homeless*?"

"Well that depends," I said, dipping my teabag sage-like, looking off into the distance, conjuring my response from the Great Beyond. "On what you mean by 'home.'"

The fam came through in time for the mama's birthday, mid month.

I whipped up a paleo choco mousse with avo, banana, maple syrup, raw cacao, vanilla extract.

Topped with a raspberry.

An anti-inflammatory bday 'cake.'

The avo a diet-cheat but OK, relatively.

———

Talked to the ole man one night for his birthday, also mid month. Walking to the water at 4 a.m.

He'd pivoted away from politics to nutrition.

Was using nutrition to feed the neurosis beast within.

To occupy his YouTube time.

He'd been preaching paleo but had one-eightied to veganism.

Was exploring fruitarianism.

"Bro I ate seven bananas today."

I was like "Bro seven? Bro that's a lotta bananas."

He was like "Dude I'll eat seven bananas tomorrow!"

I was like "Fock yeah. Get it."

Started hitting the park daily.

Re-remembering my inner baller.

Getting shots up.

Using shot-quotas to quell the hatred of neoliberal feminism I'd been cultivating.

It was lowkey working!

Was still reading Houellebecq, working through his corpus, but with less fanaticism than before.

More like Damn bruh, those some thought-provoking insights.

Those some hot takes!

Less like Wow this why my ex left if I see her new boo I'ma skull fuck her.

Y'know…progress!

•

One day went to the park to get up my 100 free throws, 100 pull-up Js, 100 3s, only to find all courts occupied save one.

221

And that one had a person on it.

A person who looked exactly like ex bae's new boo Z.

Or looked exactly like how I remembered Z.

Which consisted of no specific features, just a general shape and hair color and seeming hatred of men.

This girl had all those things.

Mid-thirties, heavyset, indignant face.

Doing form shooting in the paint.

I started with free throws.

When I got to mid-range pull-ups, she was doing alternating baselines.

Both of us not speaking, but gradually finding the rhythm.

Shooting when the other wasn't.

Moving towards the unoccupied portion of the court.

Shagging for the other when it was on our route, or could be done with a slight alteration of it.

But otherwise.

Otherwise, on our own waves.

Doing our own things.

When a couple times one ball back-ironed high and doinked the other's out.

We sorta half-smile acknowledged it.

Bc she had headphones in.

Was actively tryna not hear me.

It wasn't till I was near the end of my 3s, doing full-court-sprint transition pull-ups, sweating goddamn missiles, and she was resting from all that baseline action doing free throws, that I said something.

That I didn't cower due to her symbolic, headphoned unapproachability and instead said what I wanted to.

"You played in college, innit," I said, ball under my arm, panting, returning from retrieving an airball that had squirted

222

off the court's edge, all the way to the bathrooms a homeless dude was shaving in the outdoor sink of.

"What was that?" she said, removing a bud.

"I said you played in college, huh?"

"I did."

"Got that FORM. That DISCIPLINE."

"I don't know about that," she said, smiling. "Just getting back into it."

"Yeah? Me too."

"You played?" She seemed surprised. And I didn't blame her — I looked busted af.

"D3! But yeah."

She nodded like OK, giving me a once-over.

"Literally my first week back at it even touching a ball since," I said.

We shot in silence some.

I switched to baseline Js, bricking one off the side of the backboard but immediately chasing after it.

Tryna get my heart rate going like the pod the ole man sent to me said to, to reduce inflammation and promote better circulation.

To get all this swelling down.

"Still not on your level of all that running!" she said outta nowhere, grinning surprisingly friendly. "But trying."

I laughed and just went Nahhh, sorta laughing with her at myself.

At how ostentatiously hard I was going.

How extra I probably looked.

"I'm trying, too!" I said, doing a James Harden double-step back on three-pointer number ninety-seven of 100 and air-balling another.

But it counted.

I didn't say 100 makes. Just 100 shots.

"Two more!" I yelled to myself, chasing after it.

The homeless dude was carving out a sweet shaving cream Fu Manchu for himself, hitting that water fountain button over and over to keep the rinse going.

6

THE MA

New Year's Eve 2018

Walking oceanward with the ma.

Firework-ward.

Along California since it was mellower.

One off the thoroughfare.

Close enough for amenities access, if needed, but without the thoroughfare-stress.

She told me about the Murakami she was reading.

It was about a portrait painter.

She told me other plot lines, and I nodded like I was following. And I sorta was.

But mainly I was thinking about writing as portrait painting.

That Murakami was exploring writing as portrait painting was mainly what I heard.

"What other types of painting are good writing analogies?" I cut in, when I could no longer follow the plot.

My mama went quiet, thinking on this.

Maybe affronted by how bluntly I'd cut in, although probably not since she did this all the time.

She who taught me to.

To prioritize no-bullshit over good manners. To, when it came time, quickly move on to and consider the next, more interesting thing.

She started listing painting types.

In Philly it was arctic; we had light jackets on. Hoods though.

When she got to Impressionism.

Coming up on Ocean Ave, first traces of NYE chatter.

Around 10 p.m., when folks would be pulling up to their parties. To this oceanside hotel-patio gathering we were passing.

"Van Gogh–type Impressionism would be like etchings. Like quick lil bars," I mused. "Like cave drawings. But a bunch of them." I laughed.

She didn't get the point of this, beyond that it meant something to me; or, she got that it didn't mean anything to her. So she redirected her attention to something that did.

Started going off about a Japanese historical novel on Van Gogh she'd recently read.

About how Van Gogh had been inspired by Japanese woodblock artists. That he had wanted to go to Japan to study with them but couldn't bc he was a broke, borderline crazy homeless person living on the charity of his brother. So he went to Arles instead — where he'd end up painting his most known works.

Didn't make a cent off his art during his lifetime.

How his brother helped him bc he loved him, and that was what family was for.

How it was OK that I was where I was. That I couldn't cave. That I had to keep going.

Seemingly encouraging a type of self-mythology, but actually it wasn't about that.

It no longer was.

Self-mythology was something one indulged in.

To be able to self-mythologize was a luxury.

There was no room for indulgence when you were unable to survive / support yourself.

She was just telling me a story to help me not hate myself / give me a reason to keep going.

That was the point of stories: to help people who needed it not hate themselves / give them a reason to keep going.

The point of the only type of stories I was interested in, in any case.

I was at the part in Knausgaard's *My Struggle: Book Six* (2018) when he finally started talking about Hitler.

About Hitler's struggle.

Finally getting around to explaining the series' title.

About damn time.

How that fool Hitler initially wanted to be an artist.

Had no idea!

How he kept getting angrier and angrier when the academy kept rejecting him.

How his pops died when he was in his teens; and then his mom, right before his twenties.

Right when he started wilding more and more.

Living in boardinghouses tryna do art getting more and more alienated.

About how all of Germany and Europe got fkng floored by WWI.

Had started thinking about Modernism differently, considering this.

About Modernism as a reaction to WWI, to this seismic shift, turn of the century's second decade.

Thinking about Wittgenstein's *Tractatus Logico-Philosophicus* (1922) differently.

Modernism was about trying to say what couldn't be said. Doing wild formal shit, for that purpose. To try to tap into that, the unsayable.

When Wittgenstein spoke of 'that which cannot be said,'

'that which eludes language,' 'that about which one must remain silent,' I used to think of trivial, navel gaze-y, philosophic stuff.

Like Aw, look at those mountains there, how pretty are those mountains, bummer we don't have more adjectives to describe em, innit. 'Pretty' don't quite do em justice.

But it wasn't about that.

Or: it wasn't only about that.

Or: that wasn't the part about it that was interesting.

Tangibly considering how gnarly WWI musta been, with the level of artillery they were dealing with. How things were still largely ground-level despite the introduction of new, industrialized weaponry. How that musta made for the biggest shitshow.

Homies getting merked, left and right.

Limbs offed, bodies busted open, your homie decapitated right before your eyes.

And then, for those who returned, no one who hadn't experienced it understanding.

How could they.

They lacked the experience to even start considering how.

And those who returned lacking the words to make them.

What were words in the face of that.

That which could not be expressed in language was physical trauma.

Was that which dealt with the opposite of language — that which dealt with the body.

With the confrontation of the utter destruction of bodies.

Of their fragility.

Their tenuousness.

It was 'about *deep, personal traumas* that one must remain silent.'

This not a theoretical claim, but a pragmatically, physically felt assertion.

There was *no use* in trying to make others understand; that which concerned the body was what completely, necessarily, belied words.

We turned left where California ended, at the ocean.

Pier-ward.

Along the gravel rather than concrete path, that snaked left, right, left again.

That ess-ed.

Through lawn, palm trees. The ocean on our right, way down there, other side of the PCH, the beach; restaurants in between.

Past the Veterans Memorial — five rectangular, upright, concrete slabs, in a row — where Wilshire intersected Ocean —

More body-groups the lower, the closer to the water you get. Coming your way. Something just ended. This route, 'to the pier and back.' Same one mama would take D on, growing up, except to a different pier. Higher up the coast. But same ocean. One slightly ahead of the other, D humming along with sunglasses, a big-ass sun hat on, head up-tilted slightly, basking in the breeze. Dog-out-the-rolled-down-car-window-like. Going Move, in her robot-voice deadpan, to stragglers in her way. Her chair's engine like a Tesla's how quiet. Just joystick-whipping. All sorts of bags and drinks and extra clothes strapped to her chair's back, real compact like. Mama carrying her curled-up body into bed before plugging in her chair each night to gas it up. D's body the same as any body just more curled up. Like a bud blooming, bursting, only stalled out mid-burst. Her speech, too. Uttering, starting to, before stalling out mid-utterance. So instead of trying to say more than she could, just thinking about a single thing to say, for longer than others, then saying that one thing. An observation. A jab. A cutting shot at someone who needed to hear it. No. One. Cawes — cutting off lil sis self-importantly lamenting middle school gossip gripes. No YOU. Awe. Cwazy — shutting down the ole man righteously venting about politicians, America, the Media. Then cackling gleeful like hik hik hik. Like suffocating but enjoying it. Before choking, forgetting to chew, that she'd been chewing. Then gagging, eyes watering, mama stepping in like Oh oh oh, oh-kay, gotta chew, back-patting and mouth-wiping with her bib-napkin. Each one of D's words taking its own amount of exertion to release, and so only shooting em off if necessary. If urgent. Not wasting others' bandwidth / her own breath saying anything other than exactly what needed to be said.

But there was a second-tier level to this, this *remaining silent.*

A meta level.

Why it took Knausgaard so long to get to addressing what he knew he had to, was inevitably gonna, but was nonetheless apprehensive to.

He was apprehensive to bc society dictated that, about these considerations — finding *Mein Kampf* (1933) in his late ole man's closet, considering how there were aspects of Hitler's bio he felt contained secrets to understanding himself — he was to remain silent.

There were things about which one *mustn't speak.*

About which it wasn't right to.

Shameful thoughts.

Things deemed — and understandably / not wrongly so — taboo.

Taboo for understandable / not wrong reasons.

But that didn't mean people didn't have these thoughts.

Didn't mean repression was the way.

Repression and shame were what created monsters.

School shooters.

Suicides.

Were what, lowkey, created Hitler.

Now that there. A sizzling take, I know.

But writing.

Writing was one way to even start tackling repression and shame of taboo thoughts/impulses and unspeakable traumas.

Writing wasn't speaking.

Wasn't 'saying.'

Writing was a silent thing.

Was 'remaining silent.'

Books required silence / concerted activity to tackle.

Books didn't force anything onto anyone.

People could stop reading a book at any time.

Not stopping — getting the reader to not — in fact, was the challenge facing books.

Facing both writers and readers of.

And even if readers managed to not stop, to read the book about the taboo/trauma, books still, despite operating within silence, still operated within language.

Within that mode through which those inexpressible things (taboos, traumas) would still remain unexpressed.

Or: expressed, but un-communicated.

Attempting to communicate things that, by definition (by the limits of language, by societal law) were incommunicable, then, was the most one could do.

Was still a worthy feat, this attempt to.

This *performance* of attempting to.

What this performance communicated was: I can't express this inexpressible thing fully, I know I can't, but that don't mean I can't try.

That you can't.

The attempt to express the inexpressible was the antidote to the other option: wallowing helplessly in repression, shame, as you grew more alienated, hateful, consumed by suffering, till eventually you became a school shooter or Hitler.

Till your body was left with no choice but to start lashing out, fighting back. Deteriorating. Expressing that which you were neglecting to in words/writing.

Bc the body knows, bro.

The body will feel what you decide, mentally, you're not gonna.

The body will say what you won't.

And when the thing you won't say/write ain't pretty, best believe how your body lashes out won't be either —

Going to Little League games posted in the backseat of D's van that had only backseats, no middle row, so D could hang a right into the passenger slot after ramping up. D and Mama pulling up late to high school b-ball games, the ref taking time so she could whip it along the baseline to the stands. D going Yay. in her robot-voice deadpan. Busting out laughing whenever someone ate shit or did a bad play or got injured. Toggling that joystick with her T-Rex arm arms. No fucks given on a ho bitch. Lmao (*crying*). Homies, baes, teammates coming over for the first time, shook by the difficulty she had keeping food, fluids in her mouth, by the slight scent of Lysol-feces emanating from the supported commode in her room downstairs. But never saying anything. Never articulating their fear. Either scared of her or wanting to treat her like a baby. Either banishing her from their sight or *talking down patronizing to her, like they knew more than her. To retain their narratives of themselves as the victimized/oppressed/ special ones —*

More bodies moving upstream — back onto land — than down. Shins splinting, steps slapping, declining the ramp. Onto the pier. Each approaching face a flesh mass, eyeholes searching, mouth-holes sucking. Gasping. Heads uptilted slightly bc the incline. You forge a path through them, overcorrecting to make room for Mama. Like leading an expedition through safari grass, slicing a machete path. Garments this close up losing their individual presentation-symbolism, morphing into contingent colors, fabric-distinguished pieces of a bigger, amalgamating patchwork-whole. Home free when the pier-entrance bottle's neck loosens. When the decline horizontalizes.

Able to speak and think again, without the constriction of other bodies touching yours.

Kettle corn, $7.

Cotton candy, $8.

Carousel-ride, $5 — but closed for the season looks like.

What it came down to was names.

Names were what most demonstrated the limits of language.

Of words.

A name was a word.

A single name place-held a person.

In many cases: countless people.

'Bill' was a word-sound that signified countless people named 'Bill.'

'Bill's currently living, dead, and yet to be born.

And not only was every 'Bill' different, but a single 'Bill' — that individual person, 'Bill' — was himself ever-changing.

Capable of.

Words/names describing inanimate, unself-conscious things alone were inadequate, since, like 'Bill,' categorical names signified groups of things, each contingent example of which individually different.

Y'know: snowflakes.

Mass-produced products that, in theory, were structurally identical were an interesting case. Their presence as things at all the last couple hundred years had implications for why things were how they were, today. But even then. Product inconsistencies. Machine malfunctions. Wonky Nike tracksuits on extreme markdown at Ross Dress for Less, the sleeves too long for the torso or the swoosh dimensions off.

But people.

People were on another level than all of that.

Than everything else.

Not only different in each individual example, but each individual example changing constantly.

Sure, snowflakes changed constantly. Melting the moment they became snowflakes.

People, though. Not only changed constantly, but were capable of rebooting.

Of living multiple lives.

Of dying and being reborn in new form.

Shedding skin entirely then regrowing an entire new set of cells while still constituting the same 'thing.'

Retaining the same 'name.'

Still the *Argo*.

I'm writing this, but don't fully understand.

Don't *physically* comprehend.

I stamp names onto shit all the time.

Table, door, jacket, cig.

Let's go, get shit done, use my *tools*.

Shiiit—I stamp names onto people.

Names that only pertain to the fixed part of them I find useful.

Ex, editor, side, autonomous, roomie.

I do this. We do this. This is *what we do.*

Like the ladies ushering home soldiers whose friends got merked, who lost limbs, who witnessed *physical* carnage in WWI. Who had no experience of what *physically* being there felt like.

No amount of saying would make them understand. Will make me understand. *Will make you.* The absurdity, the inadequacy, of stamping a name onto a person and fixing them as that name-thing.

Only those with a *physical experience* of creating a person understand.

Shoot—of *carrying* the first traces of one, if only for a time.

Dads go Here, here's your name, here are your *papers* confirming this.

OK. There. You're this now.

Make me proud.

Mothers, on the other hand.

You were a thing in my tummy. A part of me. A collection of my cells.

I fkng made you, bro.

PHYSICALLY.

You were me, and now you're you.

Calling your own shots making your own calls like the fuck?

I don't even have the mental recourse to fix you in my name, to assume your okayness bc you have my name, when the strangeness of this rears its head.

Bc you didn't even get my name.

Shit, I didn't even keep my name.

How baffling, living through this disconnect. Continually.

I can't even.

Childbirth, its termination, are the WWIs every mom and almost-mom exist with.

A chasm of incommunicable privacy.

The site of *fertility… of damp caves and rich soil, of the womb… where life begins.*

The creation of a person-thing with your body/cells that society calls a fixed thing but you know is, physically feel to be, just a cell-thing capable of growing but equally at risk of dying, at any moment.

The epitome of that *about which one must remain silent —*

You decide on a spot far out but not all the way out. Decide this without speaking, but instinctively. Reading each other's bodies for where is right. Out of earshot of the pier ruckus, beyond the spotlight illuminating the pier's side stairs — illuminating an exit, a way down, so folks won't trip. But shy of the water. Well shy. To right where evidence of higher tides has padded the sand solid. Smoothened it smooth. To where, you can see, the highest tide reached, before calling it and heading back. Before going: That's far enough; time to retreat. Abort. Lil mini ridge there, where. Elevated, just past the dividing lip, by comfy, squishy sand, since no water, no salt, has hit it. Outta the salt, the water's range. Not going anywhere. Good where it is. Fkn chillin. The sea, the waves, the wind like a cave. A sonic whorl. You are the eye of the whorl. You zip up the lightweight Uniqlo clamshell mama/Santa brought. Mama zips up hers, her Patagonia drip. But you're not cold.

You sit, knees together, arms hooked around em to support your backs. Your uprightness.

You want to tell her what you've been thinking, reading.

Knausgaard and Hitler and Hitler's mid-twenties. How uncannily they mirror yours, so far. How his ole man died in his early teens; how yours did, too, effectively. Although that 'effectively' is significant. Still.

But how alienating his boardinghouse-to-boardinghouse mode, his inability to settle on an 'occupation'—a name of what he 'was.' What use he provided. How the nail was his mom dying. How when that happened, shit went way left. But you still have yours—

"So this guy, 'Karl Ove,' he doin this thing where he sorta writing unabashedly about himself, his deepest secrets. His shameful memories/feelings. The effect of reading it feels calming for me. Seeing someone else doing that. Someone not scared to."

My mama got quiet when I said that last part. Her body did.

Looking out at the ocean, the sky, the stars.

She didn't say anything immediately.

Like she'd been fully feeling these things already, or already had these feeling-ideas stashed. Dormant. Like what I'd said didn't communicate anything in words, only nudged their activation.

Once she spoke, she pointed out that Murakami's protagonists sorta did that. Divulged their secrets. Their shameful, taboo feelings/thoughts/impulses.

Why Murakami's societal rep was having 'weird/funny cringey-but-satisfying-somehow sexual elements' in all his novels.

"That's true!" I said, feeling that.

"Sounds like *shishosetsu*," she said.

"Come again?"

"Murakami is known for his American influences, like *The Great Gatsby*, but he's also part of the *shishosetsu* tradition. The I-novel."

The I-novel, my mama explained, was a Japanese literary genre dating back to the turn of the century. To the Meiji era.

A type of confessional literature where the events of the story corresponded to the events in the author's life. Meant to expose the 'dark side' of society / the author's life. Its foremost formal requirement being that it was written in the first person. An early attempt for Japanese writers to strive for a more Western form of individualism and authenticity.

"Early examples concerned the *burakumin*."

"*Burakumin?*" I said, leaning forward so my exhaled smoke wouldn't hit her. Ashamed to be smoking in front of her but trusting she'd understand. Doing what I could to not fuck up her shit by doing it, if I was gonna do it.

The *burakumin* were, literally, 'hamlet/village people.'

An outcast group, lowest on the social rungs.

Discriminated against and ostracized, relegated to impure jobs tainted by death.

Executioners, undertakers, slaughterhouse workers.

Tanners.

Like Kenji Nakagami, who dropped *The Cape* (1976) when my mama was in her twenties, and who was the first/only post-war writer to publicly identify himself as being born into the *burakumin*.

And the wild thing about him and a lot of *burakumin* was that they were born illegitimately, since if a dude wasn't *burakumin* but banged a *burakumin*, he'd bounce and the child would be born not only fatherless but nameless.

Without a name, one wasn't, technically, a person.

Not without papers.

Wasn't recognized in the system.

"Goddamn," I said, stubbing out my cig in the sand and coughing. Inhaling my lungs full of air.

238

Wondering how she knew this was exactly relevant to what I'd been thinking.

"But that's not just *burakumin,* Sean. If you guys happened earlier, during the war, like happened with a lot of American soldiers and Japanese prostitutes, there was a time when, if the baby was born in Japan, the Japanese government wouldn't recognize the Western name. So they'd be denied papers. And, until Naturalization passed, America wouldn't grant them papers either! Since they weren't born in the U.S. They'd be in limbo! No names."

"Goddamn," I said. "And I got both!"

"You got both," my mama said, laugh-sighing like Oh my.

V

Winter

*From such severe sickness... one returns
newborn, having shed one's skin, more ticklish
and malicious.*

—NIETZSCHE

1

WEE LAD

January 2019: Los Angeles

In a week it would be back to Philly. To the cold.

To a nebulous plan of 'mish it belligerently, in my van, to NYC.' To 'make something happen.'

Don't think I actually thought I was home free; there was still some cycle I was caught in: all the old skin would shed, then I'd have this new layer, but the new layer was never fully ready to face the day; it would be, for some days, but then it'd be so sensitive, so thin, the slightest scratching would slightly irritate it, slightly disrupt its surface; this wasn't a biggie till it wouldn't follow through, wouldn't commit to regenerating.

Would jump ship last minute and start shedding again.

Abort the mission and flake to the floor.

If somehow still unclear: ex bae's abortion was what fucked everything.

What made me no longer able to outdo the ole man.

What made me no different than the ole man.

Ex bae had been my ticket to not becoming the ole man.

The idea of the inevitability of us eventually procreating had been.

———

Day of my last flight out here, autonomous bae hit me with her copy of Sheila Heti's *Motherhood*.

Surprising me at the departures gate, after learning of my departure time on the low from the homie N, who'd driven me out there — she'd just landed in Philly, at the arrivals gate, from a Thanksgiving fam hang back home.

Such sweeties, the both of them.

Read it over the month I was out here; I was about to head back, so had to commemorate what it had made me think, in the place I'd thought the thoughts it birthed, before I did.

To log it.

Reading *Motherhood* while posted at the ma's was part of whatever *Motherhood* had made me think.

The ideas inextricably tied to the reading-event site.

It was January 2nd but LA so pristine out.

After the day's lone coffee, I knew I had maybe an hour of semi-coherent thinking.

Semi-coherent speaking.

Geared up for a stroll and, equipped with my voice recorder, got to walking-talking.

Went over what I had.

Sheila, to me, was Jesus — her birthday, after all, was literally Christmas — meaning I was gonna fully consider everything she said, even if it ran counter to everything I'd been saying.

Which it did.

I'd been saying: All this self-cancelling renunciation of baby-having — under the guise of man-cancelling feminism — was a dark, dark nihilism.

Neoliberal feminism nothing more than a savage, ruthless careerism.

Overlooking how/why we were all here in the first place. Namely, those individuals, our parents, who'd chosen to procreate.

Overlooking the frivolousness of the money-making/power-grabbing/reactionary flex.

Like, OK, yes—dudes have been shitty for all time; but so, what, now the move was to...out-shitty them?

I don't know, bro.

Didn't know whether that was the move.

Whether that would provide long-term satisfaction, once that hit of reactionary 'clapback' power wore off.

Like, in a Nietzschean, *ressentiment*-type way.

Not that I wasn't operating within Nietzschean-type *ressentiment,* thinking this.

Shoot, saying—*writing*—it.

But still.

I walked away from where I usually walked. Away from Wilshire.

Up the back, sloped parking area behind the ma's, away from the Whole Foods back alley, to residential alleys north. Towards where seemed quieter.

Concentric spiraling outward, onto new alleys; then back inward, retracing them.

Rambling and riffing until the strangeness of hearing my own voice—of imagining how it would sound, later, on the internet—faded. Till I forgot that whatever I was saying would go on the internet.

———

But Sheila.

Sheila wudn't tryna have a kid.

Wudn't tryna be a mom.

Or, she had been. At first.

Then she no longer was.

Then she was again; only, this second time, pivoting mom-hood's meaning.

Shifting her definition of 'momhood.'

Momhood, eventually, meant being an art-mom.

Having an art-baby.

A book-babe.

Book babies.

I mean, I got it. For her, as a late-thirties woman, an established, late-thirties writer, this move was the *different thing.*

The *counterintuitive/interesting thing.*

Why limit parenting to the nuclear family?

Mad orphans out here.

She/me orphans! Lowkey. Her book seemed to imply.

This, essentially, how I justified all my fuckshit leading to ex bae dipping.

Why limit love to the monogamous pair?

I loved V like I loved editor bae like I loved side — *along with* ex.

It wasn't ex bae personally, but the societal conventions of bae-hood, that said I couldn't love them the same if I was to love ex.

An either/or thing.

Sheila's take seemed to echo this — my initial stance that led to ex bae leaving. A love ethic that was pan-amorous, care-oriented, non-ownership-based.

Inclusive.

And counterintuitively, given it contradicted the stance I'd taken after — once ex bae left. Of wanting suddenly to procreate, do marriage, be the family guy.

That after-the-fact fidelity.

That much-too-late loyalty.

I'd been a ho; I hadn't been, like Chris Brown says hoes ain't, loyal.

But now I was! I'd been tryna say.

This was the fourth pod I'd recorded on Sheila Heti over the past four years — with ex and two subsequent baes — only they'd all been on *How Should a Person Be?* (2010).

And this pod was with no baes; this pod was dolo.

All those previous pods had been unabashedly, excessively positive; bc, let's face it, that book was fire.

Not that *Motherhood* wasn't.

It was just that...

Last June, rather than ramble, to ex bae, everything ex bae bringing up Sheila Heti's pod had made me think, I instead wrote down and emailed all those thoughts directly to Sheila herself.

Slept on and edited em over and everything.

Only — she'd never responded!

Hanging a left at the next alley to avoid a dude going to town with a leaf-blower, I explained all this into my voice recorder. That, given she hadn't, I'd be pulling no punches. Follow-through-ing all jabs.

Would dwell fully in both sides of how the book made me feel.

Wouldn't solely dick-ride.

Things were more interesting that way, when you didn't solely dick-ride.

•

That night, I walked to the park on 15th and California, where I'd been running to.

Walking, bc whatever happened to my hip when I ate shit balling out the other day.

Listening over the *Motherhood* pod.

Thinking about what my ole man's ole man wrote me in a long, rambly, honestly worrisome (for both his and my health) email this morning. From his bunker-cabin somewhere in Mendocino County none of his kids had ever been to, even seen.

About how making it through whatever I was dealing with skin-wise might require a deeper sort of treatment.

Medicine from a medical breakthrough that had yet to break.

Or, in any case, one that surpassed what every doc I'd seen so far had prescribed.

I mean, this skin shit. Wasn't anything new.

For every one of my earliest memories of running around playing footie saying things like "bloody ace!" as a wee lad in Scotland, I had an equal number of memories of laying up, unable to sleep, scratching my skin all skressed, the Aberdeen sun's refusal to set for hours after 'bedtime' not helping things.

The mama having to tend to me damn near as much as she had to the villagers.

Like Malcolm, who'd go up to whoever was closest to him and go *Mahn?* or, to me, *Dahn?* ('Sean') *Ahn ah gah tah-lit,* whenever he 'needed to go to the toilet.' Then spazz out, spastically sieg heil-ing with one arm raised while biting his other arm's hand and yelling/stomping, till someone—usually my dad—took him to the toilet.

Roderick, who'd go Bicky! I want bicky! till my dad'd go Bicky-what, Roderick? and he'd go Bicky, plee? and my dad'd go OK Roderick, bicky please is right, giving him a biscuit.

Michael Gallagher, who'd always be stressing about his hair, going How's my hair, Edick? in thick Glaswegian, till someone, usually my dad ('Eric'), told him your hair's great, Michael, looking good.

Like I was equally a villager.

And the mama's lil bro, my uncle N, had the same shit. The same condition.

On my walk back, I tried to write a description for the pod. To summarize it.

There were so many ways to write it.

So many voices.

The ole man's restlessness, his insistence on continually *fleeing,* growing up, turning those early years, for me, into a slang-learning, accent-adopting gauntlet.

Ages 1–5 Japanese; 5–8 Gaelic-Scottish accent, UK slang; 8–9 upstate New York, insulated American white folk talk; 9–11 Sactown Latino-Black hood speak; 11 onwards Santa Cruz surfer speak.

And tone aside, the what of the writing.

To condense all I'd said in that hour into two paragraphs…

To say nothing of everything I *hadn't* said — couldn't say — on the pod.

How there was some knot in my gut *Motherhood* had tapped into, that I was only able to slightly loosen by ranting about it.

Ex bae getting Winnie-kitty so shortly after the abortion, right before moving into our spot together, in Oakland.

249

How I agreed to move into that spot in Oakland with ex bae, with Winnie-kitty, even though I was allergic. Bc why.

How meeting, hooking up with editor bae so shortly after ex bae got Winnie-kitty.

How that once, in Scotland, when Isabelle crushed that kitten —

Orr recently moved into Juniper house across the way up the hill by the farm by where they sheared the sheep holding it down so it wouldn't wriggle. Moved from Is-rah-el. His mom the Juniper house parent, so he unscared of Malcolm stomping or Wally's no thumbs, like Michael (Mich-a-el, like Is-rah-el) is when he comes over to play footie. Michael is scared so I keep him out on the field with the wooden goals the orange rope nets playing PK contest then 2 v. 1 when Andrew shows. Me the 1 bc I'm faster. Isabelle Andrew's sis but different than Andrew. Different than me I think bc Michael is scared by her but not by Andrew by me. I wait till nap hour before going into Silverbirch to get water so Michael won't scare.

Orr's cat made kittens but they can't see yet. There are as many as my fingers, all sleeping on top of each other all suckling. Fuzzy like the azuki bean mochi Baba brought only these you can't eat. Like toys in my hand. Big as my hand. I can see them but they can't me yet. Upstairs with Orr in Orr's room after Michael leaves Isabelle comes. Wants to play, too. Orr in the bathroom and me looking at the footie cards Michael left me the shiny West Ham one the Alan Shearer one from when he had all his hair. Isabelle playing going Aww petting. She knows they aren't toys I think bc she's talking to them although we talk to toys also. She wants to play with to hold them so badly. To love them. Holding petting one like it's her baby. It can't see doesn't have hair yet when it happens. I never see what they do with it, I think bury it in the garden up by the farm where they sheared the sheep. Lil sis crying when she sees it no longer seeing nor breathing so I say at least there are nine fingers left. Lil sis wants one but Mama says no bc my allergies.

I wanted to write everything *Motherhood* had made me feel.

Everything I'd said, and couldn't say, on the pod.

But you can't write everything.

Not if it was really gonna hit.

For it to really hit, you could only write a few things.

I wrote two things:

Motherhood was the book-baby Sheila birthed instead of her actual baby. The gift she bore for the world, for current and future humans, out of her body.

Sheila discovered this *while writing it,* or communicated this gradual discovery *in the text itself.* The realization, seemingly discovered mid-sentence, that 'maybe this book was a prophylactic.'

Back at the spot, the mama was ziplocking up a bunch of stuff she wanted me to take back with me.

Two freezer bags of Yogi teas.

Sammie bags of deer-turd Tibetan medicine pellets.

Broccoli sprouts.

My skin, this entire stint, had been leaking out, reeking rotten-smelling. And according to Google search results for 'weird smell eczema,' prolonged antihistamine use weakened the liver, till eventually it couldn't process toxins and so simply bled em outta your pores, resulting in a faint smell like 'rotting meat or cheese.'

I'd been hitting the Claritins or Benadryls or Zyrtecs

minimum twice daily since adopting Winnie that year three years ago.

Had become an antihistamine addict.

Strung out on em bennies bruh.

Plus sugar; sugar fed yeast which heightened the smell.

The blog 'Skin Friend' we found, their solution was:

Nix sugar.

Cut the Claritins.

Hit hella broccoli sprouts, the most alkalizing of all veggies.

But so the mama went *in* at the farmer's market when we learned this; we were stocked with enough broccoli sprouts for an apocalypse.

She was constructing an elaborate Russian-doll piñata of broccoli sprouts and ice packs in bigger and bigger ziplocks.

"Mama," I said. "I'm not gonna have refrigeration in my van when I mish it to New York," I said. "Plus I can just get more once I'm back," setting my pack down.

"Seanie," my mama said, holding up and inspecting the sprout piñata, as if for leaks. "You're not going to get more once you get out there."

She was right.

"You're right," I said. "OK I'll take it."

My mama looked at me pained.

"You're really gonna move back into your van?"

"Yeah!" I said, too quickly/defensively for it to be believable.

•

On my final morning in LA, I woke up on the mama's pullout futon, made a coffee, and went down to the Whole Foods alley for a cig.

Opened my email.

Saw this.

Dear Sean,

I just listened to your podcast about Motherhood and then came back and read this email. First of all, let me say that I'm so sorry I didn't reply.... A week after I posted my podcast, my father, my favourite person in the world, died. And everything I talked about on the podcast felt so so incredibly far away from me. And I just fell behind in all my correspondence, and everything.

Second, I loved your podcast. I felt like I was walking alongside you, and I really liked hearing all your thoughts about the book, including the things you disagreed about, and had questions about, and doubts about. It just was really beautiful also for me to hear you talk about loving one's body, which is something that always feels like such a chore to me, but is really important I know, so I'm going to take your inspiration to try to cut down on all the things which make me physically feel bad, and try to do more of the things which make my body feel better. I can live so much in my mind and forget how beautiful it is to have a body that works, that can be strong, if you let it be....

I just really appreciated your whole tone, and am very grateful for your appreciation of my writing. I listened to the podcast in the car, and then at home again, after spending much of the day with my mother who broke her ankle (at the gym!) yesterday.

I hope you are well and happy and enjoying creating whatever you're creating. I think the analogy of writing slower like sometimes one walks slower on a run is a really good one. I really like your perspective. Thank you for your letter and your podcast and everything.

yours truly,
Sheila

•

I called my ole man later that day.

Actually I didn't. I would have had too much packing, and we don't have that type of relationship. Don't just call each other at random.

Or maybe I did.

Let's say I did.

Let's say I called him at the airport, while waiting for my flight to board.

Nighttime my time, morning his.

He'd just wrapped up a workout.

Tryna beat his consecutive push-up record.

He had. Eighty-five.

While doing some wild Wim Hof breath-deprivation method, not breathing the whole time.

"Wild, bro. Careful," I said.

He was posted in his spot sipping coffee looking out at the Sea of Japan North Korea had been shooting test missiles into.

Short-arming them, dropping em just shy of the shore. But in his direction.

He was ratcheting up his English teaching shit, printing flyers for and hosting home-based weekend lessons to supplement his weekday school lessons at the Waldorf School there.

"Damn, you really the plug for these English bars, innit."

Only white dude around for miles, way tf up there in Hokkaido.

"Well these kids don't have many impressions of Americans. Only what they see on TV," he said. "And there's still some cultural resentment there.

"It's important to provide other references of America for these kids — that's the next generation, ya know."

"Provide alternate reference points," I said. "I like that."

He mumbled something in Japanese.

254

Like Oh, no, you can have some, it sounded like.

Then went Ah, guess you can't! laughing.

His wife's son had come into the kitchen for coffee, he'd told him he'd make some for him, but then had spaced out and drank it all.

Gomen! Sorry!

His wife's son was eighteen. Was eleven when his birth dad and mom broke up. When my dad swooped in and took over.

I also eleven when my parents split. When my dad dipped.

Like my dad was picking up where he left off.

Round 2.

Second try.

Hell yeah, bud. Giving it another shot.

Not everyone got one.

"He actually sorta reminds me of you," my dad said. "Very… sensitive."

"Bitch who you callin sensitive."

"No—it's a good thing!" my dad said. "It's because you're sensitive you're a writer."

"Alright, bro. Careful."

Could hear the coffeemaker gurgling as he put on a new pot, for his new son.

When I dropped the I-novel *burakumin* bars on him he already knew all about em.

"Oh yeah, completely rejected by society, the *buraku*," he said.

"Seems relevant to all the handicapped folks, growing up. How we hide the deformed, cast out the outcast," I mused.

They were boarding priority seating. I had a sec; I was Group D.

I gathered my things, swept off all the skin scales I'd scraped off my face, that had fallen onto my lap.

"Malcolm was such a sweetie, always biting his hand, yelling like that. I still think of him," my dad said, when I listed whom I remembered. "Roderick always dressed like a gentleman, his dad was from some like royal lineage. He'd always do these crazy like ballet spins, super fast — "

"Pirouettes."

"Pirouettes. But it was like they were spiritual. Like he was tryna tap into a higher level."

"Tryna spin his ass to God!"

"And Michael Gallagher, he was a sweetie but he'd get violent. When he kicked that chair at dinner, snapped the leg off and sent it flying across the room. Coulda hit one of you guys. I remember I grabbed him by the shoulder, took him outside, sorta pinched the nerve real hard. Looked him in the eye and said If you EVER do anything like that again, you're fkn out. Fkng gone."

"For real. What he say."

"Oh he went Sorry, sorry Edick, never again."

"Damn."

"He was out of line."

"When someone outta line, you gotta snap on em," I said. "Expect the same respect from others that you give them. No matter who."

"Gotta."

2

NURSE DADDY

January 2019: Philly

The first nurse, the first night in there.

Flamboyant dude Roberto.

While still in the first-floor ER, after initially hitting the Urgent Care up in Manayunk and the Urgent Care doc there having no clue what to do and so sending me over.

Autonomous bae and roomie bae doing the soccer-player shoulder-carry outta autonomous bae's car, before a nurse rushed over to receive me with a wheelchair.

Me going I mean I'm good, I can walk, but thanks, but I mean I'm probably good. Autonomous bae and roomie bae going Sh sh sh, you're fine, we got you.

Then posting up in the ER with me all that night, nibbling on snacks roomie bae's boo biked over with like a champ. I don't even know how, how icy out it was.

Roberto turning everything into a joke, in a way I didn't know how I felt about but had no way/means of resisting. Making everyone leave the room when he turned me on my side, held me down, and penetrated me rectally with a thermometer. Which he needed to, there was no way around it, to get an accurate reading.

One oh four.

———

The Sunday before flying back, I hit the park and hopped into a full-court 5-on-5 game since it was Sunday and folks were balling full court.

'Taking it easy' bc all the internal roids I'd been on, and internal roids weakened the bones.

Only we won. So played another.

Had to.

The second game I took it to the rack, took the contact, only when I hit the defender mid-air we jackknifed each other and my feet swung out from under me.

Landed like thwack on the edge of the court, where it switched to gravel, on my spine.

Was so keyed up I not only finished the game but played another.

My first weekend back, last weekend.

Mished it out to NYC for big cuz E's bday hang with autonomous bae and N.

Autonomous bae for the ride; N so it wouldn't seem like anything it wasn't to autonomous bae.

Broke all my dietary rules at E's party drinking and eating whatever the fuck.

Barely slept—N crashed with autonomous bae at autonomous bae's friend's, I crashed in E's guest room / dusty-ass tool closet—and then the next day we went all the way out to the Bronx for artist bae's art show.

Limping, flared tf up, skin looking like a cracked lobster's.

Telling everyone I was 'about to move back into my van, to live out of it in NYC,' going so far as arranging for roomie bae's cousin to move into my Philly room once I did.

Despite being lowkey unable to walk.

Losing my shit all week, not being able to.

Back in my shitshow room, crashed out, layer of dead skin on the floor, clothes and papers everywhere.

Till finally, the night before roomie bae found me, railing three Advils just so I could stand.

Then walking all the way out to CVS and back, bundled like the damn Michelin Man.

Before waking up fucked, feverish, unable to sit up even bc my hip.

Skin open.

So damn dehydrated but unable to get up to get water.

Roomie bae at her boo's so unable to hear my SOS laments.

The morning after my first night in the ER, got wheeled to the MRI room.

'Sacrum fracture.'

Tip of my spine, by my butthole.

"You just been walking around the last two weeks?" the nurse asked as I re-gowned.

"I mean. I thought. If I just waited it out."

He looked at me like Dude, massaging Purell into his palms.

It was on Day 3 that I first saw dermatologist bae. That we stumbled into each other's lives.

So pretty, so put together.

Skin immaculate.

Hair so straight, like she straightened it. Although did she actually.

She could not have.

She coulda just been made that way.

———

I initially couldn't tell whether she was the actual derm or the assistant.

This didn't matter.

She was dermatologist bae to me regardless.

But there were two derm-assistant duos who pulled up to inspect me, on separate visits, Days 2 and 3.

And in the first duo, the young/pretty one was the assistant, while the older, doc-looking dude was the doc.

Although was derm bae's assistant even an older, doc-looking dude?

Honestly can't even remember, how wet off of derm bae I was.

As wet off someone as one could be in that state, how gnarly shit was.

Had gotten.

Gowned/cut up, hydration IV in my arm, on one of those recliner beds hospitals have.

Muhfuckers coming through taking blood samples, inspecting me like I was some eczema anomaly.

A rare eczema leper.

In a lowkey fugue state from not being able to smoke once in there.

In a room on Floor 11, overlooking the inner courtyard.

Not even realizing till I peeled out, evening of Day 5, against the nurse's rec, that I'd been right there on 38th, a block south of the Green Line by ex bae's where ex bae and I always met.

And it wasn't till I actually started to heal, till derm bae figured out how, found the drug to get me to, till she witnessed my gradual progress from a leprous to a functional human, in each monthly meeting telling me to strip, that she'd give me a sec, that she'd be right back, like she was going to the bathroom to 'freshen up' before a casual, habitual fuck, except I was the one freshening up, she was good to go gowned up with her clipboard, her authority, till she came back and touched me like she did, unflinching at however bad my skin, touching all the parts except the parts parts, all the parts women never touched, exhilarating—

It wasn't until all this transpired, in the following months, that derm bae became the one.

•

Both derm-assistant duos in there together, the fourth day. To compare findings.

"Never seen eczema so completely from head to toe. Behind the elbows, knees, yeah. But down to the soles, the palms, up to your face? Infected like this?"

Like This some other shit.

Taking my hand, stroking its sandpaper surface like a geologist a rare fossil.

Jotting down archeological deets of their findings.

Convening out in the hallway like during a time-out, devising a plan.

That quick derm-team huddle.

"This is our ultimate challenge," they announced when they returned, sounding excited.

We were tryna lather my bod with triamcinolone, the fourth nurse and I.

Hard to get my left arm, around the IV.

Barely able to sleep, maybe it was all the roid cream, but was so keyed up.

The fourth nurse an Asian American dude around my age, who'd done tech or science research all his twenties, something technical and lucrative.

Now 'giving back.'

I started getting all these texts that night, it was a lunar eclipse, from randos who didn't know I was locked up or who were asking whether I was out yet, whether I was seeing this, whether I was doing anything to commemorate it, based mostly on the weird flex / confusing virtuesignal I did in pod intros, commenting on and claiming secret knowledge about the moon and its cycles.

Limping over to my window, tryna see it.

Unable to.

Lone window facing the wrong way.

Later that night, wanting to see the blacked-out moon, or mainly to smoke, so damn badly.

Thinking I'd be able to convince Asian dude to let me bc we had a vibe, were broing out sorta.

He went No way.

Instead let me walk around the circular, or oval, or in any case not rectangular hallway that led around the floor, to all rooms.

Shuffling with a walker.

Accompanying me to ensure I didn't make a run for it.

All sorts of wailing coming outta the rooms.

Blood-curdling, kill-me-now wails.

Middle-aged heavyset smocked lady, the penultimate morn, to wheel me to X-rays.

Pulling up like Up with ya.

Hop on.

Me wanting to be like *You* give *me* a ride? Naaah.

Apologizing the whole time, going I'm sorry, I appreciate it, aw nice turn.

Up ramps, around corners, in-n-outta elevators.

Whippin.

Her going Oh you're OK, it's no worries, all nice and all.

Later thinking all that appreciation I was doling out mighta been condescending. Implying she wasn't a pro. That this wasn't *what she did.*

The final morning. Athletic PT guy. To re-teach me to walk.

To sit.

To step.

Had to relearn hips.

No leg-crossing, either sitting or lying.

Only straightforward sitting, feet planted.

No ankle-to-ankle reading-lounging even.

That spine-tip fracture was hairline enough to heal without surgery, but only if sustained symmetrically. No twisting.

My two legs no longer enough to move me.

Needed a third.

To syncopate, outside of my good side, with the steps of my bad.

One of those candycane-handled, rubber-tipped, hospital-issued guys I recognized older ladies around the block half walking with, half carrying on a novelty basis.

One half of crutches.

Not devolving to all fours.

But almost.

To all three-fours.

———

We practiced steps on one of those adjustable box-jump boxes.

Did stairs.

Same idea as the cane, only in the stair context the railing was the cane.

The most lowkey workout.

Athletic PT dude the most mellow/supportive personal trainer.

Was honestly lowkey stoked about my cane.

That new swag that cane swag.

Martyred out.

The last evening. What mighta made me abruptly dip, the following one.

Autonomous bae texted *Hey, need snacks, anything?*

Told her They feeding me good in here, although could do a juice. Mainly need nail clippers.

My nails were too long. Were digging into my open wounds, at night, while I slept. Or didn't sleep. Half-slept, bc the scratching.

Body following mind, going reptilian.

Growing talons.

Autonomous bae said I got you, gimme thirty.

It was after standard visiting hours. I was propped up watching the Eagles. Sunday night game.

They ended up confiscating the nail clipper at the first-floor, metal-detecting security entrance.

Autonomous bae said Surprise I brought P.

P poked his head in next to hers.

They were both so chipper, that shit pissed me off.

Why did it.

They were *too* caring.

Asking me how I was and shit.

How tf you think I am bro.

Suddenly seeing myself through them, not liking what I saw.

Not one bit.

Then when they diverted from me, once it became clear I didn't want their attention, and started ranting cheerily about other shit, getting annoyed that they weren't paying full attention to me.

Talking way too loud.

Like Yo there're muhfuckers two rooms over yelling in non-stop pain their lives their prospects fucked, tf outta here y'all wilding.

This ain't a fkn party bro.

I didn't ask for y'all to pull up.

Except I did.

I needed to stop that shit.

Stop accepting affection/care from others just bc they offered it.

After autonomous bae and P dipped, lowkey panicking.

Not digging being in here all gowned all fucked.

Needed to rally.

To get tf out.

"K first thing next morning gonna."

Tried to conk, telling the nurse Kill the light.

Lay on my side, tryna calm my tits but sweating scratching.

Rubbed my left arm, suddenly everything warm wet.

Metal smell everywhere.

Hit the nurse button, she came back, flipped the light, red everywhere, a fkng massacre, my IV needle all tangled in my twisted sheets somewhere.

Puddle pooling on the tile floor next to my bed, dripping off the side.

Except it wasn't the actual nurse.

The last nurse had just left and the next had yet to show.

Only one there the receptionist lady in training.

A novice nurse-to-be, all shook.

Not ready for this gore.

Another of the receptionist ladies mopping all around me, dabbing my mattress of blood.

Me going Aw fuck, aw sheesh, I'm sorry, I don't even know what.

The training nurse fiddling with the IV, struggling with the package like an overeager teenboy rushing to crack that rubber-wrapper before she changed her mind.

Visibly shook.

Going OK, OK, we got this, I got this.

Something about that energy making me shook.

Recoil.

Go dry.

Like she ain't gonna be the one to lead me.

She ain't a daddy, bro.

This bitch wilding.

Then her tryna penetrate me, it not taking.

The more she tried to jam it in, the more my arm, my vein, bein like Nah.

Not into this anymore.

I changed my mind!

I revoke consent.

———

After butchering her third vein on the same arm, just bellig-erently blasting all potential holes, the next nurse showed, thank fuck.

    She hit me with that calm energy.

    True daddy energy is calm.

    It says: It's all good. I got you.

    I'ma take the stress so you needn't.

    This time we hit the other side.

    Oatmeal for my breakfast take them IVs ambidextrous.

    Got it in first try.

•

The last time ex bae let me inside, two winters ago —

    Already seeing Z.

    Not 'together' yet but 'hanging with.'

    Ghosting for up to 48 between question-texts.

    Only responding when baited.

    Addies, trees, rolls.

    Resources her program-mates wouldn't know where to even start locating.

    Couldn't provide.

    I was Man Bun Weed Guy.

    The plug.

    Nah: the mfkn surge protector.

But this night was one of those.

    Tryna hit these pure rocks roam west? It's so nice out.

    That got her. Too many flashbacks to fight off.

These were the circumstances that led to that most euphoric mode;
a mode the drugs furnished, but that we too were key pieces to.
That above/isolated-from-the-world mode.
Isolated, yet not alone. Bc of each other.
Finally talking.
Really talking.
Saying whatever the fuck.
Everything a gem.
Everything straight bars.

Still, wasn't like how we used to mish it around, back west. In Cali.
Santa Cruz; Berkeley.
This terrain didn't allow for it. No variation in elevation,
step to step.
You couldn't mish it down the rocks, to sand. Feeling your way
with your feet in the moonlight.
Angles revealing themselves according to perspective.
According to your relation to the water, which itself never
stopped moving.
Was ever shifting.
This vertigo part of the intoxication.

Here and now though.
Had to content ourselves with directional variation.
That diagonal from 34th and Walnut to 32nd and Chestnut.
Grass and benches and trees, but sterilized the sheen of campus.
Of academic transplantation.
Muhfuckers carrying backpacks and briefcases and tote bags,
going to or from meetings or classes or the library.
Killing our buzz.

Not killing; these rocks were too fire to kill.
But detract-from.
Prevent optimization-of.

Back on Market, realized Market was too far. Too city-ward.
Center City energy leaking out all the way to here, across the
water. Some ten blocks. Not tryna go west; west was where the
Oldness was. And north. Up 36th. Where home was. We weren't
tryna head home yet. But were already walking towards it
before we realized. So stalled out mid-block, in the shadows of a
warehouse-y service entrance nook. Sat. Alternated playing songs
for each other on our phone speakers.

"K this one's a little gnarly and I don't mean everything it says,"
she said. "But I've been obsessed and it's also funny. It's called
'Bloody Mother Fucking Asshole.'"

I wish I was born a man
So I could learn how to stand
Up for myself
Like those guys with guitars…
I will not pretend
I will not put on a smile
I will not say I'm alright for you!
You bloody mother fucking asshole (x like 20).

She was so giggly but looked at me funny. Like I sorry? Like
Luh ya bb!!
But also like But nah this some straight up real shit.
This how it is now bruh.

269

———

We didn't wanna go any places we'd already been, so typed 'bars near me' into Google Maps. Picked one we didn't recognize and started walking towards it. Way down 41st. Still in West but further south than I'd ever walked. South of Baltimore south. In that weird purgatorial area sorta by the medical school, sorta by the tracks. We'd never been down there since it wasn't one of the 'cool' bars young educated twentysomethings went to. It was an OG West Philly dive. One black folks frequented sorta exclusively, seemingly. Although almost no one was frequenting it currently. Drinks mad cheap, juke box blasting current rap. Ordered some whiskey gingers that were like $3 and came in these lil skinny glasses with crosshatch zigzag indentations, all scratched up. Re-upped on the beans out front, after our first round. Sat at the bar. I said funny/interesting/charming things and got joke-handsy with her, in ways I usually did while out and lit, to make her say Stoppp, laterrr; and she did eventually say these things, only much later than usual.

At some point we went upstairs bc we heard there was pool. Tiny room with a big-ass pool table that took up almost the whole floor. All broody and weirdly lit and Lynchian in there. No music of its own, just the distant thumping of 808s from downstairs.

A little while later this rando, white, twentysomething couple wandered in. Like We heard there was pool. All awkward and wide-eyed full of wonder, I couldn't tell whether only bc of the drugs. Everything so strange and surreal, I think bc the drugs. They asked if they could get next. The dude kept going How weird is this place, this place is so random, sorta snickering. It was, but I didn't like how he said it. Didn't give him the

270

agreement he sought. Despite the euphoria of the molly, you'da thought I woulda. Maybe it was fading. Maybe it had stopped working, how much I'd been taking. Just sorta big-bro sonned him, like Sure brah, whatever you say. Shot my shot. Eight-balled tryna do a tricky double-bounce thing, on my last solid. We forfeited our sticks. Retreated to the back tables, into the shadowed area the dim lights didn't reach. Spoke quietly and got nuzzly. But the other couple didn't start playing. The dude was salty I hadn't reciprocated his energy so was like over-compensating by having an exaggeratedly good time, ignoring us. Ignoring the quarters he'd stacked on the table. Some-one threw on Rae Sremmurd downstairs and cranked it some notches. Wanna get outta here? I said, watching the dude sorta dancing weird and making out sloppily with his girl. We got outta there.

Back at hers. She still gave everything. But turned away. No longer took me in her arms. Into her bosom. Just faced the wall and waited for me to finish.

•

On my final evening, I put on all my clothes, over my hospital gown. Donned the kicks, grabbed my cane, and peeled outta there.

Derm bae would be in touch, she'd said earlier, when she pulled up to check in on me.

Looking too fly.

This maybe part of it. The sudden need to flee.

Autonomous bae seeing me was one thing.

But derm bae.

Derm bae was someone new. Someone to impress.

"First impressions are everything," I reminded myself, pulling my gown down over my bare ass — I'd been lying on my side, siesta-ing — when she, knocking before entering, poked her head into my room.

I was closer to home than expected. Over on Powelton three blocks, a half mile up 41st.

Today two days after the year's coldest.

Wind whipping. *Stinging.*

Cane clicking on the cobblestony sidewalk park-side there.

Sun just set.

Not telling anyone I was peeling out, so surprising roomie bae when I showed.

Once home, I texted N Come thru. To help me get sorted.

Caught him on his way back from his adjunct teaching gig.

While waiting for him, checked my email and saw that Sheila had emailed me back.

Asking *Have you made it out to NYC in your van yet?*

Lol.

Fuck dude, I'd really been talking that talk. Fractured hip, skin diseases and all.

But it was almost like Sheila could sense I'd just gotten out, how the timing went.

I read N her email, psyched.

I wish I could come up with a way to write that encouraged being in your body, she wrote. *That's the only trouble with writing: all the sitting.*

And parents, siblings: you think they're part of the landscape, like trees, or mountains. Then it turns out they're people just like you who die.

Reading those parts over and over, limping-pacing, amped.

Yeah what about *your* body though, N said. Your room.

We went up there to see what was good, N telling me to take it easy up the stairs.

Seeing the state of it, he said OK, let's get this sorted.

Helped me sweep up all the skin, the rolling papers, the random crap strewn everywhere.

Redid my sheets, me doing a tarot read for him while waiting for them to dry.

His present-future was nine of wands. I told him this was the Energy card. Fire card. That he was about to go in on his dissertation, his writing.

That it was time to *work*.

N was like Alright dude, that all sounds great. But howabout now we get that sleep-spot sorted.

3

GAL PAL

February 2019

Linked for drinks with some gal pals of autonomous bae's at Fiume.

Pulled up early in the evening, at as brisk a clip as my hip allowed.

They'd commandeered the corner, bay window table one had to commandeer in order for this upstairs-of-Victorian saloon-spot to not feel claustrophobic.

Roomie bae was there. As was C, ex-coworker of autonomous bae I'd met before. Plus others I peripherally knew.

Felt woke being included in this circle-powwow as the only dude.

Well, at one point, two peripheral, newly transplanted baes showed, each with their respective dude-baes. Although each dude-bae rocked eye shadow and 'female-presenting' attire, so.

I had on a Champion hoodie, cuffed sweats, Nike Dri-Fit cap and Huarache's.

In this context: hella bro-ed out.

But protected from West Philly ostracization by their acceptance of me.

Hadn't intended for it to be a full-on turn-up night; was only recently on this new skin drug dupilumab, and it had only recently started hitting.

Still a lil tenuous.

The biopsy results had come in. I didn't have the rare, leprous condition PRP like Dr. Botox thought I had. Just extreme eczema with inflammation levels so high I was on skin cancer watch.

Infection caused by compromised immune functioning, from the cyclosporine maybe.

Derm bae would be keeping an eye on all this.

But so it went how it always seemed to: the minute I got a glimmer of a functional bod, I started wilding.

Testing its limits.

And this, tonight, meant boozing.

How we got all the way from Fiume (45th x Locust) to the Barn (49th x Baltimore) — on foot? an Uber? — is, now, unclear to me.

But get there we did.

The Barn meant $2 draft PBRs meant all bets were off.

Vibe festive like we were celebrating something, although I can't think of what.

Maybe my health.

Maybe the fact we were, each of us, still alive.

Maybe the simple fact of our togetherness, here and now, in this place, on this night.

Unbelievably!

If you really thought about it...

Which let's face it we weren't, how lit we were.

———

Rolling deep with this whole gal crew was cool and all, don't get me wrong.

But I still had to interact.

Find things in common to talk.

I gravitated towards autonomous bae's ex-coworker, C.

C older, mid-thirties. Engaged. Set to move cross-country with her fiancé in some months.

More 'masculine' demeanor, maybe.

Or maybe the fact of her being rigidly booed made her less distractingly objectifiable.

We got somehow to talking the gender wage gap.

How did we get on the gender wage gap.

Musta been from talking marriage.

Her engagement.

Musta made a dowry joke, while probing how long they'd been together, asking how he threw down popping the question.

Said something like Fuck dude, woulda been married to my ex, only I was too broke. I didn't have enough goats for a dowry. I lacked the requisite dowry goats.

Then she musta went something like No, yeah, that element of marriage is still weird. Since we're still so discriminated against in the workforce.

Mhm…come again? I musta said.

She and autonomous bae had been managers at this food distribution company together, before autonomous bae decided to switch it up. Become an EMT.

C still managed the company.

"Well yeah, people paying women 70% what they pay men for the same work," she continued.

I'd just spent the last month unable to walk. The last six

unable to work. Holed up, stalled out, body fucked. Watching lowkey red-pill videos on this exact thing.

"Well that doesn't really make sense, does it. Wouldn't that incentivize employers to hire women? If they could do that?"

Needless to say, we were no longer homies.

Looking at me like I'd just dropped a hard-R N-bomb.

Doing an exasperated rage-screech and looking away from me for autonomous bae, hand gesturing like Yo *whose* mans *is this, somebody come get this* —

Pushing me away, cutting me off.

"I'm not saying that's true necessarily," I said, going small. "Just saying that's what I heard.

"What my anecdotal experience suggests.

"Like, dudes are fucking idiots, bro. There are less jobs, today, for fucking idiots. No?"

"Well why are you just spewing random stats that you heard?" she said.

"Well isn't that what you're doing?"

Outside, to cool off. Pacing-limping with my cane.

Autonomous bae following me out to calm/chastise me.

Or honestly just calm me.

Speaking in a conspiratorial undertone, going I know you got a point, we been over this, but you can't say it why you gotta say it.

Ex-roomie bro pulling up at some point, speaking over me when I explained my side, speaking directly to the women present like I wasn't there, like apologizing collectively for our gender, me getting in his face like Talk to me myself ya got something to say you bitch, you virtuesignalling fuck.

Then autonomous bae mad at me all night, even when she came back with and fucked me, going You're so trash, you're terrible, but either that fact (my trashness), or the power she felt saying it, or that she thought it but was fucking me anyway making her wetter.

4

BOSS MAN

Late Last Winter (2018)

When my big cuz E's boss asked him, at midnight on a Sunday, whether he knew anyone able to be in DC by sunup for a weeklong job, he had to have been joking.

Been sorta thinking aloud. Vocalizing his wishful thoughts.

Y'know *musing*.

But big cuz E's boss, he didn't know about this guy.

He didn't know I'd be just risen, drinking my first coffee of the waking cycle, when that call came in.

That I'd just had a convo with the ma, earlier that day, before I passed out, about how, if nothing gave within the next seventy-two, I'd be left with no choice but to start over.

To give up my spot in Philly, fly back to Cali, and move into her living room.

Credit maxed out, debit down to double digits.

Postmates impossible due to snow.

Last week tried to go out mid-blizzard and got stuck in — literally slowed to a stop, had to dismount, and wade out of — the middle of a snowed-in intersection.

To deliver a calzone — a single calzone! — to a grad student who — this muhfucker saw me balaclava'd up, slipping and sliding in a snowsuit — didn't even tip.

Four dollars even for an hour-long mish that left me damn near hypothermic.

So yeah.

When I got that 1 a.m. call, to be in DC by 6, I was down.

Wasn't tryna move back in with the ma.

That hit way too many mid-twenties-artist-guy-sensitive-bro-broken-by-a-breakup tropes.

Plus — all I heard was the $500 day rate.

All I needed to hear.

First thing was getting the box on the road.

Outta the makeshift back driveway I'd solo-jimmied last fall.

My backyard's back gate formerly a fence separated from the residential one-way back there by a two-dumpsters'-worth pile of trash, branches, random debris.

Plastic bags of human shit.

Syringes.

But I had, late last fall, when no longer wanting to deal with having to park the thing come first snow, noticed tire treads back there.

Had figured I could get the van up, into the yard, and stash it off-road, if I could clear the way.

So hazmatted up and went to town on the trash mountain, clearing what I could. Then sawing the fence off at its contact points. Before reattaching it, with hinges, so it swung out like a driveway gate.

Everything smooth sailing till, while tryna flatten out the inclined 'driveway' — uneven dirt and rocks and glass shards — I hit this huge concrete slab that looked like it had just been dumped there.

Like someone had started building a legit driveway, then abandoned it.

No cap — a pair of Champion tear-away sweatpants molded into the center of the block.

Like they were like *Yo, let's build this driveway. Here, dump this concrete. Oh wait. We got that b-ball game to get to. Fuck this, warm-ups starting, we out!*

tears away tearaways, throws em in the wet concrete, dips

Tried pickaxing down the concrete mogul, kept pickaxing it, chipping off shards, till I couldn't anymore. Till pickaxing it further would require a jackhammer.

I didn't have a jackhammer.

Probably coulda just left it.

Aborted the mish.

Maybe shoulda.

But nah. At this point.

After all those bricks and rocks and slabs I'd dug up, arranged.

I was a road-building peasant-slave from Roman times; I couldn't stop now.

So rammed the van up there, wedging plywood/rocks beneath the tires for traction and scraping tf out of my van's underbelly.

But got it in!

Only — I hadn't even considered moving it all winter. And now I needed to. To drive it to DC. At 1 a.m.

2 a.m now.

Did end up shattering my driver-side mirror backing out too close to the driveway-side tree — it had grown, apparently, since I'd last trimmed it back. But managed to find enough mirror shards, in the dirt, by head-lamplight, to reaffix with moving tape so I could see.

E texted *Bring all the tools you got.*

I had an impact driver. A bit set. A tape. Gloves.

On the road, after blowing my last almost-hundo on gas, by 3.

•

The jobsite was this spot the Gaylord National Resort & Convention Center. On the Potomac, south of DC.

From the Google Maps image, U.S. government–related, seemingly.

Got led along this weird stretch, on the final leg, by the FBI or Homeland Security HQs that had all these signs restricting exiting without clearance.

No shoulders, no lane-switching.

Gas gauge tweaking, tryna blend my U.S. Air Force utility box van with expired California plates in with pre-dawn, rush-hour, U.S. government traffic.

Keyed tf up off gas station coffee, blasting X on the Bluetooth.

Pillared awning with a white-gloved doorman, upon arrival, who directed me where to park.

E had told me 6 a.m. It was 6:05.

But he'd worked till 3 that morning, I'd later learn. They'd gotten delayed waiting for the National Youth Division Cheerleading Competition to wrap in the event space our job was in.

He picked up his phone at 6:20.

Elaborately pile-woven-carpeted hallway leading into a circular balcony overlooking a central, all-glass, arched atrium. Huge fountain in the middle.

Wall-encompassing oil paintings of dead presidents all over.

Winding, ornamented staircases leading up to conference rooms and event spaces at the end of the hall, past the check-in desk.

"We'll drop your shit later, we're already late," E said, handing me an extra room key.

"Yo — is there anywhere I could grab a Clif Bar or something?"

"Oh right. Let's eat first."

"Also — unless we get paid out at the end of the week, I'ma need money for gas back to Philly."

E said I got you.

Gloved butler-type dudes in the catered eating area with plastered-on smiles, attending to Sterno-lit chafing dishes of every breakfast item you could think of.

Couple carpentry bros in there — our coworkers. But otherwise. Folks in suits typing into phones, arranging meetings, nibbling on eggs.

I went in on so much shit — French toast, an omelet, Canadian bacon. All that.

Immediately exposing myself as poor.

The job was an install for Intel.

Some Intel conference.

Setting up two football fields' worth of booths and rooms and display areas, where Intel reps would sell new technology to...potential buyers?

I didn't even know.

This would take Monday, Tuesday. For the event on Wednesday. Before tearing it all down Thurs–Friday.

Not even sure whether we were scabs.

I got the sense the wild day rate was in order to avoid going through the labor union.

So they could get it done with less people incentivized to work harder.

But I mean, fuck.

I had to fkng eat bro.

I checked in with the project managers, middle-aged dudes who'd flown in from Toronto, where the production company was based.

"Appreciate you making it down here on such short notice," the main dude said. "You get him set up in a room yet?" he said to E.

"Oh. I mean," I said. "I brought my sleeping bag. I can crash on E's floor. Or in my van."

Homie looked at me like What.

"We'll get you a room, bud," he said, looking at E a bit like Yo *who tf is this guy you brought.*

Although I don't think we were totally scabs. Because there were some union-type dudes on site also.

Hood kids from outer DC—not DC DC, but the hood part, they said—who were just sorta there helping out.

None of whom had tools or were geared up or anything, and were just sorta hanging.

The main Canadian dude explained that the trucks were just pulling up now with the skids.

He handed me a map.

"Here's what we'll be doing. These are the small booths. These are the medium. These are the walls. The tables. We'll assemble, then lay em out."

The map looked like a whole damn city.

"Didn't really realize the scale of this thing till last night, when we laid out the carpet. Why we called ya!"

I looked out at the space. Fully carpeted. Little pieces of masking tape all over, outlining the edges of the layout. Bisected by a hundred-foot-tall, interlocking, moveable wall separating the football field–sized expanses. Couple forklifts moored randomly, like they'd conked out mid-task. Entire west-facing wall glass-paned, letting in the first traces of sunlight.

I surveyed the map again. Looked up at boss man. Nodded like Easy enough.

The two other dudes on the team were bros from NYC: one, W, hapa boy about my age who'd gone to school for this type of shit; and D, who was jacked af. Looking like a half–Native American, half-Black Incredible Hulk.

It was sorta like an insane IKEA furniture assembly project, but on roids. With a moving element.

Minus the relationship fight at the end, when you didn't assemble it right.

There was no room for mistakes; our relationship was with the Intel execs, and they would be slanging their products come Wednesday at 9 a.m. no matter what the fuck.

I just acted like I knew what I was doing; and, once I learned to do a thing, I fkng went in and did it over and over.

Still keyed up from the drive and all that French toast and coffee.

Just so happy to be doing something other than lying on my side all night in my freezing-ass room, next to my space heater, deep in a YouTube rabbit hole, debating whether or not to turn Postmates on.

Looking out the window at all the snow and deciding: No, I'm not gonna turn Postmates on.

Waiting to hear back on my next round of edits editor bae was supposed to send me on my Walk Book manuscript.

Ignoring the likelihood that, any minute now, she'd abandon it. Abandon me.

That she was only acting like she was editing it bc she still wanted the D.

Once she learned who I really was, she'd move on.

But 'unable to write new stuff' till I knew for sure.

I was able to help check that the masking tape was laid out right since I had a measuring tape.

Arms cracking like they did every winter, from the dryness and cold; so when I went to nab my tape, I quickly lathered when no one was looking.

Railed a Claritin.

It was unpacking these huge desk things from the skids, carrying them over to where they went, and connecting them to a right-angled wall with an Allen key.

Basic.

Got like half of em up by lunch.

E told me I was killing it and that head Canadian dude told him that I, specifically, was killing it.

I'd forgotten about this: working in a group and getting approval from older, paternal-type dudes.

I'd been, since late 2016, working alone and getting no approval from anyone.

Not even from maternal-type people since ex bae dipped.

Why there was so much at stake with editor bae.

286

———

Right before lunch I snuck out one of the doors of the win-dowpaned wall, with W, for a smoke.

Looking out onto the National Harbor. Alexandria, VA, across the way.

Windy af.

Hadn't spoken to him much since he was doing the tasks that didn't only require lifting and an Allen key. The tasks that required actual skills and power tools.

He asked if I did this type work often.

"Not often," I said.

"Ever?"

"Something like."

He said Fasho and Bet and This nigga this and This nigga that in a way that made me feel at ease.

In a way you could tell was just how he talked.

How people where he came up did.

I asked him about Brooklyn. How much his spot was.

How he even managed to survive in Brooklyn, how much his spot was.

"Just working," he said. "Always working."

I didn't even learn he was hapa till much later. Thought he was Dominican or Puerto Rican or some shit.

What people always assumed about me.

But then also why did it matter.

It didn't fkng matter bro.

•

That night we turned up at the one bar in town even though I was burnt af.

I wanted to pass out, but E was like Nah, you gotta come turn up.

Turning up with the boys part of the job.

Head honcho Canadian dude said Order whatever, on us.

This town wasn't even a town; it was an extension of the hotel.

This whole town there to facilitate the hotel.

The hotel was for the government, to house like foreign dignitaries, it seemed.

Half U.S. government, half Disneyland.

All of us rowdy bowdy talking shit doing gay jokes disrespecting women from afar.

The one woman on crew, hella zatted mid-thirties girl who gave no fucks — that was her vibe — just smirking and shaking her head when we said sus shit.

Like you fucking monkeys.

You cavemen.

I'd forgotten how to talk like this, but picked it up fairly quickly.

Doing so was the price of admission.

It brought us closer.

It unified the squad.

I'd been so bitter towards professional groups going out drinking together, wearing their uniforms, whom I'd pass on my bike while delivering things. Whom I'd deliver to once they, drunk, got home from their professional gatherings.

Like you fucking simps.

You basic fucks.

Probably thinking y'all are doing good for the world by not saying un-PC things and drinking outta metal straws when y'all are just participating in organized classism.

288

And not only that, but sedating yourself with that most savage, unrefined, un-nuanced Western drug, alcohol.

Especially insidious since it wasn't even seen as such, wasn't even seen as a drug.

Fkng understanding school shooters, biking past and delivering to these fucks.

How they had no clue what lay outside their sphere.

How they looked at those outside their sphere as human garbage.

Like they couldn't grasp how/why anyone, had they the motivation, wouldn't live like them.

But I guess I understood it.

The drinking part at least.

That shit was fun af!

Went to the bathroom like three beers in and took a bathroom selfie and posted it on the gram.

Six beers in I checked the gram and noticed editor bae had liked it.

Got so fkng happy, I was giddy.

There was hope yet!

More of the same the next morning, making good progress.

What I started to realize was, I didn't have to go so in on my own and could still get the same results.

Employing dollies, when applicable.

Rallying dudes who'd be on their phones bullshitting if no one rallied them.

Yo gimme a hand with that end of this, would ya.

Yo y'all hit that quadrant, we'll hit this.

Felt fkng good dude.

PARTICIPATING.

———

All the Intel fucks were arriving for the conference the next day, so lunch was blown af.

All tables in the lunchroom filled. The new ones they'd put out in the hallway surrounding the lunchroom also.

Joined a communal roundtable out in the hall.

Glass panes facing out on the National Harbor, like down in the showroom, but five stories up.

A glass atrium, way up in the corner, where the L-shaped hallways met.

Wild chandeliers everywhere.

Couldn't sleep much on the cot in E's room last night, plus had been going in harder than I had in years, so was irritable sorta.

The gay jokes were fun and all, but to a point.

And D, D was my guy; we'd gone in tandeming a whole bunch of shit this morning.

But my brain was accustomed to nocturnal solitude and half-hourly cigs and IV-rate coffee all waking hours.

This was a lot. Was why I wasn't cut out for steady work like these guys. Like all these Intel fucks everywhere, making plans on their tablets fkng networking.

Tough realization pills to swallow.

So when I was swallowing a big-ass hunk of bratwurst they'd served up, just tryna re-up the energy reserves in peace, and D tried to say some shit like "Oh how's that sausage taste, I bet you love that sausage deep down your throat—" I snapped and went "Dude are you ever gonna say anything that actually means anything or are you just gonna keep spewing fuckshit."

E and W looked up from their plates.

D mumbled something about just messing around.

E laughed.

W went "Well damn. This nigga ain't playin."

∙

We got a couple more reinforcements that afternoon, since we were on a time crunch to get things done by night.

At this point mostly cosmetic stuff.

Mounting TVs, ensuring they all had power. Concealing electrical cords. Putting up signs and stickers directing folks where to go and what brands were selling what.

The signs we read and followed daily were just things people with money typed up and printed out and displayed strategically.

Nothing printed and elevated was sacred.

These weren't new insights. But putting the signs up myself made them tangible.

One of the guys who got called in was a 30s or 40s Black dude decked out in John Deere. Ex–Special Forces.

Had two kids.

Had driven here from somewhere far but somewhere not that far to have been able to drive here just for the afternoon.

Part of what we were getting paid for, I realized, was our availability.

I felt like this dude should have gotten the call I got, what if he needed the bands more than me, given the kids.

Although I don't know how he could've needed them more than me bc I had literally zero.

Negative 7, counting credit card debt.

We worked on applying embossed fabrics onto and elevating these huge like 30-foot panels.

The panels had the Intel logo and images of differently raced and gendered folks smiling, holding Intel gadgets.

He said this type of work was all he'd done since his last deployment, although usually not with this type day rate.

Freelance hourly handyman stuff, unless one of these gigs came up.

We were like two dads assembling an IKEA crib, tryna figure out what screwed into where, consulting the assembly instructions.

"Ayo you got a gun on you? Think we gotta stake this," he said, showing how one we'd erected was wobbling.

"A gun?" I said.

He made a shooting motion.

I was such a noob. A gun was a drill.

"Oh word. Yeah there's one over there," I said. "But think he said we just gotta weigh em down with sandbags, we don't need a gun we got sandbags."

At dinner that night we ate out in the hallway again, by the window. D doing dick jokes to whoever would listen. E harassing local folks tryna find someone with trees — going through similar withdrawals, apparently.

I was just looking around so content, taking it all in. When I noticed a weird flicker at the corner of my sightline.

I looked up.

A lil bird perched on the chandelier, way up in the atrium.

Flying up, fluttering its wings, bumping into the glass. Confused. Then catching itself, flying in circles some, before returning to its chandelier perch.

Kept doing that.

I went Guys, look, a bird, sorta quietly, sorta to myself.

There were like fifteen people at the big-ass table we were sitting at.

And like fifty other similar tables all around us, in a row. All humming with Intel-related chatter.

No one was listening.

I watched it do the same thing a few times. Fly into the glass, get confused, then return.

Couldn't figure out how it even got in.

Or how it would fly out.

I wanted to help it.

How could I.

It was so high up, I couldn't reach that high. A ladder couldn't, even. And who was to say it would even accept my help, if I tried.

Boss man came over from another table. Said Five minutes boys, gotta mount the last of the TVs by walk-through at 9.

I killed the last of my chicken parm.

Looked back up at the bird.

Realized I couldn't help it, so just zoomed in on it on my Instagram story, took a video, added a funny caption, and posted it.

5

NEW LEAF

March 2019

"So no. This drug is different," derm bae explained at our intake appointment, last month. "How dupilumab works is, it's an antibody. So neither a steroid nor an immunosuppressant: it neither tries to override the problem nor shut it down."

Derm bae was only three years older than me — I'd stalked her LinkedIn and deduced this from her graduation years — but was already the head derm at UPenn's dermatology center.

"So what's happening is," she continued, "your body keeps flaring up, getting inflamed, bc it thinks a foreign antibody is attacking. Thinks a bad thing is invading. When really nothing is. So dupilumab, since it's *also* an antibody, essentially *replaces* those imaginary, malignant antibodies your system was convinced were attacking, and signals to your body that...No, nothing foreign/bad is invading!"

"Fkng crazy. Fkng WILD," I said, staring up googly-eyed at her from my examination chair.

They taught me to administer the stuff myself, that first appointment.

It came in an ice-packed box, monthly. To be injected fortnightly.

Plastic syringe filled with a clear, viscous fluid. Spring mechanism in the handle.

294

Cost hundreds per dose, but Medicaid somehow covered it for $3 per two-pack.

Jabbed into bunched-up tummy fat, squeezed in. Band-Aided. Lil bubble on my tummy till the fluid dispersed.

Last I'd seen her, at our one-month check-in, last week. She'd given me her personal line. Had told me—as I got dressed, pulling my shirt down over my, sure, lil flared but nonetheless fkn CUT UP (and not in the eczema way, if in that way also) torso, after she'd touched me how she had, both of us breathless at the intimacy—to call her for anything.

"If you need *anything*," looking at me significantly.

Things seemed to settle a sec after that first injection.

Could hardly believe my gooped up, conjunctivitis-ed out eyes—which, conjunctivitis, was the one side effect, the one downside. This would, however, subside with time, derm bae assured me. Once my body adjusted.

But then, a few days into my second round of injections, my skin started doing that weird skin thing it had been doing before.

Cracking then dying then shedding.

Like the most OD sunburn.

An entire layer of skin deciding: Eh, we're over it.

Flaking to the floor.

Fucking up roomie bae's socks again.

I panicked. And this panic made my skin spazz even more.

Tryna get all the dead skin off in one go and, in so trying, further irritating it.

But then remembered. Derm bae. Personal line.

Only, before I even had a chance to call, right when I was about to, like 8 p.m. that evening, *she* called *me*! Right when shit was getting fucked.

Her knowing this how I knew she really loved me.

Sounding so sultry, so sexy on the phone.

Like she'd just gotten home from a long day giving out orders, healing the masses. Had poured herself a, say…I don't know…Merlot? Had taken off her dress, kicked off her stilettos —

Wait. What am I saying. She a doctor.

OK whatever. Taken off her…smock?

Look she was taking off her clothes for me! how she sounded.

Anyway.

I told her, frantic, what was going on. How nothing was gonna work. How it was bc I had no discipline, had sinned, had had a beer, some beers, the other night. How I'd been railing Kettle Chips too goddamn much, that was why my skin was spazzing. How I didn't just have eczema, I had other undiscovered diseases the tests hadn't picked up on. I was a leper, clearly. There was nothing she nor anyone could do —

"Sh sh sh," she said. "I want you to listen to me. What you're experiencing is *perfectly natural*. In fact, there's a *medical term* for it. 'Sloughing.' This happens after your body experiences an inflammation outbreak, and has calmed down. What happens is, all that flared-up, panicky skin, essentially, dies. So once the new skin is ready, your body decides to LET GO of all that old skin. This is why it's happening now. Because your body is calm.

"This is good.

"It's not anything you're doing or eating or drinking. And it's not another disease. We've done the tests. We know everything you have, and it's not that. You're fine. Just keep doing the sweatsuit bleach method I told you to, till the dupilumab starts kicking in."

I hung up. Went upstairs. Did as I was told.

Capful of cleaning bleach in a lukewarm bath. Soak for fifteen. Then full-body triamcinolone lather while skin still wet, sealing in the water / splash o' bleach. Bleach to kill the potential for any bacterial development—what happened when the skin was open/didn't heal right. What caused the spread of not only eczema but infection. Infection, cuts not healing, what had led to the fever, hospitalization. Cuts' inability to heal on their own the first sign of cancer.

Once lubed, I slid into the Everlast, extra-thick rubber sweatsuit I'd copped—the kind boxers ran in to cut weight, cuffed at ankles and wrists and waistband. To seal in the moisture.

Then straight to bed.

•

The next morning I got awoken by the birds out back, who stayed posted in the driveway-side tree my van's mirror always got snagged on.

Who got to chirping, into my window, first thing.

That avian alarm.

Got the coffee water going, rolled a cig, and popped out back. In search of a patch of direct sun.

The only goal now was going daytime.

Getting em daily rays.

Lack of sunlight from being full nocturnal an auxiliary if nonetheless critical piece.

It went, in the ma's esoteric, Waldorf-teacher view: rock,

plant, animal, human. The 'kingdoms' did. In that evolutionary order.

My year of stationary nocturnality had turned me full fossil. Worshipping the moon so long had turned me rock, fkn cratered out. Skin no longer photosynthesizing. Just hardening, cracking, and flaking off like layers of sedimentary strata.

And it was still on that.

I was getting ahead of myself, tryna fuck/go-animal before I'd become-plant.

I had to become a plant again.

The thing with tools was, you had to use em.

You neglected em, they stopped working.

Tools enjoyed being used; you stopped using em they stopped being tools.

My van was a tool.

I needed to start using it again.

To find a use for it.

How my van was presently situated, the side sliding door — the side my desk faced — was flush against the fence separating mine and my neighbor's yards. Faced out into its overgrown, trash-strewn expanse. Away from the sun.

But if I could get it in head first, I could booty-first, too, I decided. That was physics.

I needed an office. Somewhere with a sun-facing window I could pack a lunch and mish it to. Even if that mish was five steps outta my back door.

The mish itself wasn't the point; the point was having a mish. A mish worth mishing.

And while this wasn't a task that was useful to anyone in society, wasn't a real job, it was something job-like I could do!

Something useful to me, my van; or, in any case, something that, while I was doing it—until I was done doing it—*felt* useful.

I rallied for this gig. Smoked more cigs, merked another coffee. While letting the engine warm.

Opened the back gate.

Trimmed the tree back.

Eased her down the sloped driveway, remembering how *me and V late that last grow cycle of the season on J's main property the one he lived on building that fence that perimeter that barrier to keep critters animals randos out how that football field of outdoors atop the hill J's house was at the base of were so ripe so bursting us waiting edging till they got as ripe as possible to max em out only we waited too long and we'd risk leaving em final-trimester vulnerable exposed to the elements losing em to a storm so when that storm started brewing the wind whipping J telling us to move camp to the top of the hill to be on emergency-harvest call only every time I tried whipping the box up that turnoff to the clearing it was so steep she kept skidding out spraying mud almost fishtailing into the upper post bounding the entry gate* jostling left-right-left down over the concrete craters/moguls back there, eying the tree in the cracked, moving-taped rearview mirror-shards *and it not until J thinking it over chewing on his nail a sec telling us Finish out the fence brb and leaving and coming back lugging that trailerful of gravel before 4-wheel driving it up the slope and easing it out pneumatically* then three-point turning into the handicapped parking spot opposite *me and V doing the frantic Jap rock garden sweep spreading out the pebbles evenly* before ramming that bitch back up, but backwards J *telling me Give her one more shot thinking it no way was gonna catch how slick the dirt how many times she'd skidded out already but then gunning it way fast* skrt-*ing onto the turnoff that the tracks caught*—

I was halfway back up but she kept getting snagged on this deepest crater, on the less cratered side but the side I hadn't lain the lone plywood plank I owned over, spraying out mud onto the tree.

Wasn't till a neighbor across the one-way back there saw me skidding out and ran up with a second piece of plywood, handing it to me like Take it, no questions asked, that I managed to get her up.

I tried to return it to her after—it was snapped down the center, barely hanging together, chipped wood-shards sticking out either side. But she just smiled at me from the fold-out chair she was posted on. Said No, that's all you *and not realizing till then that you could just move natural materials around like that, to accommodate your needs, provided you had the horsepower to.*

Back in my backyard, I hopped up into the back of the box *how J had been right and later that night, at almost midnight, the clouds did break.* Opened both the back swing-out and side sliding doors, the windows on either side.

Dusted off my baby-blue Brother manual typewriter I copped in Oakland, the year ex bae and I lived together in Oakland *me almost KO'd in the box, in my sleeping bag, tryna decipher, through the spliffs, by candlelight, what Calvino was* actually saying tho *in* Invisible Cities *(1974) when J banged on the side sliding door and said Get geared, we gotta move.*

Placed it onto the now sun-facing desk and tried to resume writing *Fuccboi*.

It was almost noon *us working all night poncho'd headlamped up chopping down and laying out on tarps as many plants as possible that hadn't gotten so exhausted, soporific, that they'd dipped heads into the mud puddles pooling all over —*

The sun had just cleared the top of the driveway-side tree, would descend below the peak of my apartment's roof around 3.

Four hours of direct rays.

Of sitting crumpled on the step of my side doorway, or at my makeshift, roadside-found, table-leaf van-desk. As much skin as possible exposed. Shuddering nonstop from that sustained, full-body, solar orgasm.

Picking up writing *Fuccboi* where I'd left off — before my LA recovery stint, my hospital crash-out — felt impossible.

So much different now.

Everything changing always, too quickly to keep up with.

I'd been stalling, waiting, listening. But waiting *too* long. No longer in a positive, patient, edging-type way.

Only stalling.

Paralyzed.

Shook.

V had sent me a handwritten letter last week.

I had it laid out next to my *Fuccboi* pages on my van desk.

He'd been fucking with this witchy hippy girl in Santa Cruz he'd met at the lower westside New Leaf juice bar, while sliding in there to shit one morning. After a night sleeping in his Vanagon, by the tracks nearby.

She had him thinking all kindsa new stuff about his horoscopic chart, his lunar leanings. His tarot tendencies.

But realizing things about his temperamental patterns, based on his concrete actions, his tangible decisions, also.

Patterns he fell into over and over.

Wanting this from women initially, recoiling when that happened, before wanting to flee when that and that happened.

This sharing permitted, even encouraged, me to consider my own patterns.

To even recognize, in the first place, that patterns were created by tangible actions.

I wanted autonomous bae when she didn't want me, pushed her away once she did, and only started wanting her again once she stopped wanting me again.

I still saw ex bae as the central star all other planetary baes orbited.

Last I'd seen autonomous bae, I'd drunkenly, bitterly ranted to her about ex bae, to which she'd snapped and went It's been two years! Get over it. I seriously think you're never gonna.

Explaining all this to V felt more urgent than writing *Fuccboi*.

Only — explaining all this to V *was* writing *Fuccboi*.

Geeked off this epiphany, I merked the coffee I was on *how late that night nearing dawn first glimmers of sun glimmering the rain mellowing the field pocked with plant carcass piles on tarps like lil pillage fires all over that late-battle battlefield surreality surrounded by fallen flower comrades mouths dry clothes rain-sweat-soaked damp and chilling—*

Nabbed a new leaf from inside my typewriter case's inner sleeve *J hopping out of his pickup he'd driven up the hill coming over saying Had to let these bitches get as fat as we could, and now we gotta save em, me and V nodding like Damn straight—*

And slid her in.

Got to typing.

Banging on those keys hard bc the ribbon so old.

Till, halfway through the first page, she crapped out.

Jammed up.

Got all up in there and started toggling nobs *we didn't save em all, but we tried* with the baby flathead I kept on deck specifically for toggling nobs with, whenever my typewriter jammed.

No dice on the toggling.

Nor with tryna *shake* her back into action.

But I knew exactly what came next in my letter. Any more stalling and I'd forget.

So yanked the leaf outta there, grabbed a uni-ball, and *the ones we couldn't save, that had fallen beyond the point of saving, we had to let go* kept handwriting on the same side, where I'd left off.

Could only say so much in the letter though, before it literally became a *Fuccboi* chapter.

A *Fuccboi* chapter meant saying everything, including things I couldn't to V.

Or—including things I would need time and consideration and editing in order to muster up the courage to.

So once I'd said enough, I folded it up, stuck it into an envelope, and stamped it.

Nabbed a new leaf and started over, this time writing the letter to the world.

Changing the names, expanding where I couldn't in the letter, and withholding the personal responses I'd written specifically to V.

But otherwise *the sun finally up us tandeming each tarpful into J's pickup to transpo down to the main house finally understanding why the work we'd done building out the drying room in J's extra garage insulating the doors hanging the fishing line mounting the dehumidifiers how these flowers had needed all that wetness that moisture that muck to get as fat as full as we'd gotten em but if they were to make it fulfill their role hit the shelves the game was now wind-flow breath-flow airing these bitches out—*

Same exact voice *sitting on J's pickup's flatbed's edge holding down the top of the tallest pile like it was a loyal dog I was reminding to stay put, that we were in transit, that this downhill was steep—*

Same exact sharing-intention *J trampling those guys that'd gotten overwhelmed by the moisture subsumed by the muck were scattered all over decapitated spines broke soaked brownish* with which I wrote my letter to V.

6

CANE GUY

Spring Equinox Eve 2019

I caught roomie bae in transit out on our stoop one day.

Me chain-smoking doing fuck all; she on her way to her second nannying gig of the day.

Tryna squeeze herself and her bike through the front door while also getting the door, all oblivious.

"Oh. Hey," she said, seeing me. "Spring Equinox hang at the new gals' spot out in West tonight. Come through."

"Yeah?" I said. "Sure I'd be welcome?"

She scoffed, rolling her eyes like Yea-ah. Clipped her helmet's clip.

"Stop being silly. Starts at 6."

I was at a weird, intermediate spot with my hip.

Unable to exert it fully—to bike, say—but no longer really in need of my cane.

Still carrying it around for the novelty, the martyr flex, the stray steep 'cline.

But catching myself setting it down and almost forgetting it places.

Last Saturday night I'd left it at self-checkout at the Fresh Grocer, while pit-stopping there for a $1, day-old pizza slice with N—he'd wanted to hit a real spot, but I'd insisted on the Fresh Grocer since I was still too broke to eat out.

We'd wandered off, walking and talking, to the Schuylkill damn near by the time I realized.

Almost 1 a.m. by the time we got back.

Soon as I walked into the Fresh Grocer, either legitimately limping or affecting one in case I'd need it for lost-and-found evidence, the Fresh Grocer lady saw me and smirked.

Like *This* muhfucker.

This fkn guy.

Cane guy.

She procured it from behind the employee counter, where she'd hung it for me, before I could even ask.

The orthopedic doc I'd last week seen, for my eight-week check-up since being hospitalized, had said things were healing on schedule. That I wouldn't need surgery.

Or that, given how tenuous my skin, doing surgery, penetrating my skin's surface like that, could risk further complications.

That, in my case, though my bones were still compromised from all the roids I'd been on, getting all up in there and tryna fix em completely would fuck with my body's larger equilibrium.

My skin had its plate full already, healing what it was tryna heal.

"So what you saying is…we good?" I said, taking a picture of the X-ray of my hips—my birth canal—when he wasn't looking.

"Good as we're gonna be."

Instead of walking up 41st till I hit the tree streets like I usually did when mishing it out west, I cut through the baseball diamond out back the Market Street projects, along the fence that bisected it and Drexel's athletic complex.

Sun all but dipped, elongating things.

Down the semblance of a path, way out in the outfield, leading into the projects proper.

Amidst all the rubble out back behind the project b-ball courts.

Along a felled telephone pole, playing the-ground-is-lava but also the-ground-is-trash-strewn, human-waste-covered, probably.

Holding on to the project b-ball court's cage-fence the pole ran along, for balance.

Wanting to keep my diagonal, off-road route going, I went right, further into the projects, rather than along the left-bending entry-drive onto Market, given the latter would be a backtrack—the new gals were out on 54th, further west.

Cop-SUV posted at the project entrance, up on the grass. Maybe eying me suspicious, although I didn't look.

Got spat out in back of the Aldi parking lot, Market and 44th, through a partially obscured, folded-up fence-gap I wouldn'ta seen had it not been for the trace of a path—bent blades made by shortcutters before me—in the high grass adjacent.

Taking it easy down the steep slope, into the lot, cane-step at a time.

This was the other side of the rectangle I always stuck to the same two sides of, I realized, spanning 40th–50th and Market–Cedar.

Was the rectangle's central Z.

Gaining energy from these streets hitherto untraversed, I zigzagged from 44th to 54th, taking the one-ways and lesser-blown ones I didn't recognize.

Keyed up off the *Fuccboi* chapter (Rittenhouse bars, last winter) I was typing into the Notes app on my phone.

Off the PBR I was merking out of a 16 oz. to-go coffee cup.

Off this new form—a bar at a time—I'd found that was flowing so seamlessly.

Texted V *Walking down your ole man's way!* with a pic of a single-block street's sign named the same as his patronym, that I'd never before walked down / seen.

Roomie bae, ex-roomie bae, autonomous bae, the new baes who'd been out the night I spazzed last month—whose house this was—plus others I vaguely knew and others I didn't, all there when I showed.

We did an herb ceremony thing on the roof.

Standing in a circle at sundown and letting the dried-out sage or whatever get lifted aloft by the breeze.

Ex-roomie bae reminding us that New Year's Eve was the end of the Gregorian year, but tonight, the end of the lunar.

Of the botanic/agricultural/floral.

Hibernation's end.

Bloom Time.

No one explicitly opposed my presence, but I wasn't taking any chances. I kept my distance.

Squadded up with T, ex-roomie bae's boo, who had slight misgivings about being here also.

We alternated between the snack table in the kitchen and out on the stoop to smoke.

I was feeling shitty about the New Year's Eve chapter I'd written, before my hospitalization, that had involved him.

Considered mentioning it, for a split second.

Before thinking Dude hell no, you're trippin.

That incident had fucked him up for months.

He'd basically stopped going to that house I used to live in, where that New Year's party had been, even though he still had homies there, just bc he couldn't see those front steps without getting triggered, lowkey having an acid flashback.

Fuck dude, I said when he told me this, feeling so guilty.

But we got to talking cortisol regulation, trauma management, and the connection between the two.

T a therapist.

In training.

Seeing Medicaid patients who couldn't afford full-on docs, getting his hours in.

"Oh no, they're for sure connected," he said when I proposed that maybe, just maybe, all the shame and self-hate and repression I felt about how everything had gone down with ex bae was tied to how crazy my bod had wilded out last year.

"You get real hot and sweaty? Then chills?"

"That's exactly what was happening."

"A hundred percent to do with cortisol levels. An inability to regulate them."

He passed me his Bilbo Baggins–ass wooden piece that drew so well bc he cleaned it so well and regularly. I'd never once cleaned mine (unless you counted cashing tf out of it for resin hits, which you shouldn't).

I drew, keeping that cherry going.

This block, 54th, four blocks west of the generally accepted gentrification line, was dark and quiet. Peaceful, so long as you were cool with the possibility of someone pulling up on you.

One of the gals who lived here had recently bought the house. This was the third instance I'd heard of people buying houses on the 5400 block.

"No I was just reading something about this," T continued. "About how 'unaddressed traumas' are the major psychic factor in cases like this. 'Uncontainable inflammation.' Your body doesn't know what to do with all that added trauma-stress and, I mean, it's gotta go somewhere!"

"Goddamn bro. *Too* fkn relevant. I can't even."

T stayed silent. Caught my eye and grinned.

"So... what does one do?" I said, passing him back the piece I'd forgotten I was still holding.

"The only thing to do! Start addressing that shit. Forgiving yourself. Letting go. You call that therapist like I told you to?"

"I did." And I actually had. "They initially said they had slots open, but then I said I had Medicaid and they said to call back in a month."

"Those fuckers."

Back inside, I looked for and found roomie bae, to see if she wanted to walk or Uber back soon. She was in back of the kitchen, nibbling on a shared snack plate with her boo, their faces right up next to each other's.

"I was just looking for you!" she said when she saw me. "This is A," indicating one of the new baes I'd met, but only distractedly. "She's a manager for Philly Foodworks, and she was just saying that they need a CSA delivery driver. I was telling her about your van!"

"Philly Foodworks?" I said.

"Where autonomous bae used to manage—where C, you know C, still manages. The food bank part," roomie bae said.

"That's right."

"They do composting, food banks, and CSA veggie distribution," roomie bae continued. Before adding, "Y'know she's who got V that composting gig, right?" referencing autonomous bae.

"Goddamn," I said, wondering how I'd missed all that. "Fkn lit."

"But so you have a van?" asked A.

I said I did.

"And it can carry a lotta boxes?"

I said it could.

"And *you* can carry boxes?"

I considered explaining how I'd just gotten *more-or-less* cleared to walk without my cane, that my van was *technically* stashed out back, and my driveway was a *lil* sketch but it *should* be all good, not to mention was filled with all sorts of crap, like could it even transport veggies like that, I'd have to clear it, air it out, which I *should* be able to do with my skin, my hip, but I mean—

Before not saying all that.

Before simply saying: "Oh hell yeah."

"Amazing," A said, lighting up. "When can you start?"

VI

Spring

Was I ill? Have I got well?
Who was my doctor? Can you tell?
Oh, my memory is rotten!

—NIETZSCHE

1

PRODUCE BRO

April 2019

I cleared out my van. Cleared the way for the veggies.

Moved her out the back, down my driveway ramp. To the front.

Nixed crates of camp stoves, backup propane canisters, empty 2-liters that once served as emergency urinals. Used and unused paper towels. Used and unused cloth towels. Boxes of books, maps, notebooks. Candles, candleholders, functional and unfunctional headlamps. Empty Red Bull cans, 5-hour Energy bottles, and Marlboro Red packs, wedged beneath my desk, from back when I used to drink Red Bulls, 5-hour Energies, and smoke Marlboro Reds.

Disassembled my makeshift, upturned, no-spill, 5-gal. Arrowhead 'sink station.' Broke down my 'closet' — the yard-long, inch-wide, wooden cylinder I'd L-bracketed into the box's upper, driver-side corner, hung hangers off.

Removed the fold-down futon. The emergency sleeping bags/blankets — garage sale–nabbed parkas, jackets.

Swept. Swiffered.

Redid the window and ceiling Reflectix insulation.

Aired that bitch out.

The box would be out in the open now.

Open to scrutiny, inspection.

Would be integral to my survival, like it had been before,

315

when I lived in it, only now from the income it, as a tool, would supply.

The veggies it would house.

I'd be making rent ($350) fortnightly.

Fkn ballin bruh.

Mom I made it.

Cracked the hood and loaded up on fluids — coolant, engine oil — that first day. Something I never did till the thing stalled out, started smoking, before.

Started reading my 8.5" x 11", 400 pp 1993 G Van Model Service Manual and my 1993 G Van Model Service Manual only.

Learning to not do all sorts of shit I'd been doing.

Did an #amreading tweet of its cover.

It didn't get any likes, but I was proud of it.

I legit never went north of my spot, in the near two years I'd lived where I lived, save for the stray Lowe's mish.

No reason to.

Not only no relevant amenities that way, but it got abruptly and drastically hood.

The warehouse HQ was straight north, up 41st, zigging and zagging to accommodate weird, one-way loopholes, to Girard. Then right, across the Schuylkill. Then fishhooking north, along the riverbank, all the way up past Strawberry Mansion, to where it linked with diagonal-ass Ridge. Where diagonal-ass Ridge curved back into the grid momentarily. Before splitting off of Ridge and onto W Hunting Park. Up W Hunting Park a ways.

Stopping at reds on those initial northbound mishes feeling like I was pulling up in a tank. Especially so at that first one, where 41st met Lancaster. Mad people posted at it, eying me like tf.

Feeling like I was a soldier doing a humanitarian aid mish.

Or maybe an offensive-invasive one.

Although, over time, less so.

Over time, with the buffer of the gig — of not pulling up stealthy, blacking out the windows, breathing outta the ceiling vent and peeing in empty water bottles for a night.

Of instead just being a guy driving.

Adhering to traffic rules, eye out for pedestrians who weren't.

Over time, noting all sorts of new spots north of me to hit.

This Chinese spot with $5 General Tso's. This beer spot with $1 tallboys. This Dollar General with the fire TP deals.

Spots I would hit, on foot, going forward.

That I wouldn'ta even known to hit, had I never had a reason to go straight north of my spot.

I had two types of routes: store pickups and home deliveries.

For store pickups, I unloaded up to a dozen boxes at a coffee shop or community center or school. For home deliveries, I delivered a single box directly to homes.

My routes, to start: North Philly home deliveries; Center City / South Philly store pickups; and Jersey 'burbs home deliveries.

Apprehensive af, early on, parking.

Certain streets drop-offs were on way blown.

Early on, circling blocks tryna find a spot, then walking

for days carrying up to fifteen boxes—two, three, four at a time—to a given drop-off.

Before, taking cues from UPS and USPS and FedEx trucks I'd implicitly entered my box into the circuit of, whose structures were in the same structure-genre as mine, quickly learning the power of hazards.

Double park that bitch, flip em.

Act decisive.

Walk, carry boxes, open-close doors like you had a job to do.

Bc I fkng did bro.

Freakin finally.

And no matter how blown the street.

Even once I learned this, stressing about cars getting backed up behind me, on residential one-lane one-ways or rush-hour thoroughfares, say.

Before realizing it didn't fkng matter.

HAZARDS.

AUTHORITATIVE MOVEMENTS.

Death staring the occasional impatient fuck getting their panties bunched when I *skrt*-ed to a stop in front of them, on their commute-route.

Like Bitch I got produce to slang, eat a bag o' dicks howbout.

The greetings from baristas, bartenders, security guards I'd get pulling up with a three-stack bursting with dino kale, green onions, beet leaves sprouting out their tops.

This was everything.

And not even the greetings *I'd* get; the greetings the role I was playing, the hat I was wearing, would.

"Veggie Guy!"

"Fruit Dude!"

"Yo — Produce Bro pulled up!"

Like eagerly digging through the café box we'd throw employees of each pickup site, as a gratitude-offering for agreeing to be a pickup site.

Blasé-blasé, hella zatted, gothed-out South Philly hipsters, who'd otherwise, if a mere customer, shade me as OBVIOUSLY AGGRO CLEARLY TOXIC for my bro-fit, my baby tees, smiling openly offering me road espressos and shit.

Fkng gang bro, so sick.

"Oh no, I got it," I'd say, snagging the ten-stack of broken-down empties customers had returned to be reused, that a lady-barista was struggling with. Tossing em into my van and hitting it.

But most of all.

My own produce game.

Juice game.

The real reason this job was my shit.

That fortnightly $50 veggie box credit.

Too clutch.

Picking out greens, fruits, root veggies. To add to the rotash.

Discovering all sorts of obscure shit I wouldn't have fucked with otherwise.

Hearing on a health pod that spiked inflammation levels had to do with improper hormone regulation — this I already knew — but that it had also to do with lack of testosterone production. Dudes crashed out, inactive, jerking it nonstop, no motivation getting flared up and spazzing out bc their body wasn't producing enough T.

That it was good to do those things — get up, get active, stop jerking it nonstop — that regulated your hormones, yeah.

But that it was also good to eat foods that contained/ encouraged T production.

That beets were one of those foods.

I didn't know whether this take was legit. Had any scientific backing.

Fully aware of this take's potential sus-ness. That bringing it up publicly could prove 'problematic.' That I thus wouldn't bring this up publicly.

Wouldn't dump my shit onto people.

No reason to.

Bc I also figured, eating beets couldn't hurt.

It didn't matter whether or not this take was sus / didn't have hard scientific backing. The only part of the take that mattered was that it encouraged me to get tf up, get active, stop jerking it nonstop.

And to start eating beets.

That this take encouraged me to start eating beets was the only part of it that was *useful*.

About everything else to do with this take, I would put a fkn lid on.

And what was sick was, now I could just add beets to my order.

My juice game was:

A leafy green (spinach or kale).

Half an apple (Pink Lady or Fuji).

An overripe, sliced then frozen banana.

A celery stalk.

A root veg (carrots or, now, beets!).

A root (ginger or turmeric).

A berry (blue or straw).

Tap water.

2

AUTONOMOUS BAE

May 2019

Coming home from work one day, noticing my plant Ryden had given me. Looking parched perched on the dining table surrounded by junk mail.

Gas bills.

Unread *New Yorkers*.

Seeing it, immediately realizing my neglect. Feeling an intuition-urge to Act.

I watered it.

Then texted autonomous bae about whether she was tryna go see Ryden anytime soon.

Last I'd heard he was moving his eyebrows some. Elevating them to signal Yes. Not elevating em when Nah. That his parents were still here, from California. Had moved into a spot near his care facility up in Manayunk, leaving their jobs and lives in San Diego in the lurch the past six months since coming out here, first Ryden went under.

That they wouldn't be around much longer.

Would be moving him back to San Diego once his work insurance ran out.

———

A had added two routes to my routes. One was Manayunk home deliveries that was sketch bc Manayunk, which sits elevated NE of the city proper and overlooks the Schuylkill, is hilly af. Engine straining to ascend those hills, e-brake creaking to stay all 6 tons put, midway up em.

But passing Ryden's care facility on this route another reminder.

A reminder I wouldn'ta had, had A not added those routes.

Autonomous bae picked me up. Drove.

Her whip a shitshow full of food wrappers, empty juice bottles, coffee cups. From all the frantic mishes out to her hospital HQs, for her nightly nightshifts.

Grinding nonstop racking up hours.

Going full nocturnal like I'd been, but for a tangible purpose. Doing a thing that actually affected others.

Ambulance-whippin like goddamn Hemingway through the war zone of the nighttime Philly EMT beat.

When we pulled up, Ryden's dad said Sean! Been a minute.

It had.

I apologized, although he ignored this. This wasn't about me.

Ryden's ex-girl was there. Or, the girl he used to be with, before his more recent, BK boo, and whom he'd started seeing again, once he'd already started seeing his more recent BK boo.

Holding it down six months after he'd gone under, visiting him daily to read and talk to and play music for.

We were in a common room adjacent to Ryden's. Long dining-type table with snacks folks had brought on it, down the middle. Four individual puffy chairs, in a circle, in the corner.

Row of windows overlooking the parking lot of the medical complex this facility was part of. Sky clouded concrete.

This facility resembled the hospital floor I'd been posted on, but homier. For longer-term patients. To move to once their hospital tenures expired.

We unbundled. Laid our jackets on two of the four corner chairs, as directed by Ryden's mom.

Ryden's mom, Ryden's partner, and autonomous bae sat. Ryden's dad talking fast, a lil manic, pacing. I crouched, then stood. Asked Ryden's dad how he was. Off to the side, once the ladies got settled.

He brought up all Ryden had told him about me before he'd gone under. Before Ryden's dad and I first met. How Ryden had sent him the pic he took of me that day we nabbed the couches, once we'd finally jimmied em into my box's box. How Ryden's dad, upon first seeing it, coulda sworn I wasn't me but Ryden.

Ryden was hanging in there, Ryden's dad said. Sleeping at the moment. There'd been a complication with his catheter, earlier that day, that he was still a little shook from. But we could see him in a minute.

He said that the most important thing was to talk to him about recent memories. The early, childhood memories had set. They were there, would still get activated when jostled. But they appealed to an older, more settled mnemonic self. It was his most recent memories, from right before the coma, that hadn't set yet and had the best chance of jostling things awake again.

After all going into Ryden's room together, taking turns having a moment with him, we started to migrate back to the common room. But I lingered by the doorway. Autonomous bae noticed this, could tell that I wanted to go back in for some one-on-one, without the pressure of others in the room. She told me to go back in. We asked and Ryden's dad said I could.

Getting real close by his bedside. I could hear his breathing. Catheter out his neck. Hair on half of his head shorter than the rest, where they'd buzzed it to operate. Eyes open a slit. Propped up slightly on the inclined bed.

I reiterated what I'd said last I'd visited, the only other time I had. On his birthday, day before mine. That this was just a deep hibernation. That I'd been in a deep hibernation, too. We were those deep winter babies. Just burrowing. Spring would come. We'd re-emerge, together.

Only spring had come. Ryden hadn't emerged.

I stalled out in my spiel, registering this. My voice cracking then stopping.

The seasons just kept going.

We only had so many seasons.

I thought about what Ryden's dad had said. Shifted my approach. This wasn't the time for symbolism. Ryden was dealing with something structural. Something neural. His situation didn't fit into my symbolic structure. Wouldn't, no matter how hard I tried to make it.

"Remember that day you saw me trolling around by that Rite Aid on Market bro? When you were headed to work? When I was headed home? You knew exactly what I was on, all that I was feeling, I felt. Your look felt so kind bc you didn't pity me. I needed that shit.

"And those couches. Those fkn couches. How impossible it seemed it'd be to get em all the way up those stairs. But how we had no choice but to. We'd lugged em all that way. And then we fkn got em up, bro. One step, one turn at a time. Each next angle its own thing, its own puzzle. And how good it felt to sit on em once we did. How dank eating those banh mis sitting on em was, bc how hard it had been getting em up."

3

FLOWER BOY

June 2019

The cherry blossoms had shed then swirled around some then gotten stomped on repeatedly and were no longer cherry blossom–colored but brownish.

Still pretty though.

Roomie bae and I were walking up 42nd, away from Market, past the football fields there. Back, from the pool. She lookin pretty in a flower-patterned something or other.

Dress thing.

Not skipping, but felt like it, how she was walking.

Rocking my old Soylent dad hat I lent her then gave her once she kept wearing it like I'd given it to rather than lent her.

Bill curved low like a trucker.

On her keep-back stay-in-your-lane fuccboi shit.

Telling the world: It's all love, you do you. But don't encroach, bro.

This floral pattern and whatever's beneath is for who *I* say it's for.

For who I say it's for and who I say it's for only.

But still — it's all love!

Just. Yeah.

BACK TF UP!

———

My loins were in sync with the flowers.

In bloom.

In HEAT.

No I was chillin, I wasn't about to do anything wild.

But yeah my loins were keyed up.

Seeing a sexy flower, a coy kitty, shoot an attractive vase and goin half chub.

Like OH WHATS GOOD VASE WHATS YOUR NAME.

You seem like Gemini — what's your sign, vase??

C'mon tell me!!

But no earlier I was out on the stoop, beatered up, guns out, getting-em-rays kicking it, when roomie bae pulled up on me.

Like Hey you know there's a pool around the corner, it's a city pool, what you doin rn.

No but actually.

Like Let's...hit this pool howabout!

"Whaaat," I said. "I don't even have a suit, yo."

"What about those shorts?"

"I do have those shorts," I said.

"So...yeah?"

"I mean...yeah!"

She said: "Gonna shower. Get changed."

Our shower was directly on the other side of the wall in my closet-room my twin bed was pressed up against.

And we were suddenly right next to each other, both naked and wet, but separated by a wall.

Suddenly so erect, taking my clothes off.

Seeing red, like Wait did she plan this.

Why she being so nice.

Why she tryna hang.

Was this a…test?

Was 'gonna shower' code for 'If you a man you'll know what that means and come join me'?

Nah dude. Chill.

She wifed.

She seen you when you was all fucked.

When you was splayed out, holed up, body broke.

The pool ended up being closed.

Lifeguard on site, to make sure no one snuck in.

When we pulled up, roomie bae asked Can't we just take a look?

Taking a look won't hurt no one, will it?

The lifeguard said Sure, come take a look.

I misinterpreted this; I thought 'taking a look' was code for 'diving in.'

That's seriously what I thought.

Y'know, that quick dip. In-n-out.

Like, why would we be tryna get that close to the pool, all ready to dive in, without diving in.

So after he led us through the vestibule hut, around its support columns, along the finger-painted mural walls and past both changing rooms — once inside the inner gate — I immediately tossed my towel aside, backed up to get a running start, and made like I was about to dive in.

Had he not been there to step in, to go Woah woah woah bud, you'll get me in trouble ya do that, I woulda.

VII

Summer

1

OLD HEAD

St. James Day 2019

Roomie bro over, the penultimate night of the lease. To see the spot off.

And nab a couple things of his I'd found, while clearing out the basement, from back when we were roomies.

An old bike he'd started fixing up, then abandoned when he couldn't find a part he needed. He thought he wouldn't be able to find the part. Only he had. So was tryna fix it up now.

Trinkets from the era preceding ours, when his ex still lived here.

An ornamental animal tusk, a crystal, a peacock feather.

These roomie bro, without hesitation, donated to the sidewalk.

Us doin an end-of-an-era thing, reminiscing on old times.

This was a thing, a vibe. So I wasn't tryna commandeer his bandwidth rehashing my recent thing with N.

With what N had recently said.

I was pretty sure I wasn't an MRA misogynist, and didn't need roomie bro to tell me I wasn't.

But then the convo flagged a sec, and roomie bro still seemed up to hang. Like I could tell him anything. Like he wasn't tryna be anywhere, do anything, anytime soon.

I proposed we go out onto the stoop to smoke. That way, I could broach what had happened without making it a whole thing.

———

Out on the stoop, I was gonna say something like,

All I did was go up to M after the show. Say Hi.

Since she happened to be there also, probably had tix from before Z, N's bro, abruptly cut her off last week.

Since she saw me see her and beckoned me over.

And, y'know, she's the homie.

This roomie bro woulda understood, since he'd just, last weekend, gone camping with M and other mutual gal-pal homies of theirs. Roomie bro and M themselves homies. From around town.

Because, I mean, what was I supposed to do, I woulda continued. *Ignore her? Just bc Z broke up with her?*

But then when Z and N and N's lady O—whom I came to the show with—came out and saw me talking to her.

When they then came over.

Z ventured a sheepish Hi.

M ignored him completely.

Like continuing to look at me, smiling uncomfortably, and going ANYway, what were you saying?

Which. A bummer. Sure.

But understandable.

Z standing there shifting, looking shook.

Like the wheels turning, unable to grasp why that reaction.

Then we're leaving, and O goes What's wrong with you? Why would you ever even think *about talking to her?*

To which I, joke-y but defensive, went Sorry! Sorry I didn't adhere completely to 'bros over hoes.'

This shocked O. She went Why would you even say that. That's so sexist.

I said I'M not saying that. YOU are!

What you just said implied that. Demonstrated that concept, 'bros over hoes.'

Which is when N stepped in, in defense of his gal, like this was too much conflict for her, like she couldn't handle this, and went Dude. That's sexist. You're a misogynist for saying that.

They all turning on me, like I was the problem.

Bc words I said.

When clearly Z was getting a firsthand look into the consequences of dropping M like he had, as if there'd be none.

With no explanation. No communication.

All one needed to do to not be sus was communicate.

Or fkn try to. At least try.

I honestly felt it was good that Z saw that. Saw her reaction.

Anyway, they no longer wanted to do drinks after like we'd planned.

Then N, the next week.

Saying all sorts of wild shit at a Clark Park hang we had.

Going I'm worried about ya bud.

You're getting lost in the men's rights tunnel.

Writing about your hatred of women.

What, bc I said 'ho'? I said.

That's what this is all about, innit?

Like, do you understand what that phrase, 'bros over hoes,' even means?

If anything, I was critical of that concept. Only said the phrase to communicate my criticism.

How are you missing that.

And you think that's what I'm writing about? Hatred of women?

N just doubled down.

Like You need help. Should talk to someone. You're listening to too much Joe Rogan.

I'm investigating myself! I cut in. You think you're never sus?! That you're all good?

INVESTIGATE YOURSELF, DOG!

O's a big girl, we were hashing it out, you stepping in like that was wild cringe-patronizing.

You think she can't speak up for herself? Needs to be babied?

And you think Z wasn't being sus?

Cutting off a bae a friend just bc he feeling a type of way that day?

Then communicating none of why?

That's wack, bro.

But nothing was hitting.

Something seismic had shifted.

Why you think you're still stuck on ex bae? N said.

You think it's bc you 'love' her?

That's not it, man.

You think you own *her.*

You don't care about her.

You just wanna take her back.

And all this 'fuckboy' self-awareness? When does that become reveling in it. Become self-fulfilling.

This made me go quiet.

Consider this.

Still considering this, today.

I was about to say some version of all this to roomie bro.

Before, outta nowhere, I noticed, in the streetlight, my neighbor R just going *in* on his girl K. Two units over, on the sidewalk. Just throwing hands so fast it looked confusing.

Like he was dancing or something.

The movement was so unnatural, it took a sec to register what was even happening.

But soon as it did, without thinking, I bounded down the steps and grabbed him off her. Then hugged him to me when he tried to hit me. He was going "I'll dog you like this for the rest of your life, bitch. Don't EVER text another man while you in my house."

Towering over her.

She a crumpled heap on the sidewalk, barefoot and tear-strewn.

I blocked his path, going Nope, nope, no dude, chill dude, breathe, walk it off, drive it off, get the fuck outta here. You'll thank me later.

Till he, finally, agreed to take off for a drive.

Roomie bro and I made sure K made it back inside OK.

Then returned to my stoop.

Panting, sweating. Keyed up off all that action.

Old heads down the block sorta cheering me for stepping in, but same time weren't about to do anything. I mean, they were old heads; stepping in wasn't their role.

After some silence, roomie bro went Wait, what were you saying?

I laughed.

"Nothing, dude. Nothing important."

— August 2020
Harlem, NY

Works Cited

The Return (2010) by Roberto Bolaño
Society of the Spectacle (1967) by Guy Debord
Motherhood (2018) by Sheila Heti
Trip (2017) by Tao Lin
Food of the Gods (1993) by Terence McKenna
Philadelphia (2017), reprinted in *Some of the Times* (2020) by Gina Myers
Evolution (2018) by Eileen Myles
The Gay Science (1887) by Friedrich Nietzsche
"Bloody Mother Fucking Asshole" (2005) by Martha Wainwright

Works Mentioned

I'm Gay (2011) by Lil B
Painting Pictures (2017) by Kodak Black
2666 (2004) by Roberto Bolaño
Invisible Cities (1974) by Italo Calvino
Don Quixote (1620) by Miguel de Cervantes
Scorpion (2018) by Drake
Chronic 2001 (1999) by Dr. Dre
Signed to the Streets (2013), *Signed to the Streets 3* (2018) by Lil Durk
The Story of a New Name: My Brilliant Friend Book 2 (2013) by Elena Ferrante
The Language of the Goddess (1989) by Marija Gimbutas
How Should a Person Be? (2010) by Sheila Heti
Mein Kampf (1933) by Adolf Hitler
The Elementary Particles (2000) by Michel Houellebecq
Blue Is the Warmest Color (2013), directed Abdellatif Kechiche
My Struggle: Book Five (2017) by Karl Ove Knausgaard
My Struggle: Book Six (2018) by Karl Ove Knausgaard
"Petty Wap" (2018) by Young M.A
"Two 16s" (2017) by Z Money
Killing Commendatore (2017) by Haruki Murakami
The Cape (1976) by Kenji Nakagami

Come Over When You're Sober, Pt. 1 (2017) by Lil Peep
Rontel (2013) by Sam Pink
Savage Mode (2016) by 21 Savage
The Marvelous Mrs. Maisel (2017), created Amy Sherman-Palladino
Infinite Jest (1996) by David Foster Wallace
"Starboy" (2016) by The Weeknd
Tractatus Logico-Philosophicus (1922) by Ludwig Wittgenstein
"RIP Roach" (2016) by XXXTENTACION, Ski Mask The Slump God

Acknowledgments

Ty ty ty to Giancarlo DiTrapano for not only letting me write how I talk, but encouraging me to.

That shit there.

Man.

I can't even.

To all the day 1s who read this shit as written each month, about the year's previous. Tren, Eric, Viva, Nick.

To Sam Pink, for the early encouragement, and for lighting the way.

Likewise to Bud Smith, and to Scott McClanahan.

To Sam Lipsyte, for seeing the slap past the sus.

To Erroll McDonald, for setting the bar so high.

To Rebecca Godfrey, for seeing it clearly so early.

To Sheila Heti, for being so warm and supportive, for no apparent reason.

To Nico Walker, for being one of the real ones.

To Tao Lin, for being Tao Lin.

To Jordan Castro, for being there.

To Julie Flanagan, for riding for the vision.

To Jean Garnett, for guiding *Fuccboi* home.

To Michael Pietsch.

To all my Philly peoples.

To Catherine and Giu.

To R.

To K, for looking directly at everything and never batting a fkn eye.

And to everyone else who done ever podded with or fucked with me.

Gang.